THE
CIRCLE
BROKEN

A NOVEL

DOROTHY CARVELLO

A REGALO PRESS BOOK
ISBN: 979-8-88845-442-8
ISBN (eBook): 979-8-88845-443-5

The Circle Broken
© 2024 by Dorothy Carvello
All Rights Reserved

Cover Design by Jim Villaflores

As part of the mission of Regalo Press, a donation is being made to The Elton John Foundation, as chosen by the author. Find out more about this organization at www.eltonjohnaidsfoundation.org.

Regalo Press
New York • Nashville
regalopress.com

Published in the United States of America
2 3 4 5 6 7 8 9 10

In loving memory of Michael Kelland Hutchence
January 22, 1960–November 22, 1997
Lead singer and lyricist of the band INXS

1

THE CIRCLE

CEE CEE PORTER BOWED HER head. Instinct made her want to genuflect, but then she came to her senses: this wasn't church. It felt like it, but it wasn't. She stood in the rotunda at the Country Music Hall of Fame. High above her head, circling the entire room in giant bold letters emblazoned on the wall were the words: "Will the circle be unbroken?" Beneath that timeless question came the answer in a hundred pictures and plaques and items of memorabilia: the circle unbroken from Hank Williams to Kitty Wells to Johnny Cash and Dolly Parton, from Roy Acuff to the Carter Family to Willy Nelson and Emmylou Harris. How appropriate, Cee Cee thought, that the actual building was a circle too, unbroken and perhaps unbreakable.

Tonight Sam Rogers would become the newest member of that circle. Cee Cee hadn't seen Sam yet, but she could hear the dull thud of musicians rehearsing his songs in the CMA Theater across the way, and she knew he'd be sitting next to the Colonel, his manager of forty-odd years, puffed up like a peacock to hear his songs sung by country music royalty. She wanted to hate him, wanted to hate the whole town for enshrining him in the halls of glory instead of punishing him for what he had done, but she couldn't feel hatred here. Not with Patsy Cline staring soulfully at her from a six-foot high picture painted on the wall; not with Buck Owens's red, white, and blue 1969 Harmony acoustic guitar hanging above her head. Besides, tonight was about peace, not war. Tonight was her triumph, too.

She checked her phone to see if Michael had texted.

Cee Cee left the rotunda and walked to the theater, where Alan Jackson had just finished rehearsing his performance of Sam's first hit, "Secondhand Guitar," while Reba McEntire stood at the wooden podium preparing her induction speech. Cee Cee climbed the stairs to the stage, wondering if anyone would stop her. No one did. She stood amongst the shuffle and hum of a dozen conversations—roadies telling road stories while they tuned guitars, soundmen changing microphones and taping down cables, and a gaggle of security guards barking into their crackling walkie talkies—and looked out into the empty seats.

In the center aisle sat Sam, his silver hair coiffed, his back straight and proud, his cheeks stretched in a grin that would stay there from tonight until the rapture. He wore a white Nudie suit with blood red roses stitched on the sleeves and down the back and blinding white cowboy boots, and a turquoise ring ornamented his pinky finger. He accepted the congratulations thrown his way with the grace of a pharaoh, but beneath that façade, Cee Cee knew, was the slobbering glee of a well-petted puppy. Sam needed this night more than he would ever admit.

Next to the speaker's podium stood Sam's bronze medallion, which would be unveiled after Reba's induction speech and hang forever after in the rotunda. Cee Cee read the inscription:

Born July 30, 1952—

With his deep, rich voice and movie-star good looks, Sam Rogers exploded on the scene in the 1970s with the number-one song "Secondhand Guitar," followed by three straight gold albums. He successfully toed the line between country outlaw and music superstar, becoming a worldwide phenomenon in the process. At the height of his career, he sold out the 100,000 seat Melbourne Cricket Ground in Australia and swept the CMA Awards in the same year. Nearly forty years after his first hit, he returned to the top of the charts, and he continues to inspire new generations of country music lovers.

Cee Cee felt a presence behind her. She turned to see Sam's manager, the Colonel, his hair dyed too black, his face Botoxed too tight, his suit cut too flamboyantly even for Nashville.

"Where's Michael?" the Colonel said, his eyes darting nervously around the room.

"He'll be here," Cee Cee answered.

"You said he'd be here," the Colonel said, straightening his cufflinks, running his hand through his hair, and straightening his cufflinks again. "That was the deal," he said.

"Colonel," Cee Cee said, grabbing him by the lapel. "He'll be here."

"He'd better," the Colonel said and paced away to solve the next crisis. He seemed miserable, but Cee Cee knew this was what kept him alive—stomping around in his big boots, knocking trouble on the head like a kid playing Whac-A-Mole.

Cee Cee walked outside and squinted in the sunlight. She called Michael. He didn't answer. She understood Michael's problems with Sam better than anyone, but their fates were tied to each other—Michael the rising future of country music, and Sam the resurrected past—and her fate had become caught in the knot. She began to sweat. Pacing the sidewalk, she texted Michael: *Where are you?* Waiting for a response that didn't come, she watched the limos roll in and disgorge the greatest living names in country music. They came dressed in their finery— leather boots, weathered cowboy hats, rhinestone-studded belts and buckles, sequined gowns, feathered hair. Despite her own brush with stardom, despite spending a decade married to Bucky Porter, owner of one of Nashville's premiere record labels, Cee Cee still lost her breath when she saw her heroes in person. They always seemed unreal, as if they had just stepped from a record cover into the street.

The sun set. Still no word from Michael.

Cee Cee ducked behind Randy Travis and Miranda Lambert on their way into the building. The air in the rotunda swirled with laughter as all the legends greeted each other like lovers after a long separation. Nearly everyone in this room had reached the height of stardom. For that reason, it was only in this room that they could let their guard down. This was part of the Hall of Fame's magic: it turned people into legends, but it also turned legends back into people.

Circling the room, Cee Cee saw Dolly glittering like a queen, hugging Reba who lit up the room with her warm smile. Beside them stood Garth and Hank Jr. so close in conversation their cowboy hats touched. She caught herself staring and ripped her gaze from the stars only to run into the Colonel's secretary, Martha Moran. Martha wobbled on her high heels and spilled her martini, then righted herself and gave Cee Cee a polite hug.

"Where's Michael?" Martha asked.

"On the way," Cee Cee said.

Martha had worked in Nashville long enough to spot a lie when she heard one, but she also knew better than to say anything. This town was built on lies. Poke a hole in one, and the whole thing might come crashing down.

"Come on, it's about to start," Cee Cee said, grabbing Martha's hand and walking into the theater. As she filed into her row, Cee Cee saw her husband (*ex-husband*...it was so hard to get used to) Bucky coming from the opposite direction. Hanging on his arm was a girl who looked like she had come from Central Casting's high school division. She had great tits; Cee Cee gave her that.

Cee Cee avoided Bucky's eyes and took her seat. The lights went down. The show began. Legend after legend climbed the stage and filled the theater with music. In the middle of the ceremony, a short film detailed Sam's life from his upbringing on a farm in rural Tennessee to his chance meeting with the Colonel in Nashville, to his rise to stardom in the 1970s, his fall from grace in the ensuing decades, his struggles with drugs and booze, and finally his triumphant resurrection.

Cee Cee checked her phone to see if Michael had responded. Nothing.

After the film, the legends returned to the stage and sang "Will the Circle Be Unbroken." Tears filled Cee Cee's eyes. It was such a beautiful metaphor, the circle of music, no beginning or end, like a wheel that kept rolling from generation to generation. Then she thought of Sam and Michael, of the Colonel and Bucky, and realized there was another circle, one that was also passed from generation to generation. Why did no one talk about it? It had touched everyone in this room as surely as music had; it had bruised them and scarred them, and it had done worse to so many others, had driven them to darkness, despair, and death. That circle, too, was unbroken and perhaps unbreakable.

The final chorus rose until it seemed the entire building had lungs. Cee Cee joined in her clear, sweet voice—"By and by, Lord, by and by." Then the room settled for Reba McEntire's heartfelt induction, followed by the unveiling of Sam's medallion, and Sam's teary acceptance speech that ran on too long. Now Cee Cee began to worry. Sam's big performance was next. Michael was supposed to be here. She texted him again: *Where are you?*

Michael Jennings lit a joint and lay back in his plush bed at the Thompson Hotel, his long hair splayed out in a halo around him on the pillow. He felt like someone had taken an axe to his head. He nearly vomited from the pain. He shook an Oxy from a yellow plastic bottle and swallowed it. He sucked on the joint and exhaled a billowing cloud of smoke. He coughed until he nearly vomited again. He heard his phone ping, but he ignored it.

He thought of the girl and wished he had slept with her. He should have let her stay. Maybe his head would have stopped hurting then. He smoked the joint down to his fingers, burning himself where the old burn had just healed. He felt nearly numb, which wasn't good enough. He heaved himself from the bed and, trailing the goose-down comforter in his wake, grabbed his phone and his snakeskin belt, then played a little run on the baby grand piano as he passed it by on his way to the bathroom. He kneeled on the cold tile, looped the belt around his neck and pulled it taut, then tied it to the door handle. He pulled up a picture of Cee Cee on his phone and let his weight fall into the belt. His neck bulged as he stroked himself, feeling the ecstasy build behind his eyes and run down his legs. Just one more moment, and his head wouldn't hurt anymore. This was the last time, he told himself. After this, he'd do everything right.

2

BABY BLUE

FOUR YEARS EARLIER: "CEE CEE, come in, please," said the counselor. "Good afternoon, Doctor Pace," Cee Cee said, rising from the waiting room chair and following the doctor down the hallway and into a room containing a plush leather couch covered with velvety pillows and soft quilts. Scarf-draped lamp shades cast a warm glow against the walls. From somewhere came the soothing sound of trickling water.

"No Bucky today?" said Dr. Pace.

"He's at home," Cee Cee said, sinking into the couch and holding a pillow across her chest like a shield. "Some sort of work party. He told me I'd only get bored, so I figured I'd keep the appointment."

"Tell me what you'd like to talk about, then," said Dr. Pace.

"I don't know. He wants me to get fertility treatment. He says it's my fault."

"And what do you say?"

"I got pregnant once before. I mean, you know…it only lasted a few months before the whole…*thing*…but it's not impossible. I know that. Still, we can't seem to make it happen again. And he's got this condition."

"Peyronie's disease. You told me about that last time."

"I think he should be the one seeing a doctor."

"Did you ask him to?"

"A hundred times," Cee Cee said, throwing the pillow aside. "He never listens." Then she added under her breath, "Unless he's taking credit for one of my ideas."

"Resentment is cancer to a relationship," the doctor said.

"I know, I know, I know," Cee Cee huffed. She dropped her eyes and her voice and continued: "But he's changed. He doesn't look at me anymore. It's like he blames me for everything that went wrong, so he doesn't have to face it."

"This is the third appointment he's missed."

"I feel like if I could just get him in here, and we could talk to each other, *hear* each other, we'd figure out how to get through this. Together."

"Is that what you want?" Dr. Pace said, making a note on a yellow legal pad.

"I don't know if it matters what I want," Cee Cee said softly.

"Why is that?"

"I come from a long line of women who settled."

"Settled for what?"

"Second best. Whatever crumbs of happiness fell from the table of the banquets they made for their husbands. It's just what's done."

"Forget about them for a second," Dr. Pace said. "Tell me what *you* want. If you had the power to make your life anything it could be, anything at all, what would you make it?"

Cee Cee sat silently for a long time. Then she spoke in a small voice: "I want a family. I want to sing again. I want people to look at me for me, not because I'm Bucky's wife. I want to be in love."

"You're not in love with your husband?" Dr. Pace asked, removing her wire frame glasses and cleaning the lenses on her shirt.

"I don't think he's in love with me anymore."

"That's not what I asked."

Cee Cee stared at her feet. The ambient sounds of the room seemed to wash over her: the gentle gurgling of water became a raging flood; the soft ticking of the clock became a pounding jackhammer. She breathed deeply and exhaled. "I don't know," she said.

"Cee Cee, I'm a couple's therapist," said Dr. Pace. "Unless Bucky starts coming to these sessions, I have to recommend once again that you see one of my colleagues who specializes in a one-on-one approach.

There are plenty of tremendously helpful options out there: inner family system, EMDR, cognitive behavioral therapy."

"Please just give us another chance."

"I'm here for you, and if you want to keep seeing me, I will see you. But I must advise what I believe is best for you. Think about it. Let me know. That's our time for today."

The doctor rose from her seat, and Cee Cee followed. They walked to the door.

"Hang on," Cee Cee said, "I forgot to pay." She rummaged in her purse, found her checkbook, and stared at the name printed in block letters on top: Mrs. Bucky Porter. "Two-hundred and fifty dollars," she wrote in a looping script then tore the check from the book and handed it to the counselor.

Cee Cee left the office, but she didn't want to go home. It was nearly half past four. Who knew how long Bucky's party would rage? She drove aimlessly around Green Hills, winding through tony neighborhoods and their two-story manor houses with little blonde children gamboling across immaculate Girl Scout-green lawns, laughing in the spray of afternoon sprinklers. Slowly the neighborhoods turned into endless strip malls full of Starbucks shops and barbecue restaurants. Without thinking, she turned into one of them, parked, and ended up standing before a movie theater box office. "Give me one for whatever's playing right now," she said and didn't even read the name of the movie on the ticket as she entered the theater and took a seat in the back, alone.

3

PARTY IN THE USA

MICHAEL FLOATED ON A RAFT in a swimming pool designed after Hugh Heffner's, complete with grotto, his brown curly hair undulating in a halo around his head. There was something Christlike about him. Something devilish too. He didn't know the girl going down on him, didn't even know her name. His lean, chiseled body bobbed up and down to the girl's rhythm. Her lips were as red as gala apples against his flesh. His toned arms played in the water, occasionally reaching to pull her bikini top to the side and squeeze her breasts. He didn't know the other girl either, the one who approached him, naked, holding a birthday cake with twenty-eight candles arranged in neat rows.

How many girls had there been before these two? How many had desired him, loved him, grasped for him since he learned to play guitar at home in Australia as a teenager, since he learned the power it gave him over women young, old, and in between, learned what it meant when they looked at him a certain way, the pupils a little too big, the stare held a little too long? He had lost count. Back then, they wanted him for what he might become. Here in Nashville, they wanted him for what he was: a star.

He wasn't sure which way he preferred.

Michael gestured to the girl with the cake. She climbed in the pool, the cold water raising goosebumps on her flesh, and held it in front of him. "Make a wish," she said. As if commanded, his mind wandered back in space and time, back to Australia. A cake shaped like a guitar sat on the table in front of him, nine candles throwing shadows on the wall. A Sam Rogers record played in the background. He heard his mother's voice: "Make a wish." He blew out the candles and then proudly told her, "I wished to meet my daddy." Worry lines creased her eyes, and she said, "Michael, you know your daddy died a long time ago." Michael noticed the strange look on Grandma Pearl's face. That night, he crept out of bed and stood outside his mother's bedroom door, listening to Grandma Pearl's stern voice: "You better tell that boy the truth."

The truth. By the time he became a teenager, Michael had stopped asking for it. His mother would say nothing of his father except that he died before Michael was born. It clearly hurt her too much to speak about it, so they didn't speak about it. But still, every year he made the same wish, and every year it didn't come true. And now that his mother was gone, he feared he was running out of birthdays.

"That must be some wish," the girl said, and Michael realized he had been silent too long. He snapped back to the party. The first girl was still going down on him. He blew out the candles, then took a love bite at the second girl's nipple. It hardened in his mouth. Southern girls are all the same, he thought. Round faces, blonde hair, and big pearly white teeth. Pious on Sunday, like everyone else in Nashville, but Saturday night they let the beast loose to prowl—like everyone else in Nashville.

He took his time with the girls, pleasing each one in turn. A small crowd gathered to watch. Michael hardly noticed them; he was so focused on the flesh at his fingertips. When he finally finished, he went inside the mansion and showered. On his way back outside, he caught the eye of a petite blonde with long hair and sculpted legs. They found an empty bedroom, and forty-five minutes later, Michael showered again and walked to the kitchen to find something to eat.

In the kitchen, Bucky Porter, a man of average height and build, of average tastes and abilities—average in everything but shrewdness, which was how he built his fortune—was busy with two girls of his own.

Born and raised in Nashville, Bucky was a Southerner down to the roots of his hair plugs. His father was a preacher, his mother a preacher's wife. He had memorized the New Testament by age thirteen. His path was set for a life of service to the Lord until one day as a freshman at Belmont University, a pretty girl saw him preaching in the campus chapel and followed him back to the dormitory, where she reached her hand down his pants and, with a deftness Bucky had never known, made him see stars.

Soon he had a harem of nubile girls with firm breasts and eager hands competing for the young preacher's favor. He consoled himself with the stories of David and Bathsheba, Timer and Amnon, all the Biblical figures who had fallen prey to sins of the flesh but retained God's favor. By the time he reached the final year of his master's program at the Vanderbilt School of Divinity, he had perfected his art. Scripture, Bucky learned, is not hard like marble, but pliable like clay. If ever a girl was hesitant, he could call to mind the precise chapter and verse and mold it to fit his needs.

He convinced Cee Cee in this way. He had to have her. She was beautiful and chaste, unpretentious and kind. She had cascading blonde hair and a petite body and big eyes the color of a clear sky in spring, and she seemed to have no idea the effect these had on men. She radiated warmth. She made him feel welcome. The more cynical and calculating Bucky became, the more he was drawn to her sincerity, if only to understand it, like taking apart an engine to learn how the pieces fit. At first he didn't trust it, but it never wavered. He could think of only two explanations: either she had never been hurt, and her sincerity was the result of immaturity, or, what scared him more, she knew the bitterness of life and still had the courage to face it with an open heart.

After bedding her, he recoiled and as a reflex went on a rampage through every girl he could get his hands on. Then came a scandal—an accident that required Bucky to bend Scripture until it nearly snapped—and although the girl took care of the problem, rumors spread. When Bucky's father found out, he gave his son an ultimatum: repent his wickedness, find a nice girl, and settle down, or be disowned, excommunicated from his family, cast into the darkness to moan and gnash his teeth.

Cee Cee was perfect on paper: stainless in body and spirit, a submissive subject, a fit helper. She played guitar and sang, in a sweet voice, songs of uncomplicated love, songs she had written but was too shy to show to anyone but Bucky, who then gave her a book of poems and inscribed it with a marriage proposal. Cee Cee, swept away, said yes.

For their first few years of marriage, Bucky didn't so much as cast a glance at another woman. He was dedicated to Cee Cee and their life together. She wrote a song on their first anniversary, and he put together the money to record it. That was the beginning of his career and the beginning of the end of hers. When the song became a fluke hit, Bucky felt his wife pulling away from him. She said it was all in his mind, that she'd never let anyone else have her, that they were a team for life. He knew she wanted a family, and he convinced her she'd never have one living on a bus with a bunch of sweaty musicians, traveling the world, away from home all the time. When she became pregnant, she canceled her future engagements and came home to build a family.

But the baby never came.

The longer Cee Cee remained barren—and Bucky was certain it was her fault—the more he felt justified in sowing his seed in other fields. As he rose through the ranks of Nashville music, first representing Christian artists, then following the money until he founded his own country label, DMG, he became more and more brazen until he didn't blink at hosting an orgy in the kitchen where his wife cooked him breakfast.

Wandering around the mansion, Michael found a room painted like a nursery, by the looks of it, never used. The crib had become a junk heap of old golf clubs, a pair of skis, a ball of tangled Christmas lights; the rest of the room was piled high with boxes and books and other junk. Michael wondered how Cee Cee lost the baby.

He wandered some more and eventually found a quiet room full of expensive guitars. He lovingly caressed a mint condition 1956 Fender

Telecaster and then lifted a 1962 Gibson acoustic from the wall. Below it hung a picture of John Lennon playing the guitar at Abbey Road during the recording of *With the Beatles*. Michael began strumming, and the noise attracted a curvaceous brunette in a bikini that hugged every curve, who said, "You're Michael, right? I'm Amber. Play me a song, and I'll suck your cock."

Michael obliged.

But the bliss turned sour like an out-of-tune chord when Martha Moran walked in the room. Martha was tall and lean and beautiful, black Irish with silken dark hair, vivid blue eyes, and a sprinkling of freckles on her cheeks and nose. She was born and raised in Brooklyn, but apart from her accent—which everyone in Nashville mocked, like they couldn't hear themselves speak—she brought little of the city's ball-busting brashness to the South. Martha was meek, believing this to be the surest way of inheriting the earth. Though it was she who brought Michael's demos to Bucky, and though Bucky promised her a promotion, and though the promotion was forgotten as soon as he had seduced her, Martha left the boat unrocked. *Wait,* she told herself. *Someday they'll give you what you deserve.*

Michael had never met a woman he couldn't read until Martha, and it tormented him the way blank maps once tormented the great explorers. Sometimes he was sure she loved him. Other times he felt like he did now, as she looked him full in the eyes while his erect penis was in a stranger's mouth: lost. Why didn't Martha even flinch? He tapped the girl on the head and said, "Will you give us a moment?" The girl wiped her mouth, adjusted her bathing suit, glared at Martha, and walked brazenly from the room.

"Bucky sent me to find you," Martha said. "He wants you to sign those headshots for the fan club."

"He can wait," Michael said. "Sit."

Martha sat opposite Michael like a secretary ready to take dictation, betraying no emotion. Michael flashed back to the first time he had met her. He had just arrived from Sydney, Australia, and was sitting at the Killebrew coffee shop in the Thompson Hotel, marveling at all the rich people who could afford to stay there, wondering how he'd ever make it in Nashville, when Martha walked in. He invited her to sit with him, just to make sure his Aussie charm worked on American girls. They made small talk until he learned she worked for the Colonel, manager of Michael's idol Sam Rogers, and then he was playing her his demos, which he had saved on his phone. He studied her face while she listened and was struck by her beauty and the way it seemed so carefully locked behind that little smile, the one she was giving him now.

"I've got a new song," Michael said. "And I was sort of hoping to sing it with...well, with Sam." He looked at her from the corner of his eye, trying to judge her reaction. This was it—this was the big ask, the reason he had come to Nashville.

"Can I hear the song?" she said, simply.

Michael began strumming and singing, pausing every few bars to say, "Now, this is where Sam would come in." As the last chord died, Michael said sheepishly, "Do you like it?"

"Have you told Bucky?" Martha asked.

"I want you to do it," Michael said, rising from his seat and sitting next to her. The smell of Martha's perfume aroused him. He held her gaze. *Maybe this is it*, he thought. *Maybe she wants me to kiss her.* He leaned forward slightly, when one of the girls from the pool peeked her head in the door and said, "Bucky wants everyone outside."

Michael broke apart from Martha like waking from a dream. They walked outside and were greeted by a cheering crowd of record executives and groupies. As Bucky pulled Michael to the center of the crowd, he whispered in his ear, "Don't forget the T.J. Martell dinner Wednesday. Sam's going to be there." Bucky knew Michael idolized Sam Rogers. Bucky idolized the man too. It was a bond they shared.

Turning to address the crowd with a perfect smile, Bucky made his voice boom across the pool deck. "One month ago, all of Nashville thought I was crazy to sign this guy." He swung his champagne flute toward Michael. "An Australian singing American country? 'Never gonna happen,' they said. Well, we are here tonight not just because of that Australian's birthday, but also because his first single, 'Don't

Change,' has just broken the record for the best-selling streaming single in country music history. And when his album comes out Tuesday, he's going to put everyone so far behind him, they'll choke on his dust."

Bucky faced Michael. "As if that weren't enough," he continued, "our little label is now the hottest thing in Nashville, which means the world. And no one is saying I'm crazy anymore. So, grab your *tinnies*, mates—to put it in language he can understand—and join me in toasting the great Michael Jennings."

4

MUSIC CITY

THE LIGHTNING FLASH OF A camera left Cee Cee momentarily blind. Blinking away the black spots, she watched Bucky schmooze his way down the red carpet and remembered five years ago, when the cameras flashed for her, back before Bucky made her believe she could be more productive from behind the scenes. He was right, in a way: she had become a major player in Nashville's charity scene, which connected her with the most powerful people in town. But they all still saw her as Bucky's wife. Every year she raised nearly all the money for the T.J. Martell gala, donating millions to cancer research. It was a consolation prize for giving up her career as a singer and songwriter. Tonight, to celebrate her contributions, they were giving an award to Bucky.

It had been a cold day between them, and the award was the least of it. She had come home last night after the movie to find her house in total darkness, moonlight streaming through the open windows and glinting off the piles of beer bottles on the floor, on the tables, on the couches, on the counters, some of them half empty and warm, some of them spilled over and staining the leather upholstery, some of them arranged in neat rows atop used pool towels. Empty pizza boxes gaped at her from the kitchen table while spent crusts sat mashed into the living room carpet. A girl she didn't recognize lay passed out on the foyer floor, her face pressed dumbly against the cold marble tile. A banner reading "Congratulations, Michael!" fluttered, half torn, over the stairs. She found Bucky sleeping in the guest bed, emitting giant snores, sounding like a lawnmower that wouldn't start. She began cleaning immediately, knowing it was her job—Bucky was too paranoid to hire a service. The only good part was a stack of headshots signed by Bucky's new boy wonder, Michael Jennings. She spent a long time looking at them, fighting the Bible verse that screamed in her head: "But I say unto you, that whosoever looketh on a woman to lust after her hath committed adultery with her already in his heart." Well, at least it didn't mention anything about a woman looking at a man. *Loopholes.*

After finishing her chores, Cee Cee slept alone in the master bedroom, where Michael's smile haunted her dreams. Come morning she could barely stand to look at Bucky's bleary red eyes or his bloated, pasty face. "What's wrong?" he said a dozen times, and she ignored him a dozen times.

But looking at him now on the red carpet, she felt grudging admiration for how effortless he made it all seem. He moved like an electrical current, lighting everyone he touched. When he looked at you, he made you feel like the only person worth talking to in the world. The truth came later, when you spent every night telling him it was okay, you enjoyed it, and then woke up in bed next to him every day and saw him put himself on, stepping into his charm like that navy Hugo Boss suit he wore tonight, buttoning up his megawatt smile like the pristine white dress shirt, knotting his piety around him like the Ferragamo necktie with red horses on it.

A pretty young blond in too much makeup stopped him on the red carpet and stuck a microphone in his face. Cee Cee watched her husband gently touch the girl's arm while he looked deeply in her eyes and answered her question. That was how he did it. The touch was nothing, not a hint of impropriety to it. And yet it was everything. It was the only true thing about him. He wanted to touch you, and he knew how to make you pretend it had never happened afterward. He knew how to make you *want* to pretend, for him, for the chance of another touch.

Cee Cee wasn't pretending, not at first, not during those golden college days when every smile from Bucky was the sun shining, and she opened herself to him with no thought of sin or damnation. But somewhere along the way, it became harder and harder to ignore his late nights, his unexplained absences, his intense interest in the career of this or that young girl with a guitar and a few songs to play.

She approached Bucky and his interviewer wondering if they'd ever slept together.

"Once again," the interviewer said into her microphone, "we're here at the Omni Hotel for the T.J. Martell Foundation gala, raising money for cancer research. And I have with me the man of the hour, Bucky Porter, chairman of DMG Records, who will receive a special award tonight for his philanthropy through the years. Bucky, how does it feel?"

Cee Cee put her hand into Bucky's as he began to answer. He snatched a glance at her, then turned back to the camera, simultaneously holding his wife's hand, touching the young woman's arm, and making those puppy dog eyes into the camera, while he spoke about how important it was to cure cancer.

The interview ended and Bucky led Cee Cee into the hotel for cocktail hour. She looked with distaste at the brown pattern carpet, the beige walls, the dozen chandeliers glittering gaudily overhead. The ballroom at the Omni wanted so badly to be more than a convention hall for used car salesmen. But it was a far cry from the Beverly Hilton, which Clive Davis once booked for his pre-Grammy bash. Hell, the bathroom there had a fish tank.

Maybe Nashville would catch up someday.

With a martini in hand, Cee Cee joined Bucky in the center of the room, where the glitterati of Nashville lined up to pay their respects and have their picture taken. An older man with a receding hairline approached with a hangdog smile. Bucky put his hand on the small of Cee Cee's back and presented her to the man the way a fisherman shows his prize catch.

"Cee Cee, you remember Dale Cunningham of Big Smoke Records," Bucky said.

"Of course," Cee Cee answered, offering her hand. "How lovely to see you again, Dale."

"Got any new songs?" he said with a pleasant smile.

Cunningham had signed Cee Cee to Big Smoke all those years ago, and he oversaw the release of her hit single "A Good Man is Hard to Find." He was the one who suggested to the press the phrase "The new Shania Twain." He was the one who bought her Dolly Parton's old Alvarez 4103 classical guitar, the very one Dolly used in performance of "Coat of Many Colors" on television in the seventies—it was Cee Cee's favorite performance, not just because it was so candid and unpretentious, like Dolly herself, but also because Dolly played while wearing two-inch long, fire hydrant-red press-on nails, and by God, that was a *woman.* Cunningham felt personally betrayed when Cee Cee gave up her career for Bucky.

All these years later, Cee Cee knew, he couldn't care less whether or not she had a new song. He was twisting the knife. Or maybe he was just being nice. Or maybe there was no difference between the two. He took Cee Cee's hand and kissed it. Then he turned and shook Bucky's hand like an old friend he hadn't seen in years. Cee Cee heard him whisper to her husband, "You prick, you don't give a fuck about kids with cancer."

"I'd give you cancer if I could, Cunningham," hissed Bucky through his smile.

"Some philanthropist. Remember when you pissed on that swan at Fan Fest?"

"Say cheese, asshole."

The camera flashed, leaving Cee Cee momentarily blinded again.

Later, sitting at the dinner table, black polka dots swimming on the white linen every time she blinked, Cee Cee began to sweat. She was crammed elbow to elbow with Bucky, Sam Rogers, and the Colonel. Next to the Colonel sat two empty seats.

"Is Michael coming?" Cee Cee asked, careful not to sound overexcited. She rarely paid attention to Bucky's work anymore, but everyone in Nashville knew about Michael. He was an outlier, a curve breaker. He stood so obviously at the pinnacle of the sexual hierarchy, other men felt honored when he flirted with their wives. He was the first artist on Bucky's roster Cee Cee had ever wanted to meet. Bucky glared at his wife, ignoring her question, and texted Martha: *Where the fuck are you?*

Over the polite din of clinking silverware, Cee Cee made small talk with the Colonel. She noted the way he took care of the crease in his Tom Ford suit pants when he crossed his legs, and the high shine on his Bruno Maglia shoes. Men in Nashville didn't dress like this. His waxy skin was pulled too taut. It lacked the lines it should have had for a man his age, giving him a look of inhuman youth.

"You're a good sport, sweetheart, letting him drag you to these dreadful dinners," the Colonel said.

"Am I?" Cee Cee said.

The Colonel smoothed his hair with a manicured hand, the nails painted with clear polish. "I guess it's just nice to be invited anywhere at this age," he said with a sad smile.

"Well, I hope it hasn't come to that," Cee Cee said. "People still love Sam, don't they?"

"Here's a secret," the Colonel said with a grimace. "In this town, love is just another name for money, and money is another name for power. The sooner you accept that, the less disappointed you'll be."

"Well," Cee Cee said, "I know people love Sam, and I know they also love Michael. You should put them together. Old country meets new country. That's love, power, and money right there."

"Oh, yeah?" the Colonel replied, looking at her with condescending approval, like she was a child who had just done long division.

"That's what I'd do. Send 'em to Europe to work out the kinks, then hit the summer circuit here and make a fortune."

"Smart little cookie," the Colonel said and patted her hand.

Cee Cee stabbed at a crouton in her salad, wondering what she had to do to make someone, anyone, take her ideas seriously, when she heard a commotion at the front of the room. She felt him before she saw him. Michael, tall and muscular and lithe, wearing black leather pants that laced up at the crotch, a black belt with a Western silver buckle the size of a tea saucer, and an ornate shirt with piping around the collar and cuffs—men didn't dress like him here, either—his hair flowing, a cigarette burning between his long fingers. He swaggered in with two girls on his arm. Martha trotted after him, his exasperated babysitter. "I hope we haven't missed the show," she said to Bucky, hurriedly taking her seat. Michael remained standing, his eyes fixed on Cee Cee. "Martha, my dear," he said, "how many times do I have to tell you the show doesn't start until I arrive?" Then he grabbed a passing waiter's arm and said, "Two chairs for my dates, please."

"Right away, sir," the waiter said. "And, um, sir, there's no smoking here, sir."

"Is that so?" Michael asked, exhaling a cloud of smoke.

The waiter slowly backed away, and Michael turned to the table.

"These are my friends, Lily and Samantha," Michael said. Everyone stood up, so Cee Cee did too. Hands were grasped all around. "Of course, you know Martha," Michael added.

As Cee Cee watched Michael shake hand after hand, she noticed an uncharacteristic stiffness come over him. All of a sudden, he looked like a little boy stuck somewhere between terror and awe. It didn't take long to understand the reason: Michael was shaking Sam Rogers's hand, and holding it like it was made of diamonds. It always amazed and delighted Cee Cee when the biggest stars turned out to be the biggest fans. It proved that, even though the business was rotten to the core, there was still something beautiful about music, something incorruptible.

She had an opening line poised on her lips waiting for Michael, but before Michael reached her, the Colonel took him and Bucky aside for an intense, whispered conversation. An awkward silence fell at the table as Michael's dates took their seats. Cee Cee tried to break the tension. "I just saw you on the cover of *Vogue*," she said to Lily. "What was that like?" Lily just smiled. Cee Cee tried again. "What's *he* like?" she said, pointing to Michael.

"Alright, I guess."

"Just alright? Come on. Spill the tea."

"Don't have any," Lily answered flatly. "He never talks about himself."

The talk had petered out again by the time Michael took his seat. Staring at Cee Cee from across the table, his eyes lingered on the deep neckline of her tight black dress. He reached over and grazed her hand as he took her wine glass.

"Do you mind?" he asked. "Hair of the dog."

Before she could answer, the lights dimmed. A portly, balding man with a head like a bulldog stepped to the podium. "For those of you who don't know me," he said and paused for effect, "how the hell did you get in here?" Polite laughter flitted around the room like butterflies. "Seriously, I'm Joel Katz, and it's an honor to be here tonight. We're here to raise money for a great cause and to celebrate a man who truly needs no introduction: Bucky Porter. Bucky changed the country music business by getting Willie Nelson the same royalty rate as a pop singer— never done before for a country artist. Wait a minute, Bucky didn't do that. I did." The polite laughter returned. "But seriously, folks, Bucky is proof that if you do enough good in this town, you'll be rewarded in kind. Unless you're Jewish." Polite, uncomfortable laughter. "Most of you in this room tonight will have to take my word on that. But Bucky deserves this tribute, and so, here is his favorite artist singing his favorite song. Ladies and gentlemen, I give you Sam Rogers."

The room erupted in applause. Sam took the stage and began to sing Neil Young's "Harvest Moon." The audience was riveted by the performance, but Cee Cee could only look at Michael. He looked like a child meeting Santa Claus. And indeed, Michael had never been so close to his idol, the man whose picture he spent hours upon hours staring at on record sleeves from the time he was a child, the man who connected him to his mother and eased the pain of her loss. This wasn't the Sam Rogers he was used to seeing, the svelte, dark haired, brooding, country heartthrob. This man was paunchy, gray, wrinkled. He was shorter than Michael expected him to be, older. But he was still Sam *fucking* Rogers.

Michael shot up from his seat and disappeared. As Sam reached the chorus, Michael appeared on stage. The roar of the crowd was so loud, Sam was shaken. He could do nothing but introduce Michael and pretend it was all planned. Michael snatched the microphone out of its cradle and stared at Cee Cee, singing only to her.

The song ended with a standing ovation. Then the crowd mobbed the stage, grabbing, touching, tearing, clutching Michael. He pushed through the throng back to the table. Sitting next to Cee Cee, ignoring the commotion around him, he said, "I don't believe we've met. I'm Michael."

"I know," she said and laughed nervously. She couldn't see Martha staring daggers at Michael, willing him to hear her thoughts: *What the fuck are you doing? That's your boss's wife.* She couldn't see the Colonel, his eyes two burning black coals, thinking behind his impassive mask, *This boy's going to be trouble.* All she could see was Michael.

Coffee service broke the spell. Cee Cee politely excused herself and put one foot in front of the other, staring at the carpet, as she walked to the bathroom. In the bathroom, she splashed water on her face. Then she heard giggling behind her. "You're not supposed to be in here," said a girl's voice. Cee Cee raised her eyes to the mirror and saw Michael standing behind her.

"What are you doing here?" she said to his reflection.

"I came to see you."

"This is the ladies' room."

"I'll leave if you want me to."

Cee Cee turned and faced him. Michael approached slowly. He backed her against the sink and leaned over her, his arms raised over her head, his hands resting on the mirror. He looked her deeply in the eyes. "Am I making you uncomfortable?" he asked. Cee Cee blushed. She couldn't speak. "I want to taste you," he said, and bent down and kissed her.

His lips were warm and soft. And then they were gone.

"Until next time," Michael said over his shoulder.

Later that night, while Bucky snored next to her in bed, Cee Cee heard a light tapping at her bedroom door. Opening her groggy eyes, she struggled to make out shapes in the darkness. Thrown over the chair next to the bed was the black dress she had worn to the gala dinner. Crumpled in the corner was Bucky's suit. She'd have to pick it up tomorrow and have it dry cleaned. She felt her stomach tighten at the thought. She was tired of being a glorified maid. What good was all that money if you were too paranoid to use it? And what secrets did Bucky fear a maid or cleaning service would uncover? Again came the tapping. The door creaked on its hinges as it slowly swung open and revealed Michael, his arm rested casually on the door frame, his white teeth glinting in the moonlight.

"How'd you get in here?" Cee Cee said, breathless.

"Same way everyone does. Through the front door."

"What are you doing here?"

"Isn't that obvious?"

In three quick strides he was at her side, his hand caressing her hair. Cee Cee sat up in bed and softly took his hand from her head. "He's right there," she said, gesturing toward Bucky. "Even if I wanted to, there's no way we can—"

"Then you don't want to?"

"I didn't say that. But this is crazy."

"Exactly."

Michael stripped off his shirt, unclasped his belt, and unlaced his leather pants, then took her hand again and placed it on his body. Feeling his arousal, Cee Cee couldn't think to speak. She lifted the sheets and pulled him toward her. Then, finding her voice, she said, "If he wakes up, he'll kill us." Michael slipped into bed next to her and ran his hand down her body, then up again to her chest, and inside her nightgown to touch her soft flesh. He turned her away from him and lay spooning her, kissing her neck. With expert deftness, he tugged her panties to the side and pressed himself against her. "You can still say no," he whispered in her ear. She turned to kiss his lips. "Yes," she whispered, then bit the pillow to stop herself from screaming with pleasure.

Somehow, Michael moved without making the slightest motion to disturb Bucky sleeping three feet away. Somehow, he produced a symphony without making a sound. Cee Cee rose and rose, higher and higher, until she fell back against Michael, panting, dizzy, quenched.

She awoke with a gasp, her right hand stuffed between her trembling legs. Bucky stirred next to her, rolled over, and began snoring again. She felt a lump against her back and turned to find nothing but a pillow. Easing out of bed, she tiptoed downstairs, poured a glass of water, drank it in one gulp, and curled up on the couch, hoping the dream would return.

5

GOOD OLE DAYS

"THIS AIN'T THE WAY IT used to be," Sam Rogers muttered, sitting in the Colonel's office the day after the T.J. Martell dinner, trying to accept the news he had just received. His latest album, *Back in the Saddle*, was a failure. No hits, low sales, little interest. His label was dropping him.

"It's just a bump in the road," said the Colonel. "Everyone saw how good you were last night. You had 'em on their feet, howlin' in the aisles."

"That wasn't for me, Colonel," Sam said. "They were howlin' for that boy."

"All they care about is digital," said the Colonel, lost in his own thoughts. "Digital this, digital that. They don't understand the way we used to do things. I'll call Jack White. He loves the old masters. He'll know what to do."

Good old Colonel, thought Sam. *He still believes.*

"It's over," Sam said, gazing at his friend's waxy Botox face and realizing how old they both had become. Then the Colonel's face turned red and he began jabbing his finger in the air, shouting that Sam didn't know what the hell he was talking about, and thank God the Colonel still had some sense in his head, or else they'd both be out on their asses. "I'm making the call," the Colonel said, finishing his tirade by punching a number into his phone.

That's how he did it all these years, Sam thought. *He scared 'em into submission.*

Sam gave his friend a grave stare. "Colonel, this ain't even the worst news I heard today." Silence filled the room as Sam worked up the nerve to say the word.

Cancer.

The Colonel's face lost all color. He dropped his phone, and it clattered to the ground. Two things scared him—death and irrelevance. In a way, they were the same thing. He moved his lips, but no words would come. Finally, he said, "What about a greatest hits compilation? I can call RCA and explain the situation. You're a legacy artist. They'll help us—for the good times."

"Goddamnit, Chance," Sam said, "we already done that." Sam hadn't called the Colonel by his real name in forty years of partnership. It snapped the Colonel to attention. "Remember when I got sick from the booze?" Sam continued. "Did they offer to help me? No, they put out a story about how I was going to die, and then they used it to sell some bullshit 'oldies but goldies' record. You know as well as I do that this business is a trap. I'm tired of getting caught in it. Can't I at least die in peace this time?"

He read the question in the Colonel's eyes. *How bad is it?*

"Nothing's certain yet," he said. "They have to do more tests."

The Colonel stared at Sam in silence. The man who always knew what to say, who relied on this gift to run circles around his opponents, who could talk a man off a ledge—or talk a man *onto* one, if needed—was finally at a loss for words.

Sam stretched his stiff legs and said, "Remind me of those good times you were talkin' about, ol' buddy."

The Colonel's mouth hung open like a dying fish. His eyes were far away. With a shake of his square head, he returned to the room. "Nonsense," he said. "You've got an interview in fifteen minutes. "We're going to turn this thing around."

"What interview?"

"Some kid is coming. Works for a blog. I can't remember the damn name, they got so many of them these days."

"I ever tell you about the time at RCA—"

"Save it for the interview," the Colonel said.

Fifteen minutes later, a young man with a peach-fuzz mustache snuck his pimpled face through the door, took out a pad and a pen, and prepared to ask Sam questions. His hands shook with nerves.

"What magazine did you say you worked for again?" Sam asked.

The kid answered, but Sam wasn't listening. He didn't even own a computer. Whoever this kid worked for, whatever story he wrote, Sam would never see it.

"So how did you get your start?" the kid asked.

This is the best the Colonel could get me, Sam thought, and with a sigh, he told the same story he had told so many times that he no longer knew if it was true.

"It was 1972. I was mopping the bathrooms at RCA and ran into Loretta Lynn crying over the sink. I said, 'Miss Lynn, can I help you?' And she said, 'Son, don't ever fall in love. You'll just get used like a secondhand guitar.' And I went into the janitor's closet and wrote my first song. When I came out, I nearly knocked over Charley Pride."

"That song was your first hit, 'Second Hand Guitar'?" the kid asked.

"You got it," Sam said and warbled a bit of the chorus:

> You can sing her a tune and then steal her little heart
>
> You can make her to swoon while you're kissin' in the car
>
> You can shoot for the moon, if you miss you'll hit the stars
>
> But if you fall in love, you'll just end up used, like a secondhand guitar

Sam seemed to speak to himself now as he told the story of how the Colonel scraped together enough money to cut a demo and took it to Diamond Management. They set up a session at RCA's hallowed Studio B, the most important room in the world as far as Sam was concerned.

The Colonel watched his old friend tell the story and noticed a gleam in his eye—*Is he crying?* He realized he hadn't allowed himself a moment to reminisce in forty years. Even when he spoke of the past, it was in carefully crafted sound bites, worn smooth like marble from the telling. Losers thought about the past. The Colonel moved forward relentlessly, like a shark. But now he followed Sam back to the summer of 1972.

Back then the Colonel was interning at Diamond Management, which handled the biggest stars in country music, when he met a gangly, dirty, tall, handsome kid with an acoustic guitar, waiting for his spot at an open mic in a dive bar on the outskirts of town. That was the first time he ever introduced himself as "The Colonel."

"Strange name," Sam said, and the Colonel explained his plan: he was going to be the biggest manager in the music business, bigger than Colonel Tom Parker was with Elvis. He just needed his Elvis. "Why don't you stay for my set?" Sam said. Though his songs needed help, and his voice needed training, his confidence was enormous. The Colonel followed Sam backstage and said, "Want to be rich and famous?"

At twenty-one, the Colonel was two years older than Sam, and Sam showed him the unthinking deference he believed were due to age and wisdom. Sam only cared for music. The Colonel only cared for power. Such was the extent of their business arrangement. The Colonel knew he could sell Sam, and he wore out a pair of boots walking from label to label trying to do it. When he wasn't thrown out of the building, he was ignored until he left on his own. But when Sam began making a name for himself in the clubs on Music Row, the labels were only too happy to welcome his wispy, effeminate manager. They mistook him for an easy mark.

But the Colonel knew the secrets buried in their hearts. The first man he ever slept with was forty and married and one of the most powerful men in the music business. They met in Riverfront Park and had sex in the woods. In college, he spent countless blackout nights on Commerce Street in the Jungle and Juanita's Place. Every night it was the same: the Music Row men entered in their business suits, pretending they didn't know where they were, scanning the room to make sure no one recognized them, then settling into a seat at the bar, drinking their courage. They talked in code like spies, talked around what they wanted, hoping he would understand them, and then followed him to the bathroom, and they trembled while he penetrated them in a dirty stall. He paid his rent with the money they exchanged for discretion.

Working at Diamond Management added a new dimension to the game: now he saw these men during the day too, and he felt their fear every time they sidled past him in the hallway or exited the elevator on the wrong floor just to get away from him. He knew them in a way their own wives and children could never know them. And he studied them too. By the time he began working with Sam, the Colonel had learned to schedule meetings late in the day, after the executives had consumed two fingers of scotch for breakfast and drained a few martinis with lunch and treated themselves to a little four o'clock pick-me-up. In his pocket he kept a running tape recorder and, after meetings, he listened and learned from his mistakes. He did this at several labels of varying sizes before approaching the one he and Sam really wanted: RCA.

The A&R man at RCA had once paid the Colonel twenty dollars to ejaculate on him in a bathroom stall at the Jungle. When he entered the man's office, the Colonel pretended he had never seen him before, and when the meeting reached a sticking point, the Colonel asked for a drink, knowing the man wouldn't let him drink alone. Watching for the moment the man turned his back to pour the drinks, the Colonel silently closed the office door and approached from behind, whispering into the man's ear, "How can we work this out so everyone is happy?" He pressed his body against the man's back, slid his arm around, and began to unbuckle his belt. "It's just business," he whispered, sliding his hand down the man's pants. "You give me something I want, and I give you something you want."

When it was done, the Colonel sauntered to the man's desk and lifted a picture showing a smiling blonde woman, her hair in a bob, holding two pink baby boys. "Technology is incredible," he said, slipping the tape recorder out of his pocket and laying it on the desk.

"When I was a young'un like those rascals there, if I wanted to hear music, I had to turn on the radio. Nowadays, it's easy to just make a tape and play it anywhere."

He walked out with a contract unprecedented in the history of country music. The Colonel, not the label, owned Sam's copyrights. Royalties would be split 40 percent to the Colonel, 50 percent to the label, and 10 percent to Sam. The Colonel would have final say on the songs Sam recorded, the singles he released, the timing of the releases, the routes of his tours—in short, everything.

Sam came to the Colonel's apartment that night, and they sat on the Colonel's scratchy tweed couch and celebrated with a twelve-pack of beer and a quart of tequila. When he saw the liquor make Sam's brooding eyes start to twinkle, the Colonel made his move. Sam was a bad kisser, so the Colonel unzipped Sam's pants and swallowed him. It was the first time he had ever known love with sex.

The next morning, Sam awoke with a terrible hangover. From the piercing, pained look in Sam's eyes, the Colonel knew he had made a mistake. Sam had a girlfriend. He had always thought of himself as straight. A man like that, the Colonel knew from experience, had to be eased into the truth. You couldn't just take him there in one night. The shock was too great. The Colonel tried to smooth the awkwardness, but Sam fled the house in shame. From that day, the Colonel locked his feelings away in the place he had kept hidden since he was a child and waited until Sam was ready. But even after Sam began openly sleeping with men, he was never ready. And so they never spoke of it again. Only once, at some dreadful industry party in the eighties, did the matter arise when a drunk CBS executive cornered the Colonel and Sam and said, "Hey Colonel, I think the reason you work so hard for Sam is because he won't let you fuck him."

The memory, and the burning shame, broke the Colonel's reverie. His attention came back to Sam and the interview in his office.

"Tell me about the album *Bicentennial*," the kid asked. "A lot of people consider it your masterpiece. You released it in 1976 at a tough time for America. How did you capture the mood of the country?"

The kid doesn't want to talk about the new music, Sam thought. *I'm a dinosaur. No present, no future—only past.*

Sam said a few scattered words about his most famous work, and then the interview ended. He sank into the chair, exhausted.

"Make sure you mention the new album," the Colonel said as he ushered the kid out the door. When the Colonel came back to the room, the two men stared at each other in uneasy silence. Just then, the intercom buzzed. "Martha wants a minute," said a tinny voice.

The Colonel exhaled, saved by the bell. He puffed out his chest as Martha stepped into the office. The lecherous twinkle in his eye was overdone. Sam felt embarrassed for his friend. "Well, sweetheart," the Colonel said, "whatcha got?"

Martha smiled her impenetrable smile, pulled up Michael's song on her phone, and pressed play. When it was over, she said, "The hottest star in country music wants to record this song with Sam."

"Hey, Sam," the Colonel said, his eyes flashing with the old bravado, "you feel like making a comeback?"

6

HOLY, HOLY, HOLY

SUNDAY MORNING, BUCKY SAT IN a stained oak pew facing a spartan altar, wearing a different navy-blue Hugo Boss suit from the night before with different Ferragamo loafers shined to a high sheen. The pew was as uncomfortable as sin.

This was the Church of Christ on Granny White Pike, and anyone who was anyone in Nashville belonged to it. Bucky found it a comforting, strange church. They attempted to worship exactly as the original Christians did, based on the accounts in the Bible, and except for the giant video screen above the altar, which gave the room the aura of a sporting event, it was the closest thing to the Last Supper this side of Jerusalem. No musical instruments, no gilded filigree, no priestly hierarchy—just man and God, toe to toe.

But there was always a hierarchy. Bucky looked at Cee Cee sitting next to him, so prim and proper, like a little girl in her Sunday dress. As a church elder, Bucky had the sacred duty of standing at the altar and reading passages from the Bible to the congregation. Often they'd get home after a service, and Cee Cee would corner him. "Why can't *I* read a passage at church? It's always *Brother* Bucky, would you lead us in prayer? *Brother* Bucky, will you share the word with us?" And Bucky would say, "Don't start with this again. 'Wives, submit yourselves unto your own husbands as unto the Lord. For the husband is the head of the wife, even as Christ is the head of the church: and he is the savior of the body. Therefore as the church is subject unto Christ, so let the wives be to their own husbands in every thing.'"

That always stopped her. The Bible offered little ammunition to a woman.

Today he was to read from his favorite book, Psalms. King David was a musician, and Bucky understood musicians. King David was unfaithful to his wife, but God forgave him because he had a good heart. Bucky believed he had a good heart.

He jogged his knee nervously. Cee Cee looked at him out of the corner of her eye and said, "Nervous? You've done this a hundred times." Bucky gave her a benevolent smile, took her hand in his, patted it, and placed it on his knee. It wasn't the reading that made him nervous. He was waiting for someone to arrive. She didn't need to know that.

As if on a silent command, the churchgoers broke into song, and the mass began. The voices of the believers rose like incense to soothe their vengeful God.

Lord, you are worthy of praise.

The melody became a living, breathing thing as more voices joined in, weaving harmonies into a rich tapestry of song. Bucky always found it a bit eerie, all those voices with no instruments behind them. He didn't quite understand the prohibition. Didn't many of the Psalms begin with specific instructions for instruments—the harp, the timbrel, the shofar, the psaltery? Then again, the first Christians worshiped without these instruments. That was in the Bible, and so it was true and good.

As Bucky sifted these thoughts, mindlessly singing, he smelled the musty brown aroma of old cigar smoke mixed with Tom Ford Oud Wood *eau de cologne* and knew the man he was waiting for had arrived. He sang a little louder as the Colonel shuffled into the pew and sat next to him. The Colonel sang too. His voice was deep and rich as if his lungs were old leather bellows dipped in whiskey.

Praise him, praise him, tell of his excellent greatness.

The church was in full throat now. No one noticed when two voices dropped out of the choir and began to whisper to each other.

"Michael's written a song he wants to sing with Sam," whispered the Colonel.

"Good boy," whispered Bucky, his eyes gleaming. "I want to buy Sam's back catalog from RCA, and I want to sign him for everything moving forward. Can you get him out of his contract?"

"Hell if I can't."

Hail him, hail him, highest archangels in glory.

"You think Sam's got another album in him?"

"I'll scare it out of him if I have to."

"Either way. We record this duet, we do a deluxe thirtieth anniversary release of *Bicentennial*, we send them out on tour together, we're gonna be very rich."

How great God's love, both strong and everlasting.

"Let's talk terms."

As Bucky began to whisper his reply, the singing ceased. He waited patiently while Brother James, a lithe man of fifty-five with the chipper air of the saved, trotted up to the altar and led the congregation in a prayer and a reading from the Bible. When the singing began again, Bucky leaned toward the Colonel and whispered, "It's a three-sixty deal: we handle record promotion, tour support, merchandise, digital, streaming, licensing, copyrights. You'll get ten percent of ninety percent."

"Hell no," the Colonel hissed. "I want all merchandise and fifty percent on physical and digital sales, plus right of refusal on licensing."

"Colonel, that's not how things are done anymore."

He will come to judge this world. He will come to exact his wrath on this world.

The Colonel sighed heavily. "You gotta sweeten this deal for me, Bucky, else Sam ain't gonna take it."

"What do you want?"

"Thirty percent. And keep Martha as Michael's babysitter."

"Done."

A mighty fortress is our God.

The collection came around. Bucky pulled out a thick wad of hundred dollar bills, peeled one off, and put it in the basket. He peeled off another and handed it to Cee Cee. She dropped it in the basket. Brother James rose to the altar again and said, "Now, we'll have a reading from Psalms from Brother Bucky. First, let us bow our heads. Father, I pray for Brother Bucky as he delivers your message, that you use him to pour out your truth to our lives...."

As Brother James prayed, Bucky nudged the Colonel with his elbow and said, "One more thing. I got this new artist, a chick, Shelby Andrews. I want her to be the opener on tour."

"Is she any good?" the Colonel asked.

"Hell of a voice. Good songwriter. Plus—" Bucky pulled out his cell phone, no longer listening to Brother James's prayer (*Father, I pray that your holy spirit will be in our church today*) and scrolled through his pictures (*Father, I hope that you will help us every day to live what we profess, that we are believers in Christ*) until he found one of Shelby in her panties (*Father, we love you so much, and we are so thankful for all you do*) laying in a disheveled bed, her hair spread on a pillow, her skin creamy white, her nipples erect (*But most of all, Father, we are thankful for Jesus, who died on the cross for our sins*) and showed it to the Colonel (*In Christ's name, we pray*).

The Colonel looked at the phone and said, "Amen."

7

WAIT, WAIT

SITTING IN THE WAITING ROOM at the Tennessee Fertility Institute, Cee Cee stared at all the couples waiting, just like her, for a miracle. She couldn't help but notice she was the only woman waiting alone. Bucky had an important meeting with Michael and the Colonel, but he said he'd try to make it in time.

Of course he didn't.

She put her earphones in, hit shuffle on her Spotify app, and felt a pleasant jolt of surprise to hear her guitar bashing out the first chords of her hit single. She could still see herself in the studio with Dave Cobb and a crack group of session musicians. The first three hours of the session she spent nearly doubled over with nerves, making mistake after mistake, until the musicians formed a circle around her, put their hands in the center, and the drummer said, "Get your hand in, Cee Cee. You're here for a reason, and we're here to back you up. Believe in yourself." They all shouted on the count of three, and the next take was the one they released.

The song still sounded fresh to her ears, although she couldn't help but smile at her naivete. She had written it for Bucky:

> *A good man is so hard to find,*
>
> *So don't you dare go stealin' mine,*
>
> *Cuz my man loves me all the time,*
>
> *And a good man is so hard to find.*

In the middle of Cee Cee's guitar solo, her phone rang. "Hi, Mom," she said. "I'm about to jump in the shower. Can I call you later?" She hated lying to her mother, but she also felt sick imagining telling her mother where she really was, hearing the disappointment and the judgment in her mother's voice because Cee Cee couldn't even do this one thing, the simplest thing, the thing every woman had done before her, the thing that made a woman a woman.

She hung up as the doctor called her into the examining room and put her through an inquisition: Are you married? Do you have sex? How often? Can your husband ejaculate? Have you ever been pregnant? What happened to the fetus?

After a brusque physical examination, the doctor explained Cee Cee's options: ovulation induction, artificial insemination, in vitro fertilization, intracytoplasmic sperm injection, intracytoplasmic morphologically selected sperm injection, donor conception. Cee Cee's head spun with the jargon, while the doctor rushed on headlong: "I recommend we put you on birth control to down regulate your cycle, plus a nasal spray to inhibit certain hormones. You're going to go on a little emotional roller coaster, but once we've got your cycle under control, there's an injection you can administer yourself into your stomach once a day to build up the follicles, grow the eggs, and hopefully produce a viable embryo. Any questions?"

Cee Cee realized she had been clutching the arms of her chair so hard her knuckles were white. She released the pressure and swallowed hard. This was what she wanted, and yet she couldn't understand why she felt so...repulsed. "I need some time to think about it," she said.

"Of course," the doctor said. "Discuss it with your husband. We're here when you need us."

Inside the Colonel's opulent office in Green Hills, Martha paced the room, tidying and straightening, preparing for the meeting to come. She took her shoes off to walk over Colonel's antique Oriental rug, fluffed the pillows on his pink velvet couch, straightened the framed picture of Jesus of the Sacred Heart on the wall and the two cowhide chairs in front of his massive oak desk where a phone, a lamp, a computer, a silver goblet full of pens and pencils sat, and an award from the chamber of commerce. She couldn't do anything about the smell of cigar smoke that oozed from the walls or the stinking, yapping, slobbering, ever-present bulldogs, Elvis and Dolly. The Colonel let them roam free like spoiled children. They barked at Martha now as she paced to their side of the room.

"Elvis, Dolly, back to bed!" the Colonel shouted, and the dogs tottered to the corner and slumped down, wheezing, into their dog beds—blue suede for Elvis and pink chenille adorned with rhinestones for Dolly. Then, turning to Martha, the Colonel snapped, "Sit down, woman."

Martha took a seat on the pink couch and surveyed the room. Dr. Robert, the Colonel's personal fixer and procurer, stood silently in the corner. He was a tall, elegant man with silver hair swept up in a high wave above his forehead. Over the years he had gained a reputation in the business for being able to get anything, anywhere, at any time.

Bucky and Sam sat in front of her, a cowhide chair apiece. She looked at the back of Bucky's head and felt a rush of disgust. At first Bucky was so kind. She had come to him four years ago, crying after some verbal lashing from the Colonel she couldn't even remember now, and poured out her heart. She told him how much she hated the Colonel's mood swings, hated the way he never took her ideas seriously, hated the way her career had stalled under his indifference. Bucky gave her gifts and promised her a job in A&R to get away from the Colonel, so she let him have what he wanted. This wasn't the way her career played out in her dreams, but then again, she understood the world. You did what you had to do. And despite Bucky's physical shortcomings, she began to look forward to their afternoon "meetings," during which Bucky would close and lock his door and sit at his desk working, while she climbed underneath it and fellated him.

But then something switched in him, and he began making lewd innuendos in the presence of artists and other executives. He said he wanted to "fuck the Brooklyn out of her." This she would not accept.

Martha returned to the Colonel because even the lowest rung on the ladder was better than no rung at all, and to her various areas of expertise she added keeping her thoughts to herself. She stared at the plaque hung on the wall that said in curly script, "To thine own self be true." *Bullshit*, she thought, looking at the Colonel with his hair dyed a ridiculous shade of brown and his puffer-fish face with its fake Botox smile. It was just another thought he'd never hear.

And yet the Colonel was true to himself in his own way. He had made the bargain long ago. He always knew he was different. As a young boy, he wasn't interested in playing sports, and he devoured his mother's fashion magazines when they came in the mail. This caught the notice of his fire-and-brimstone preacher father, who spared not the rod lest he spoil the child. Many was the night the boy was forced to kneel on the hardwood floor and recite Leviticus 18:22: If a man also lie with mankind, as he lieth with a woman, both of them have committed an abomination: they shall surely be put to death; their blood shall be upon them.

The Colonel learned how to please his father, outwardly erasing any trace of his true self, while carrying on a secret inner life the old man would never know about. This capacity to be two opposite people at once served him well in the music business. He knew how to be whatever the person in front of him wanted him to be while behind his eyes, he pursued his own ends and desires. He knew the most powerful kind of control was letting others believe they were in control.

After years of great pain and shame, he acquiesced to his father's insistence that he attend Lipscomb University, an evangelical college that was so strict, dancing was forbidden. He signed a vow of abstinence until marriage. He married a stunning blonde, a former Miss Tennessee. They set up house at Belle Meade. They shared a love of Jesus.

All the while, the Colonel carried on torrid love affairs with men. Managing a touring musician made it easy—nothing but one-night-stands. Dr. Robert made it easy, supplying an endless buffet of eager young men. The Colonel made sure to call his wife every night. An hour on the phone was a small sacrifice for an evening alone. Not alone, of course, but unreachable, untrackable, unwatchable, as he sampled the doctor's offerings.

When he'd come home from the road, his wife always found receipts in his pocket for Swinging Richards, the gay gentlemen's club in Atlanta. One night, she confronted him, receipts in hand. "Don't be ridiculous; they belong to one of the roadies," he lied and quoted Kings 15:12: "He took away all the Sodomites out of the land and removed all the idols his father had made." She believed him. But the next time, it was harder to believe. And the next time. And the next time. And the tenth time, she backed up a U-Haul, emptied out the furniture, packed her belongings, and ran off with the pastor of the church, never to be heard from again. The only thing she left was a tacky reproduction of da Vinci's *The Last Supper* hanging above the dining room table.

The Colonel pretended to be heartbroken, and in a way he was. The marriage was a perfect cover. But his father was dead, and with that came freedom. Now the inner life, which for so long had been jailed inside, began to escape through the cracks. In public he blamed his wife for breaking up the marriage, and his lips formed the right words: "Whoremongers and adulterers God will judge." No one believed him, but the Colonel didn't care. He had become the most powerful manager in Nashville. He was a Goliath in a town of Davids. He dared them all to sling the first stone.

Martha knew all of this, knew things the Colonel didn't want her to know and didn't know she knew. She waited for her advantage, though she wasn't sure it would ever come.

"Where's that boy?" the Colonel said, looking at his watch. "He's an hour and a half late."

"The show doesn't start until I arrive," Martha said in a cartoonish Australian accent that broke the room into laughter. Just then the door swung open, and Michael waltzed in wearing a white Hanro T-shirt, Levi's blue jeans, and brown Lucchese boots. His long hair was tucked beneath a baseball cap. He wore thick-rimmed Armani glasses. It cost money to look so casual.

The Colonel shot daggers at him with his eyes, but as usual, Michael seemed to walk on air, impervious to all feelings but his own. "Morning, mates," he said, and although it was half past two, no one corrected him. He plopped down on the couch next to Martha and reclined with his hands laced behind his head.

"Everyone knows why we're here," the Colonel said. "Michael's got a song he'd like to sing with Sam. Well, Sam is mighty pleased and interested to do it. But he ain't heard the song yet, and he don't just sing anything." The Colonel was laying on the Southern schtick heavier than usual, Martha thought. It seemed he was trying to say to Michael without saying it: "You're not one of us, Aussie boy, and this isn't your show anymore." He turned to Martha and said, "Sweetheart, hit play there, will you, and let us hear the song now."

When the song ended, all eyes turned to Sam. Martha could feel Michael holding his breath next to her. Sam gave one small nod of his head, and the Colonel began handing out cigars, skipping Martha— "This ain't nothing for a little lady such as yourself," he said. He held one out for Michael, and Michael took it, feeling like he had just signed an unwritten contract. As the room filled with smoke, Bucky grinned and said, "Michael, tell me about those girls you brought to the dinner."

"A gentleman doesn't kiss and tell," Michael said.

"What the hell does that have to do with us?" Bucky burst into lascivious laughter. "Come on, I'm a married man. I gotta live vicariously."

"Like that ever stopped you," the Colonel muttered.

"What was that one chick's name?" Bucky continued, ignoring the Colonel. "The model. Lily? And her friend. You fucked them both, I bet."

Michael smiled.

"You dog," Bucky growled. "Come on. Details! Details!"

"You'd be surprised, Bucky," Michael said. "Sex with a model isn't all it's cracked up to be."

"Hot on the runway, cold in the sheets, huh? Then why do you keep her around?"

"She finds other girls," Michael said quietly, a grin playing at the edges of his lips. "Models are great at that, you know."

Michael could see he had Bucky dangling at the end of a string, and he enjoyed watching him squirm as he toyed with the string. But Bucky continued to demand blow-by-blow accounts of his escapades, and Michael, feeling Martha stiffen next to him, said, "Come on, Bucky," with air of finality in his voice.

"Alright big shot," Bucky said, "here's a little wager for you. I know a guy runs a modeling agency around here. I bet you a thousand bucks you can't fuck 'em all within the month."

"Ah, Bucky," Michael sighed, "I don't want to take your money."

Bucky and the Colonel burst out laughing. Martha sat as still and silent as a statue.

"Well, shit, I propose a celebration," Bucky said. He took out his phone and hit a button. The harsh ringing on the speakerphone gave way to a honey-sweet voice. "Yes, hello," said Cee Cee.

Michael's guts quivered at the sound.

"Cee Cee, what would you say to a dinner party tonight, say six o'clock?" Bucky said.

"You can't keep doing this to me," Cee Cee said, exasperated. "This is going to ruin my whole day."

"Honey, you're on speaker," Bucky said.

"Oh…sorry. Well, what do you want?"

"I'll leave that up to you, dear. Just make sure you get enough food. It'll be me, Sam, the Colonel, and Michael."

The line went silent. "Hello?" Bucky said. "Did we lose you?"

Cee Cee's voice came back sweet and eager: "Six o'clock then."

Bucky hung up. With a gleam in his eye, he leaned back, put his feet on the Colonel's desk, puffed his cigar, and intoned, "'Wives, submit yourselves unto your own husbands, as unto the Lord.' Ephesians 5:22." The last thing Michael heard as he left the office was the sound of men laughing.

8

DINNER AND
A SONG

THAT EVENING, CEE CEE SPENT an hour in her closet trying to find the right outfit. She had noticed Michael looking down her dress at the T.J. Martell dinner, so she picked a white dress tailored to follow the curves of her hips and ass, with three-quarter sleeves, cut conservatively just past the knees, and a neckline that plunged just far enough to leave a man speechless.

At half past seven, Michael knocked at the door. He was surprised when no one answered. He stood on the portico, marveling at the Doric columns, which led the eye up to the second-floor balustrades. He didn't understand Nashville's obsession with ancient Greece.

He knocked again and heard a harried voice from inside, "Coming!" The door opened, and Cee Cee appeared with an apron covering her dress, her hair charmingly disheveled. Michael felt his guts quiver again. "Won't you come in?" she said and lingered for a moment to give him a chance to see her.

Michael followed Cee Cee through the foyer and into the empty dining room. "They're running late," she said apologetically. "Take a seat. I'll bring out the wine." Michael, intoxicated by her scent, followed her into the kitchen. She nearly jumped when she realized he was behind her. "I'm glad none of you knows how to be on time," she said, regaining her composure. "Gives me a chance to get all this ready," and she gestured at the messy kitchen, the sink piled high with grimy saucepans.

Michael approached her the way he had done in the Omni bathroom and backed her against the kitchen counter. "You know, this is my home, not a hotel bathroom," she said, holding his gaze, a hand resting lightly at his elbow. Then, grabbing a handful of silverware and cloth napkins, she went to set the table, Michael following at her heels.

"So, how did the meeting go?" Cee Cee asked.

"Gangbusters," he said. "We've got a deal. Can I help with that?"

"No, I've got it," she said, laying out the last of the napkins and brushing against him as she walked into the living room to place a bouquet of flowers in a vase.

Michael chased her to the living room. "Beautiful flowers," he said, picking one from the vase and inhaling its scent. "What are they?"

"Peonies," Cee Cee said. "My favorite." She took off her apron and excused herself back into the kitchen to check on the dinner, walking slowly so Michael had time to study her. Needing stronger ammunition for the battle, Michael entered Bucky's guitar room, selected a 1937 Martin D-28, and went looking for Cee Cee. He found her back in the living room, sitting on the couch, checking her phone.

"You know how much Bucky paid for that guitar you're holding?" she said. "Two and a half million. And he can't even play."

"Pity," Michael said, sitting on a plush leather chair opposite her and laying the guitar across his body. "All the better for me, though. It just so happens that I *can* play. Don't you want to hear the song?"

"The song?" Cee Cee said.

"The one that made this night necessary."

Michael began to strum a slow waltz. "It's a Christmas song," he said and began to sing.

> *The presents are under the tree,*
>
> *The children all sleep in heavenly peace,*
>
> *They're nestled up tight in their beds,*
>
> *While visions of sugarplums dance through their heads,*
>
> *And the snow starts to fall,*

Friends come to call,

Their noses all rosy and red,

They're all happy Christmas is here,

Hear them singing of love and of cheer,

Bells are ringing to bring in the year,

I just wish you were here.

When he sang, his Australian accent disappeared. He performed with his eyes closed, only opening them to steal looks at her. He had done this a hundred times with a hundred girls, and it always ended the same way: they melted. But Cee Cee didn't melt. By the end of the performance, Cee Cee was still sitting on the edge of the couch, spine straight, hands folded primly in her lap, face arranged into a small smile that said neither yes nor no.

"Well?" Michael said sheepishly when the guitar stopped ringing and silence filled the room.

"You should get Dave Cobb."

"Who?"

"Great producer. He worked on my first...well, my only album. He'd know just how to record that song."

"I'll tell Bucky."

"You'd better. God only knows what he'd do if left to his own devices."

Michael loved her grit. He fought the urge to take her in his arms, carry her to the nearest bed, and ravish her. Instead, he began speaking to fill the silence. "You didn't say you liked it, though."

"It was beautiful, Michael."

"Thank you. I wrote it for my mum. She raised me alone. Well, we had Grandma Pearl too." Without quite knowing what he was doing, Michael began to pour out his story to Cee Cee. He told her about his mother, how he lived for her and she for him, how he inherited his love of country music from her, how he lost her. In his mind, he was back in Sydney, halfway through his final year of university, just home for Christmas break, walking into his mother's house with his arms full of presents. He could still see her stretching to put the star atop the tree, could still hear Sam Rogers's voice singing "Silent Night" on a small record player in the corner. This was what Christmas always meant to him—being with Mum and Grandma Pearl, decorating the tree, listening to Mum's favorite country singers sing the same ten Christmas songs over and over. He still had the albums: Willie Nelson's *Pretty Paper*, Loretta Lynn's *Country Christmas*, *Elvis' Christmas Album*, and of course Mum's favorite, Sam Rogers's *Silent Night*.

Cee Cee, overcome by Michael's accent, thought back to the gala dinner and heard Lily's voice say, "He never talks about himself." She wondered what made her special enough to get the stories Michael wouldn't tell his supermodel girlfriend.

"It was hot that year in Australia," Michael said. "Mum had the oven blasting, and we couldn't take it. So we went for a swim in the pool. I did a cannonball, splashing Mum and Grandma Pearl, who pretended to be angry. Then Mum started crying. I never thought a splash could make such a strong woman cry. But it wasn't that. She had found a lump on her breast. The doctor said she didn't have long. She was all I had in the world. My father died before I was born, and Mum always refused to speak of him. I never even learned his name. As a teenager, after years of asking about it, I finally accepted that, for whatever reason, she couldn't speak about it. I forgave her, although I never stopped wishing I could know who he was."

As Cee Cee listened in silence, she noticed Michael transform before her eyes. The cocksure aura dissipated like smoke, leaving in its place a sad, scared little boy. Michael told her how he spent months going to doctor's appointments and chemotherapy treatments with his mother, singing to her when the pain was unbearable, force-feeding her pancakes when she couldn't eat; he told her about the funeral, how lost and alone he felt, and she was overcome with the desire to take him in her arms and mother him.

And then, Michael's eyes filled with tears as he told Cee Cee about the day after the funeral, as he was packing his mother's things in boxes, when he noticed a strange looking yellow paper—a carbon copy of a letter written in her hand. He laughed at the memory. It was just like her to keep carbon copies of her letters. She was the type of woman who alphabetized her records and books and sorted them by genre, the type of woman who saved every postcard she had ever received. The letter was dated August 1987. The vagaries of time and storage in a damp attic had ruined several pages. "I still don't know who it was meant for," he said. "I think it was a letter to my father. She wrote stuff like, 'Why won't you take my calls? Why won't you return my letters? I just want you to know that you have a son. I don't expect you to leave Nashville, but I think you should be part of his life.' I haven't told anyone, but that's the reason I came here. I want to find him and ask him why he left her alone, why he never wanted to meet me."

A tear rolled down his cheek. As if in a trance, Cee Cee rose and walked to Michael, sitting on the arm of his chair. She held his face in her hands and wiped the tear away with her thumb. Michael took her hand gently and licked the tear from the tip of her thumb. His blood rose. He wanted to undress Cee Cee, to possess her totally. He pulled her to him and kissed her, then hesitated for a moment, wondering whether he should throw her over his shoulder and carry her to the bedroom or just do it right there on the couch, and in that moment, Bucky, Sam, and the Colonel came in drunk, smelling like a strip club.

Cee Cee jumped like she had been shocked by a live wire. She wiped her eyes quickly, straightened her dress, and walked to the door to greet the party.

"Dinner ready?" Bucky said, pecking her on the cheek.

"I'll set it out," she said and turned to the kitchen.

"Good girl," said Bucky, and he slapped her on the ass as she walked away.

As they ate, Michael tried to be awed by Sam's presence, tried to imagine what his mother would have said had she known her son would be eating dinner with not just Sam but the Colonel too, tried to share the excitement as Bucky laid out his plans: "I've set up a recording date tomorrow. A little surprise for you both." His eyes twinkled. "We'll announce the duet. Since it's a holiday song, we have to wait until at least November for release, but the announcement should get a buzz going. March is the twentieth anniversary of Sam's *Full Moon*, so we're going to release a deluxe remaster and send you both on tour in Europe. You'll be the biggest thing to hit country music since the fiddle."

All of this should have been terribly exciting to Michael. His wildest dream was coming true. But he couldn't concentrate on anything except the woman across the table. After dessert, coffee, and another bottle of wine, Sam and the Colonel stood and excused themselves. "Mighty fine dinner," Sam said to Cee Cee. Then, turning to Michael, he held out his hand and said, "Looking forward to working with you, son." For the first time, Michael looked directly into Sam's watery blue eyes and felt a jolt. He still wasn't used to seeing the man in the flesh. "Cheers, mate," Michael said nervously.

Now it was just Michael, Cee Cee, and Bucky at the table. Michael looked at Cee Cee without blinking, trying to catch her eye. She would not be caught. Bucky chattered away, oblivious. After what felt like an hour of silent staring, Michael rose, his eyes still on Cee Cee, and said, "I should be leaving."

"Walk Michael to the door, will you dear?" said Bucky.

As Michael exited the mansion, he grasped Cee Cee's hand and gave it a small tug so that she had no choice but to follow him. Outside, he breathed her in and tried to kiss her. She turned so that his lips landed on the top of her head. He tried again.

"Michael," she said.

"Tell me you don't feel this, and I'll leave you alone."

She stared at him hard. A pregnant moment passed. She kissed him on the cheek and went inside.

9

STUDIO B

THE SMELL HIT SAM FIRST. It came from the walls, from the scuffed checkerboard floor, from the battered piano in the corner. He hadn't been in this room in four decades. Everything was still there as he had left it in 1975, but most of all the smell: stale cigarettes, quarter-inch tape, and magic.

Sam stopped short at the entrance. Michael, scrolling through his phone as he walked, bumped into Sam's back. "Sorry, mate," Michael murmured, but Sam could not hear him. He was time traveling. He was a kid again, walking in the footsteps of his idols. The smell of the room brought back other smells, ghosts of smells, memories of smells: Elvis's pomade and Dolly Parton's perfume; Johnny Cash's sweat and Loretta Lynn's hairspray. RCA's Studio B. Was it really in this room all those years ago? And could it happen here again? For the first time in as long as he could remember, Sam itched with excitement.

It was Cee Cee's idea to record here. She recommended it to Bucky, who recommended it to the Colonel. Unlike Studio A, this one had never been renovated. And although it was more a museum than a working studio these days, it still worked. Cee Cee thought it would evoke the memories in Sam's voice and the wonder in Michael's.

While the studio musicians shuffled in and began setting up their equipment, Michael and Sam stood in the corner rehearsing the song "Happy Christmas." Michael played his Charcoal Burst Guild acoustic guitar. Even though he could afford any guitar he wanted, Michael refused to part with the Guild. It was the last present his mother had given him before she died. She picked up extra shifts at work, sick as she was, to scrape together the money. It was a beginner's guitar, but to Michael it was priceless. It was especially meaningful for this song, which Michael had written for her.

The engineer placed the microphones and ducked back into the control room to fiddle with the knobs as the Colonel tiptoed through the studio door. He stood silently watching Sam and Michael rehearse. Both were left-handed, and as they played together, they formed a mirror image. The Colonel focused on Michael's face. He was a beautiful man, as beautiful as Sam in his prime. The way his lip curled when he sang, the way he tilted his head to the side and closed his eyes, the way his body moved behind the guitar—clearly the kid had been watching Sam, idolizing him, copying him. It gave the Colonel an eerie feeling, like when his father used to take him fishing and made him stick his hand in a bucket of live worms.

Sam and Michael didn't even notice him, enraptured as they were at the sound of their voices intertwined. The Colonel had no musical skill, but he loved the sound of musicians speaking their own language: "You're a little flat;" "Try singing the note under me—not the third, the fifth;" "The rhythm of those notes is wrong...sing it like a triplet." And he had been around long enough to know when the magic had entered the room. He felt it now, picking his way through the guitar cables and microphone stands, leaving the air heavy with cologne in his wake, and entering the control room. He nodded at producer Dave Cobb, who spoke through the monitors, "Shall we try a take?"

Michael picked the opening riff, and they were off and singing:

> The shoppers are bustlin' downtown
>
> But it ain't the same since you're not around
>
> While the lovers perspire and dream by the fire
>
> The carolers join in the choir
>
> They're all happy Christmas is here
>
> Hear them singing of love and of cheer
>
> Bells are ringing to bring in the year
>
> I just wish you were here.

The hairs on the Colonel's arms stood on end. In his head he began counting the money they were going to make. Christmas music was big business in Nashville. His eyes gleamed. He smiled secretly to himself. Sam was back. They had done it again.

When the take ended, Sam and Michael tumbled into the control room like excited schoolboys to hear the playback. They listened in rapt silence to their voices coming from the speakers.

"It's a beautiful song," Sam said.

"Thanks, mate," Michael said, his eyes glassy with tears.

"I think your mama's gonna love it."

Michael smiled sadly. "She's gone," he said.

Sam put his rough hand on Michael's shoulder. "Well," he said, "I'm sure she would've been proud."

"You don't know what it would have meant to her, me singing with you. She was your biggest fan."

"Yeah? What was her name?"

"Rosemary."

"Wish I could have met her."

After a few slight adjustments to the arrangement, Michael returned to the studio floor. But Sam, passing the Colonel on the way out of the control room, stopped and said, "What's the matter? You look like you seen a ghost."

"It's nothing," the Colonel said.

"Oh, so you don't want to tell me?"

"I said it's nothing," the Colonel hissed.

Sam gave the Colonel a long look, then sighed and walked away. At the door, he turned and said, "Seems like the kid got everything from me." With a wink, he was gone.

The Colonel took a seat in the corner of the control room, lost in thought. What was the strange fear that had gripped him? A memory, long forgotten, tickled the edges of his mind, but every time he tried to catch it, it slithered away like a snake.

10

A STAR IS MADE

MONTHS PASSED, MONTHS IN WHICH each man—Sam, the Colonel, Bucky, and Michael—became enveloped in his own life again, his own concerns, his own problems, his own schemes and plans. Sam spent his days seeking alternative cancer treatments or swimming laps in the gym pool in a desperate attempt to lose his gut and look trim and fit come Christmas, when the duet with Michael would require him to appear in front of the camera again. The Colonel worked the phones, sniffing out his colleagues and their interest in Sam, should the plan with Bucky fall apart, all the while rolling the name Rosemary around in the back of his head. Bucky spent so much time with his gorgeous protégé Shelby; heads turned in the office whenever she arrived, but no one had the courage to say a word.

Michael spent the summer and all of the fall crisscrossing the country, from New York to Los Angeles and back. Sometimes Lily accompanied him; sometimes he found company with one of the girls who lined up outside his dressing room. His days were a nonstop carousel of interviews: *Rolling Stone, Billboard, Country Music People,* the *New York Times, GQ, Esquire.* Then came the photo shoots, the endless clothes fittings and sittings under hot lights, the occasional taking of a model into a dressing room to let off some steam while everyone waited outside.

He also appeared on every talk show to promote his album. Michael had no idea there were so many. He couldn't keep them straight. There was *The Late Show, Late Night,* and *The Late Late Show,* to say nothing of *The Daily Show* and *The Tonight Show.* Bucky had hired a band of top guns to back Michael, and with every performance of "Don't Change," they grew tighter, and the screams from the crowd grew louder.

Then came the first royalty check. Michael could barely read it. How many zeroes? Five? Six? He called Martha.

"Martha, my dear," he cooed into the phone, "I feel like spending some money."

"You don't need me for that," Martha said.

"*Au contraire, mon chérie,*" Michael said. "I need you for everything, of course."

"What do you want to buy?" Martha said flatly, not rising to his bait.

"Horses. A maid. I want two dogs. A man to keep the stables."

Martha sighed and said, "Okay, Michael. I'll get on it right away."

Meanwhile, Cee Cee returned to the life of a housewife. She bought groceries. She made beds. She straightened pictures and dusted surfaces. She attended one more couple's counseling session, alone, and decided not to return, then did the same at the fertility doctor. She had nearly put Michael and his sensual kiss out of her mind, but one night, lying in bed with Bucky, idly reading a book with the television on low in the background, she heard the Roots playing the opening music to *The Tonight Show* and heard the announcer say, "Tonight: country music superstar Michael Jennings," and even with the air conditioner in the house set to seventy-two, and even with the ceiling fan on medium above her head, she began to sweat. When Michael and his band appeared for their slot, Cee Cee nearly fell out of bed reaching for the controller and turned the volume up until Bucky complained. "He's your artist," she said. "Don't you want to hear him?" Cee Cee watched, rapt, as the camera luxuriated over Michael's face, his full, sensuous lips parted in singing, and his long, elegant fingers dancing over the frets of his guitar. As a songwriter, she admired the way Michael had hidden a slow ballad inside an up-tempo country foot-tapper. She appreciated the way he followed country music's simple three-chord structure but snuck in a jazzy diminished chord in the chorus. She loved that his lyrics went beyond the typical blue-jeans-and-Budweiser country fare, that he dared to reach for something a bit more cosmic:

Some say time is the foe of desire

But my love, it still burns like a fire

So until the planets rearrange

Don't change, don't change, don't change.

After the performance, Jimmy Fallon invited Michael to the couch, where Michael announced his upcoming single with Sam. Then he and Fallon played a silly game where they shot squirt guns in each other's mouths. Watching Michael outcharm even Jimmy Fallon, Cee Cee realized with a mixture of lust and shame that he had his claws in her, and no amount of distance would remove them.

By November, *Don't Change* became the first album since Garth Brooks's *Ropin' the Wind* to hit the top of the country and pop charts. It went straight to number one in Australia and entered the top ten throughout Europe. Michael had no time to consider what it all meant. Every second of his day was spoken for, every detail of his life fodder for the star-making machine.

The bigger Michael got, the smaller his world became. He no longer heard the word *no*, but the people saying *yes* were strangers. He loved being in a band, but as much as he tried to make his bandmates his friends, there was a wall between them he could not cross. At the end of every concert, he'd sing "Don't Change," then he'd climb on the bus and lay in his bunk while the rest of his band played cards in the back. Some nights in the twilight of sleep, Michael would dream of his old life. He didn't miss it. It was better to be rich and famous. But there was a feeling buried deep within him, a feeling only half felt and less understood, that fame was a sort of penetration, and when it happened so quickly and violently, it was impossible to weigh what it had taken against what it had given.

The tour broke for Thanksgiving. When Michael returned to his house, two giant mastiffs careened toward the fence and barked bloody murder at him. "Who the hell are you?" Michael said.

A man wearing Wellington boots and a straw sun hat tramped through the yard toward the gate. "Who the hell are you?" Michael said again.

"Name's George. I keep the stables."

"Stables?"

"Stables. Want to meet the horses?"

"Horses?"

"Horses."

Michael texted Martha: *You've been busy.*

Two dogs, two horses, and a man to keep the stables, Martha replied. *Working on the housekeeper. Oh, and by the way, you didn't have enough room for it all, so you know those woods around your house? You own them now. P.S. We need to discuss your finances. You officially have too much money.*

Walking to meet his horses, Michael's feet crunched on the dead leaves, but he did not hear it. He shivered in his thin shirt but did not feel it. He had spent so long dreaming, wishing, hoping for success. Now that he had it, he was the dog who caught the car. He shuffled through a hundred emotions like a deck of cards. Elation, anxiety, cockiness, inconsequentiality. He felt the strange sort of survivor's guilt that comes with a dizzying change in fortune, and then he thought of Sam, who had lived through it all and was now living through it again.

He reached the stable, where two Australian stock horses stood, their chocolate brown coats glistening in the morning sun. One lowered its head as Michael approached. He patted the wide nose and breathed in the sour sweet smell of hay and manure. "What's his name?" he asked.

"*Her* name is for you to decide," said George.

"Pearl," Michael said softly.

"They're Australian," said George. "Like you."

George saddled the horse, and Michael climbed on gingerly.

"I haven't done this since I was a kid," he said, taking Pearl on a slow walk around the stable.

"Take her easy," said George. "Plenty of time to get back in the saddle. So to speak."

Michael laughed and dismounted the horse. "I have a feeling we're going to get along just fine," he said. "Isn't that so, Pearl?" Pearl gave a loving snort and rubbed her neck against Michael. George handed him an apple, and Michael held it out for Pearl, laughing as her bristly nose tickled his wrist, and her teeth nibbled his hand.

Michael walked back to the house and shuffled through a pile of mail on the table, lifting one envelope and opening it carefully. "Royalty Statement," the heading read. His eyes scanned the sheet until he saw his earnings from "Don't Change" to date. Again, the number barely registered. He called Martha.

"I want a motorcycle," he said. "Mum never let me have one."

Martha sighed and said, "Okay, Michael. I'll get on it right away."

"Leave it to me," he said. "I just wanted to warn you. I assume we have an accountant. Tell him to expect a call about payment."

"Michael, you don't need an accountant for that. What could it cost? A couple hundred bucks?"

"Martha, Martha, Martha," Michael said. "Are we speaking the same language? I want a Harley, my darling manager."

"Right, of course you do."

"I'll be going to Boswell's Harley. The one on Fesslers Lane."

"Anything else?"

"Send a car round to get me."

Michael hung up and felt better. There was one thing to make him complete. He pulled up Cee Cee's number and texted: *Want to go shopping?*

11

KING OF THE ROAD

CEE CEE SAT IN A leather chair at the salon, her feet in a bucket of warm water while a small woman prepared a tray of emery boards and nail polish. She heard the ping on her phone, read the message, and blushed scarlet. "You like the color?" asked the woman working at her feet. Cee Cee muttered a *Yes* without looking away from her phone. Her entire body felt like it was on fire. What Michael did to her, no man had ever done. The mere mention of his name sent her world reeling. But she had made a vow before God to be true to Bucky.

"I'm sorry, but I have to go," she said breathlessly to the woman painting her toenails. She wobbled to her feet, dropped a wad of cash on the counter as payment, and pushed the door open. It rang *ding-dong*. The sun pounded on the parking lot asphalt, making Cee Cee dizzy as she walked to her car. She turned the key in the ignition, blasted the air conditioner, and sat staring at her phone, wondering what to do. She began a dozen different replies and deleted them all. Finally, she threw her phone on the passenger seat, closed her eyes, and with a deep breath, recited from Corinthians: "God is faithful, and will not suffer you to be tempted above that ye are able; but will with the temptation also make a way to escape, that ye may be able to bear it."

When Cee Cee returned home, Bucky was standing over the kitchen sink finishing lunch. He was dressed for work in a polo shirt and khaki pants. "Important meeting tonight," he said, pecking her on the cheek. "Don't wait up for me." He jumped into his Lexus convertible and sped off. With the quiet of the house ringing in her ears, Cee Cee sat at the kitchen table, picking up her phone, putting it down again, picking it up, putting it down. Needing something to occupy her hands, she noticed a shiny, new copy of Walt Whitman's *Leaves of Grass*. She opened it and read the inscription: "Shelby, read this for inspiration and think of me. Love, Bucky."

Cee Cee threw the book down when she heard Bucky's key in the door. "Nearly forgot this," he said, grabbing the book and turning to leave.

"Who's Shelby?" Cee Cee said.

"New artist," Bucky replied. "I'm trying to get her to finish her album so we can put her on tour with Michael." He waved the book and said, "I'm hoping this will spark a few song ideas." He was through the door and into his car before she could reply.

Cee Cee watched Bucky speed down the road and forced away the jealous feeling in her gut. But who was she jealous of? Toward Bucky, she felt only vague contempt. His moves hadn't changed in ten years—the book of poems, the romantic inscription. How many women had received that poison apple? No, the jealousy was not for her husband. It was for Michael, with those pretty young starlets all to himself. Just then her phone buzzed with a text from Michael: *Meet me in half an hour*, he wrote, along with a map to the Harley Davidson retailer.

Cee Cee looked at herself in the mirror. She had on old blue jeans, a simple white shirt, and sandals. Her hair was pulled back in a ponytail. She decided to stay as she was. Somehow, not getting dressed up made it feel better, safer. She retouched her eye makeup and lipstick—she would have done that no matter where she was going or who she was meeting—and drove to the address Michael had texted her.

When she arrived, Michael was nowhere to be found. Her pride wouldn't let her text him. She waited and waited in the parking lot, her anger rising. An hour and a half later, she saw him tumble out of a hired car. He had on sunglasses and a baseball cap pulled low over his face, trying to avoid a scene. Shaking with anger, she walked to him. He threw his arms around her and said, "I'm so glad you're here." But she did not return the hug. Michael noticed the red rims of her eyes and said, "What's wrong?"

Cee Cee felt a tumble of emotions: lust, guilt, anger, shame, pride. She looked down at the ground as she said softly, "Where I come from, you don't keep a lady waiting almost two hours."

"You're right," Michael said. "It'll never happen again. Can you forgive me?" He smiled his boyish smile and held out his hand. Cee Cee forgot her anger and took it. She let him lead her inside to the showroom, where the gorgeous bikes gleamed. Michael slung his leg around a navy blue, five speed, 1,202cc Roadster. A moment later, the salesman came by and introduced himself.

"Want to take it for a spin?" said the salesman.

Outside, the salesman handed Michael the keys and two helmets. Michael put one helmet on his head, and the other he held out to Cee Cee. "I don't...I don't think so," she stammered. But Michael's smile made it all seem so safe, so natural, so right. "Hop on," he said, and she found herself obeying. "Put your arms around me and hold on tight," Michael said. He gunned the engine and peeled out.

Cee Cee held on for dear life as Michael took to the back streets, testing the bike. He hit Interstate 65 and opened it up to sixty. He would have gone faster, but he could tell by Cee Cee's death grip around his torso that she was afraid. When he turned off the highway exit and back toward the dealership, he felt her grip slacken. "You okay back there?" he yelled, and she gave him a little squeeze as an answer. She had begun to enjoy the wind ripping through her hair and against her arms. She savored the excuse to touch Michael, to feel his muscular body, to be intertwined as closely as lovers. She put away her fear and let him take her wherever he wanted to go.

Back at the dealership, Michael put the kickstand down, turned off the motor, and helped Cee Cee off the bike. Her legs seemed to pulse with the vibrations of the road. She wanted him more than anything in the world, wanted him to take her right there in the parking lot. For a moment, they looked each other deeply in the eyes. Michael bent his head toward her. She closed her eyes.

"How was it?" said the salesman.

Michael and Cee Cee parted, the moment ruined. Shaking himself out of his ardor, Michael looked at Cee Cee and said, "Better than I ever imagined."

"I'll draw up the paperwork," said the salesman. "You two lovebirds have time for one more quick spin. If you want."

Lovebirds. Something about the word gave Cee Cee chills.

"All good, mate," Michael said. "We have other business to attend to."

When the salesman walked away, Michael leaned close to Cee Cee and whispered "My place?" in her ear. He felt the goosebumps rise on her arm.

"I can't," she said in a low voice. "I have to go."

Michael watched her walk away, imagining her body in his hands, then paid for the motorcycle and drove home with the wind in his hair.

12

THE LABEL HEAD

LEANING BACK IN HIS LEATHER office chair, Bucky took out his phone and stared at the screen. He had sent Shelby the text an hour ago: *I have good news. What time tonight?*

Why hadn't she responded?

As if he had willed it into being, the phone buzzed with Shelby's reply: *Gotta take my husband to the airport at six. Be free by seven at the latest.*

Bucky smiled and began composing his response. He didn't want to seem overeager, but then again, this girl barely had a high school education. She hung on his every word. He thought about Cee Cee. It was always the same with these women. They wanted everything done for them. They thought stardom should be handed out like candy on Halloween. At least with Shelby the game was new. He was her mentor, her leader, her master. He had the power to make or break her dreams. He texted: *All things work together for good to them that love God, to them who are called according to his purpose. Romans 8:28.*

Your place or mine? she responded.

Yours. Give me the address, and I'll see you at 7:01.

She replied with an address in East Nashville and a winky-face emoji.

What are you wearing? Bucky texted.

Black panties.

The answer made him hard.

Pics or it didn't happen, he texted.

In her reply, she was stretched out on black satin sheets, her hair splayed over the pillow, her legs open to show the black panties, her left arm raised above her head, and her right arm just barely covering her naked breasts. Bucky pressed a button on his desk and his office door locked. He unzipped his pants and, with difficulty, pulled out his crooked penis. Cee Cee was the first girl to ever have the guts to ask him about it. She had never heard of Peyronie's disease, and he secretly thought she blamed his disfigurement for her inability to conceive a child.

As he neared orgasm, he grabbed the tissue box on the edge of his desk. It was empty. Looking frantically around for a napkin, a cloth, anything, he saw Shelby's contract on a pile of papers. The idea itself almost made him finish. He grabbed the contract just in time, defiled it, then crumpled it and threw it in the trash. He sat slumped over, breathing heavily, until he regained his composure, zipped his pants, and paged his secretary. "I'm going to need another copy of Shelby's contract," he said. "I spilled coffee on mine."

At one minute past seven, as promised, Bucky arrived at Shelby's house, a rundown little bungalow in East Nashville. The place needed a coat of paint and a good landscaper. Bucky felt an odd mixture of disgust and power. He could take her out of this place. Then again, it was good she had a house way out here. He didn't have to worry about running into anyone he knew, and he didn't have to rent a hotel room. Bucky loved being rich, but he hated spending money.

Shelby opened the door and let Bucky in. It was an artist's house: messy but not dirty with guitars hanging on the walls and leaning against the futon, colorful scarves hung over the lights, the faint smell of last night's bong water and weed smoke in the air, and a battered piano in the corner next to a drum set. "I didn't know you played drums," Bucky said.

"My husband," Shelby said with an exasperated wave of her hand. "Never stops. I can't stand it."

"Maybe you just haven't heard the right drummer," Bucky said, sitting on the stool and lifting the sticks. He played a passable beat.

"The multitalented Bucky Porter," Shelby said with a grin, then picked up a guitar and said, "I'm having trouble finishing this one.

Maybe you can help me." She began strumming a song, and Bucky played along as best he could, never taking his eyes off of her. "Now, here's where I don't know what to do," she said. "It needs a bridge."

"Funny you should say that," Bucky said, opening his satchel and handing Shelby the book. "I bought this for you. For inspiration."

Shelby opened the book and read the inscription. "How sweet," she said. "*Leaves of Grass*...is it any good?"

Bucky laughed. "You've got a lot to learn, darling."

"I'll need a good teacher," Shelby said, placing the book on the chaotic kitchen counter and rummaging in the refrigerator for two beers. "Want one?" she asked Bucky.

"Let me tell you the good news first." As Shelby cracked the beers, Bucky said, "One: Dave Cobb just signed on to produce your album." Shelby let out a squeal of delight. "Two, we need to finish it within the month, because three: you're going on tour with Michael Jennings and Sam Rogers." Shelby jumped into Bucky's arms. He swung her around in a circle, laughing, triumphing. And then his lips were on hers, and after the slightest moment of hesitation, she returned the kiss. Then her top was off, and her bra was off, and her tits pressed into Bucky's chest. He lowered her to the kitchen floor, and her pants were off, and her panties were off, and his pants and underwear were off, and he climbed on top of her. She let out a small gasp when he shoved his fingers inside her, and she said, "Bucky, I'm married."

Bucky, panting, said, "It's okay. I'm married too. We won't have sex. It's not cheating." As he clumsily touched her with his left hand, he began masturbating with his right. Soon it was over, and they both lay in silence on the floor.

Bucky stroked Shelby's hair as she rested her head in the crook of his arm. Finally, he spoke. "Michael and Sam are going to be on the cover of *Rolling Stone* in June," he said. "I'm going to get you on there with them." Then Bucky fell asleep, for how long he didn't know, until he felt Shelby stir. He looked at the clock on her greasy stove. Half past nine. Watching her walk naked to the bathroom, Bucky became hard again. He heard the shower start and followed her in. He kissed her neck under the hot water. He whispered a verse from Song of Solomon in her ear—"Blow upon my garden, that the spices thereof may flow out"—and with the slightest pressure on her shoulder, pushed her to her knees.

As they toweled off, Bucky grabbed Shelby and hoisted her, and walked, her legs wrapped around him, to the bed. "Not on me this time," Shelby said. "I don't want to take another shower." Bucky ran back to the bathroom and grabbed his towel, then straddled Shelby on the bed. A minute later, with a wrenching groan, he flopped down beside her.

When the sun came streaming through the window the next morning, Bucky slit open one bleary eye and grabbed his watch from the bedside table. Half past seven. *Shit*, Bucky thought. He crept out of bed, careful not to wake Shelby, and tiptoed to the kitchen, where he found his clothes. He checked his phone. Thirteen missed notifications, including a text from Cee Cee a minute before midnight: *Is everything okay?*

Sorry, Bucky texted his wife, as he drove home. *Fell asleep on the couch in my office. Didn't mean to worry you. Be home soon. What's for breakfast?*

13

THY WILL BE DONE

COME SUNDAY, CEE CEE AND Bucky sat again in the hard wooden pews of the Church of Christ, listening to a sermon on faithfulness. For his text, Brother James selected Luke 16: "He that is faithful in that which is least is faithful also in much: and he that is unjust in the least is unjust also in much....No servant can serve two masters, for either he will love the one and hate the other; or else he will hold to the one and despise the other....Ye are they which justify yourselves before men, but God knoweth your hearts....Whosoever putteth away his wife and marry another committeth adultery: and whosoever marrieth her that is put away from her husband committeth adultery."

Cee Cee squirmed in her seat. Every time she questioned her faith, God always seemed to have the exact response ready, chapter and verse. This made her feel both comforted and terrified. For if God truly watched her that closely, then He surely clocked the slight rise in blood pressure every time she thought of Michael, and He surely felt the intimate wetness between her legs every morning as she dreamed of him, and He surely recorded in his ledger every time she looked at Bucky and for the briefest of moments wished he would die, so she could let Michael possess her body while keeping her soul spotless. Yes, somehow He always knew. This was proof of her faith. But it was also a prison. She had committed adultery, she knew, in her heart, and whether she climbed to the top of Mount Everest or sunk to the bottom of the Mariana Trench, she could not escape judgment. In college, she had taken a women's studies class and learned about feminism and the concept of the male gaze. Well, there was no male gaze quite like God's.

Bucky, meanwhile, barely listened. He toyed on his phone, scrolling through his texts with Shelby, wondering when he should propose their next tryst. He kept one ear out for the sound of his name, which meant the time had come for the reading of the Psalms. Otherwise, he had no need for the wisdom of Luke Chapter Sixteen. He'd read it before, and though he had sinned, he felt final confidence in God's forgiveness. As long as he asked for it before he died, Bucky knew it would be granted.

And then came the Psalm, and the eerie singing, naked of all accompaniment, and the final blessing. Before Brother James dismissed his flock, he said, "We have an announcement before you leave," and called Brother Bucky to the pulpit again. Even though the announcement, in truth, should have come from Cee Cee, since she did most of the planning and the work, Bucky hopped up to the pulpit with a smug smile on his face and said, "I hope to see you all this Thursday at the Thanksgiving meal for the homeless."

Every year Bucky and Cee Cee presided over the Nashville Rescue Mission's charity Thanksgiving meal for the homeless. Every year, the local news came to document the good and great Bucky Porter proving that, though he had summited the mountain, he had not forgotten those who wallowed in the valley. Every year, Bucky stayed just long enough for the cameras to capture him serving the wretched with a sanctified gleam in his eye, then, once the cameras left, he eased himself into the heated seat of his Mercedes and drove away.

This tradition meant more to Cee Cee. She spent the day before prepping for the meal, selecting the turkey and roasting it so that it only had to be warmed through the next day. On Thanksgiving, she arrived early and stayed late, piously fulfilling her Christian duty to feed the poor and care for the meek.

Knowing of the tradition, Michael had called the Church of Christ and asked the details. "We arrive at six-thirty to make the food," said an old woman. "The bus comes with the homeless at nine." Her lilting Southern accent made it sound like *naahn*. Then he typed "flower shop" into his map app, drove to the nearest one, and bought a bouquet of peonies.

The next day, Thanksgiving Day, at six-thirty a.m. on the dot, Michael knocked on the church door. Waiting for an answer, he blew warmth into his hands, and stamped his numb feet against the ground. Finally, he heard the lock being drawn, and with a creak, the door opened.

"Michael," Cee Cee gasped. "What are you doing here?"

He noticed she had dressed with a perfect sense of propriety, not flaunting her wealth but also not going out of her way to hide it. Her jeans were neither new nor old, her plaid shirt was rolled up at the sleeves, her hair was swept up in a high ponytail. Michael wanted to throw her over his shoulder and carry her away.

"I want to help," he said, struggling to control his arousal. He handed her the flowers. "I brought these."

Her smile was shelter from the cold. She led him into the kitchen, where half a dozen pious souls worked around a steaming stove. "Where's Bucky?" Michael asked.

"He doesn't usually get here until it starts. So what was it you wanted to do?"

"Whatever you're doing."

As she led Michael into the kitchen, Cee Cee saw the heads of the other workers turning in her direction. She read the judgment in their eyes. Was she being obvious? Then again, she could no more hide her attraction to Michael than she could hide the scent of roasting turkey. A hot flush rose to her cheeks. *Not here*, she thought. *Don't do this here.*

She led Michael to a side counter piled high with potatoes. "Can you peel these?" she asked.

"Never done it before," he said. "But I'm a quick study."

Cee Cee walked away desperate to find something, anything, that would lead her from temptation, but Michael called to her, "Aren't you going to help me?" and looking over her shoulder at his gorgeous face, she surrendered.

Michael and Cee Cee worked together in silence, communicating only with the slight brush of his hand on hers as he passed each peeled potato for her to dice and throw in the boiling water. Soon, the rhythm—peel, pass, *brush*—lulled them into a trance, until with each touch, slight as it was, Cee Cee felt as though Michael's hands were on her entire body. She felt the fire of passion spiked with the heat of guilt and recognized the devil's temptation. Then again, she reminded the judging voice in her head that God had commanded her to feed the hungry. She was merely obeying orders. She didn't invite Michael here. It wasn't her fault. And what was she supposed to do, make him leave? Surely it was a sin to turn away a worker in the Lord's cause.

Through the kitchen doors, Cee Cee and Michael heard the cafeteria come alive with hungry voices and shuffling chairs. An array of news vans pulled up outside: Fox 17, NewsChannel 5, WKRN News 2. Then came an even more unwelcome intrusion. Bucky entered through the back door, wearing Berluti brown leather loafers, crisp Gucci blue jeans, a white Ralph Lauren dress shirt, and Cartier aviator sunglasses. His pungent cologne clashed with the smell of turkey and stuffing. He whipped off his sunglasses like a movie star and bounded into the fray, all energy and good will. Michael and Cee Cee froze like two fugitives caught in the searchlight.

"Michael," Bucky boomed, extending his hand. Leaning in close, he said into Michael's ear, "Is this what I think it is?" Michael set his jaw and tensed his torso. His hands balled into fists. "A little promotional opportunity?" Bucky continued. "Let's get the cameras on you. Do you have a guitar?"

The tension drained from Michael's body. Of course Bucky's first thought would be business. Michael realized he had been silent too long, but before he could speak, Bucky took his silence as an assent. "Perfect!" Bucky boomed, and with a few bold strides was through the kitchen doors and in the cafeteria seeking the cameras.

Michael followed him, trying to stop whatever he was about to do. As he pushed through the kitchen doors, everything in the bustling cafeteria came to a stop. A gasp of recognition rose from the crowd, and then all eyes, all cameras, were on him.

Bucky was used to being the one at the center of the fuss, but he knew he couldn't compete with Michael, and he didn't need to. Let Michael do the work. Let Michael charm the room. Bucky would shine with the reflected light. He spent the morning in Michael's hip pocket, subtly positioning himself, so he was always in the conversation. For the first time, he stayed after the meal was served.

After the turkey, but before the pie, a satisfied hush covered the room. Bucky cornered a cameraman packing up his equipment for the day. "Before you go," Bucky said, "ask Michael what's next for him."

"Come on, man, it's Thanksgiving," the cameraman said. "I got to get home to the kids."

"Trust me," Bucky pressed. Then, to Michael, he whispered, "Get your guitar."

"I don't have it."

"Why did you say you did?" Bucky hissed through a smile.

"I didn't."

The camera pointed at Michael and the red light blinked. "Tell them what's coming," Bucky said, improvising.

"Come on, Bucky," Michael muttered.

"Oh, he's just being shy," Bucky said. Putting on his snake oil sales-man voice, he bellowed, "Tomorrow, ladies and gentlemen, you will get to hear for the first time ever the greatest Christmas song since 'Silent Night,' sung by the greatest country duet since Waylon and Willie."

He had everyone's attention now. All the reporters bustled over to the table to get a shot. Somehow, Bucky had made a scoop out of thin air. "Come on, Michael, why don't you sing them a verse or two?"

Half a dozen microphones pointed at Michael's face. He blinked in the sudden frenzy. "They'll just have to wait," he said, laying on his most charming smile. Amidst a hail of questions shouted from every side, he slid out of his seat and retreated to the kitchen, looking for Cee Cee but not finding her.

Cee Cee stood outside in the cold heaving trash bags full of turkey carcasses, potato peels, and empty cans of cranberry sauce onto her shoulder and throwing them in the dumpster, where they landed with a metallic clang. She saw Michael walk to his Jeep, his head swiveling in search of something. *Is he looking for me?* she thought with a desperate lurch in her stomach and began to call to him, but the sound caught in her throat as Brother James's voice echoed in her head: *God knoweth your heart.*

14

CHRISTMAS TIME
IS HERE

"HAPPY CHRISTMAS" DEBUTED AT NUMBER one on both the country and pop charts and set Michael running again on the endless hamster wheel of success. Bucky packed Michael's schedule with concerts from the day after Thanksgiving to the night before Christmas Eve, and even Christmas Eve was spoken for with a taping of the CMA Country Christmas special.

On tour, Michael texted Cee Cee every night and wondered why she responded so sporadically, so formally. But the road provided enough distractions between the pre-show meet-and-greets and the post-show trysts with a woman or two, or three, whose names he never knew. And when all else failed, he had winter, glorious winter, to watch. The world wore a mantle of white, and the snowflakes fell just like they did in all the Christmas songs he loved as a boy. Back then, living in Australia where the temperature rarely fell below sixty, he could only imagine it. But now, for the first time in his life, he made a snowball and threw it at his tour manager and scampered away howling with laughter. Now, for the first time in his life, he saw the moonlight glint off the endless American countryside covered in snow. Now, for the first time in his life, as he took a piss on the side of the road halfway between last night and tomorrow night, he watched his breath steam from his nose and mouth. He couldn't get enough of it.

At each show the screams begging him to perform "Happy Christmas" grew louder, and at each show, he told the crowd, "Sam ain't even here. You'll just have to wait." And then finally the bus took him back to Nashville, where he found himself next to Sam on a television soundstage preparing to tape the CMA Country Christmas special.

The stage had been transformed into a TV producer's idea of a normal American home. A fake staircase led down to a fake living room. A fake Christmas tree, decorated within an inch of its life, stood next to a plush white couch, in front of which was a stained oak coffee table, upon which sat a glass bowl full of red and green baubles. Fake windows with fake frost had been set up at the back of the stage. The walls were festooned with garland and ornate wreaths covered in twinkling white lights. A real fire burned in a fake fireplace—Michael wondered how they did it—and the mantle was covered with garland and lights. In the midst of this Christmas miracle stood Kacey Musgraves in a sparkling silver hula skirt, singing "Mele Kalikimaka."

A man carrying a clipboard, a headset in his ear, approached Sam and Michael and whispered, "You're on next."

Sam grabbed Michael's hand. "You ready, boy?" he said, a twinkle in his eye. Let's go sell another million copies." In a whirl, they stood before the audience singing together. Michael struggled to sing through the lump in his throat. He wished his mother was there watching her son sing with the great Sam Rogers. Michael's mother always said she loved Sam because it felt like he was singing to her. Well, now he was.

They finished the song, but the crowd wouldn't let them leave the stage. Everyone in the room seemed to know they had just witnessed music history in the making, and no one wanted it to end. As Sam and Michael stood arm in arm soaking in the ovation, Sam leaned in and said, "Join me for Christmas dinner tomorrow, won't you?"

Michael could barely find his voice to say yes.

Christmas Day, Michael spun his mother's old records while he decorated the house, like always, but this year a new record had joined the pile. He finished hanging the lights and garland, walked to the kitchen, and lifted the record carefully from a box of promotional copies. "Happy Christmas from Michael and Sam," it said in red and green block letters above a picture of the two men smiling. The cover was shiny and new. It looked out of place on the stack of old records, but time would take care of that, Michael thought, as he eased the vinyl from its sleeve and placed it on the turntable.

He stood motionless as his voice came from the speakers, singing with Sam. It would never feel real, he thought. Michael dug in his bin of decorations, found the star, climbed on a chair, and placed the star at the top of the tree. He whispered, "Happy Christmas, Mum."

That evening, he drove his Jeep past the towering white gates in front of Sam's white Victorian mansion on the hill, parked on the long driveway, and walked to the door, gravel crunching beneath his boots. Betty the housekeeper showed him inside.

Sam's house made Bucky's look like a shotgun shack. First there was the front door itself, tall enough for a herd of giraffes to walk through without bending their necks. Then came the foyer, and another foyer, each one wallpapered with framed gold records. The second foyer led into a large sitting room, complete with a fireplace the size of a small car and a glittering chandelier overhead. Two staircases, one at either side of the room, led up to the second floor, their ornately carved and highly polished balustrades softly reflecting the firelight. Past the sitting room was the dining room, where at a comically long and spotlessly polished mahogany dinner table, Sam and the Colonel sat opposite each other.

"Merry Christmas," Sam bellowed when he noticed Michael enter. "Sit, boy, sit! Is it just you? No model girlfriend?"

"She's in Bavaria with her folks—or something," Michael said, sitting next to the Colonel.

Betty served three plates stacked high with roasted pheasant, mashed potatoes, sweet potato casserole, green bean almondine, and cranberry sauce. Sam patted the chair next to him and said, "Betty, I want you to join us and enjoy the fine meal you've made." She served one more plate, then took her seat next to Sam. "I'd like to say a short prayer," Sam said. He bowed his head. Michael followed. "Thank you Lord for the blessings," Sam intoned, his voice catching on the word "blessings." He spoke thickly through a tear-choked voice. "For

Michael," he said. "For this meal. For everything." Then he fell silent. No one knew what to do. They kept their heads bowed, waiting for Sam to finish.

Sam had run out of words to count his blessings. As the silence stretched, he saw the whole thing in a flash through his mind: "Happy Christmas" was the song of the season, replacing "Don't Change" atop the charts. Interview requests poured in for Sam, good ones, not obscure blogs but national media. The repackaging of *Full Moon* had just been announced, and it had enough advance orders to go Gold, maybe even Platinum. Sam was about to perform the hardest trick for an old artist. He was about to make the jump between generations, from *has been* to *is again*. His past was no longer a shackle; it was a legacy.

The hush in the room became, in its way, holy. Michael stole a glimpse at Sam, and seeing the old man sitting there, his face contorted in a mixture of agony and ecstasy, tears trickling from his shut eyes, a wave of emotion ran through Michael as well. He saw his mother. He saw Grandma Pearl. He saw Cee Cee. He saw the crowds, ever growing, until it seemed his future, his destiny, was already written: he would join the immortals.

Inside the Colonel's mind, other calculations prevailed. Michael was a blessing and a curse. Yes, he made Sam relevant again. Yes, he would earn the Colonel truckloads of money. But power was a zero-sum game, and anyone who thought different was a sucker. The more power Michael had with Sam, the less power there was for the Colonel. And then there was the mother: Rosemary. *Rosemary.* If life had taught the Colonel anything, it was to recognize a threat with enough time to protect himself. It was like a sixth sense, a tightening in his gut that always warned him. He felt it as a child when his father came home and caught him with his nose in a fashion magazine. He felt it in high school when the beef-headed bullies sauntered down the hall shouting, "Fag!" And he felt it that day in the studio when Michael said the name Rosemary. Ever since, the Colonel had wracked his mind to understand it.

"Amen," Sam finally said, breaking the spell.

The meal eaten, the wine drunk, the pumpkin pie and coffee served and enjoyed, Betty stood and cleared the plates. Sam walked to the lounge and placed "Happy Christmas" on the turntable, and he and Michael sang along with their own record. As the sound suffused the air, something twisted inside the Colonel, and the memory that refused to be caught revealed itself with all the power and terror of a religious conversion. "Betty," he said, "thanks for the wonderful meal." Then, throwing his wadded napkin on the table, he said: "I'm off to visit dear old mother." Before Sam could object, the Colonel was at the door, donning his snow boots, and gone.

As the candles burned down and left pools of wax on the table, Michael and Sam fell into an easy silence. The fire crackled. In the next room, Sam had left his hundred-inch HD television tuned to a football game, and it murmured in the background. Michael busied himself on his phone, feeling perfectly drunk. He texted Cee Cee: *Come over.*

It's Christmas, she replied.

I know. And I must have been a good boy, because Santa brought me everything I asked for. Except you.

Michael, my parents are here. I can't...

Well, I don't know what I'm going to tell the horses.

?

I got two horses, and I can only ride one at a time. I need someone who knows how to ride.

Tonight?

Yes. A moonlight ride.

Michael stared at the three dots dancing on his screen as Cee Cee composed a reply, then he watched the dots disappear as she deleted it, then they danced again, disappeared again, and the phone went silent. He sighed sadly and scrolled through his contacts, trying to remember the name of the girl from Bucky's party. Andrea? Amelia? *Amber.* He excused himself from the table. In Sam's bathroom he took off his shirt, snapped a photo of his naked torso, and texted it to Amber with the message, *Your turn.* A heartbeat later, his phone buzzed with her response. She was a tall brunette with long, straight hair and tits so perfect Michael would have sworn they were fake if he hadn't touched them himself. She had carefully cropped the picture, so it ended just below her navel, cutting off her left hand, inviting Michael to imagine what it was doing down there.

"Gotta go," he told Sam. "Thanks for everything."

"Call a car," Sam said, rising from his easy chair and wrapping Michael in a warm embrace. "Don't need you driving drunk on these roads." Sam held Michael at arm's length and looked him full in the face. He felt a sense of responsibility, of protection, which he had never felt before. *Must be getting soft in my old age*, he thought, walking Michael to the door. As he watched Michael get into the Uber, he called, "Text me when you get home, so I know you're safe."

Cee Cee avoided her mother's eyes across the table. The turkey was cold. It had been a strange Christmas. Bucky had gone out earlier that afternoon saying he had to run an errand—although Cee Cee couldn't fathom what errand a man *had* to run on Christmas Day—and never returned. Cee Cee spent half the day becoming increasingly angry and the other half worrying. He was, after all, still her husband. Her mind taunted her with morbid fantasies: Bucky dead in a ditch; Bucky spinning out of control on the ice-slick highway into oncoming traffic; Bucky shot in the back and left to die while the thieves emptied his pockets. She called the police. She called the hospitals. And then, not knowing what else to do, she carved the turkey and set out the plates. As soon as she sat down at the table, he called.

"Sorry, I got held up," he said. "Be home soon. Don't make your parents wait. Eat."

Then Cee Cee had different fantasies: stabbing Bucky with the carving knife; slicing him up like canned cranberry sauce; pulverizing him into mashed potatoes. She hardly touched her food. Every word from her mother's mouth came barbed with criticism and disappointment, as though it was Cee Cee's fault Bucky left, as though he might have stayed had the turkey not been a bit too dry, and the wine glasses marked with water spots, and the napkins folded imprecisely, and lurking behind it all, the ultimate failure: no baby.

"I don't judge people," her mother said, after having spent fifteen unbroken minutes judging Cee Cee. "I guess your father and I just did things differently, that's all."

In the middle of this cloaked assault, Cee Cee's phone buzzed. She lifted it with dread, wondering what excuse Bucky had cooked up this time, but then her cheeks flushed as she read Michael's message: *Come over.* Then came the invitation to a moonlight horse ride. Horses were her first love. She had competed in dressage all the way through high school. Bucky was allergic, so she gave them up a long time ago. But she never stopped yearning for that connection. *I'll be there*, she typed, then deleted it, then typed, *Not tonight, but maybe soon?* then deleted it. Her mother issued a stern warning about using the phone at the table, and Cee Cee obeyed.

Dinner over, they cleaned the dishes in uneasy silence. Cee Cee dipped them in the suds and rinsed them, then handed them to her mother, who dried them, alternating between two fluffy white towels slung over her shoulder, working with knobby, arthritic hands, her gray hair swept up in a ponytail, her blue eyes dulled from long years spent with her back bent to a woman's solemn duty. As they worked, the smell of cigar smoke and the sound of her father snoring wafted from the living room.

Near eleven o'clock, with Christmas all but over and still no sign of Bucky, Cee Cee climbed the stairs, dug in the closet for her old riding boots, put them on with a pair of jeans, a thick cashmere sweater, and a plush overcoat—no bra, no panties—and tried to tiptoe to the garage without being noticed.

Her mother caught her and demanded to know where she planned on going at nearly midnight. "Bucky's having car trouble," Cee Cee lied. She climbed in her black BMW and pulled up her maps app and typed in Michael's address, then backed out of the driveway, her headlights illuminating the angry, confused look on her mother's face.

15

ORIGINAL SIN

BACK HOME, MICHAEL LET SAM know he was safe, then sent Amber his address along with an artistically cropped picture of his abs, and the words, "Door's open." He lay naked in bed, scrolling through his trove of pictures of past conquests, until he heard the front door open softly, and the sound of high heels clicking on the floor, and then the shoes came off and bare feet padded through the kitchen, searching. Michael let her search. When she appeared in his bedroom doorway, he rose from the bed and undressed her without a word.

Amber was taller than Michael liked. He hadn't noticed that when she was on her knees before him at Bucky's house. She was taller than Lily even. He lifted her against the wall, but soon his arms became tired with the strain, so he threw her on the bed. She lay naked in a pool of yellow light streaming through the open blinds from the streetlamp outside. Michael took her left foot gently in his hand and admired each toe. His lips searched down the inside of her leg and stopped just short of her hip joint until she begged him to continue. He waited a cruel moment and said, "What do I get in return?"

"Anything you want," she said.

"Anything?"

Her hand was around him, pushing him inside. He held her legs as they trembled, then flipped her over until they trembled again. Only when he was certain of her satisfaction did he finish and collapse on the sweaty sheets next to her, sated but unfulfilled.

As he lay stroking Amber's back, he heard a car pull in the driveway. The dogs rustled themselves like grumpy old men from their blankets and, with chains jangling, half trotted, half staggered to the door to fulfill their canine duty. Michael eased himself from the bed, pulled a robe around his nakedness and went out to investigate. "Easy, boys," he said to the snorting, growling dogs. Standing at the front window, he peeled back a corner of the curtain and peered outside to see Cee Cee getting out of her car. Turning on his heel, he sprinted back to the bedroom and roused Amber. "I'm really sorry about this, but you can't stay here tonight."

"Aw, come on," she said, yawning beneath Michael's plush blanket.

"I mean it," he said, picking up her clothes from the floor and folding them neatly for her at the foot of the bed. Then he dressed in a sweater and slacks, keeping the robe on for extra warmth.

"Is that your wife or something?" Amber asked, sliding one perfectly sculpted leg from beneath the covers.

"It's not like that. But hurry, please."

"Whatever," Amber said.

Michael helped her dress and ushered her out the back door. "It's safer this way," he explained. "No hard feelings?"

She laughed and left him with a soft, haunting kiss.

Michael made a note in his phone to have Martha send Amber flowers tomorrow. Then, when he saw her disappear around the side of the house, he rushed to the front door and opened it.

"Cee Cee," he said, "Merry Christmas."

"Did you have company?" she said.

"No, no, no," Michael said, pulling her inside before Amber could turn the corner. "I'm so glad you came."

Cee Cee smelled the lingering ghost of a woman's perfume inside the house, and she felt a thrill that Michael would end his date for her. The thrill spread goosebumps over her entire body as she wondered if Michael had stamina left for her too. A surge of guilt spiked the thrill like a flask of rum poured in a punchbowl at a high school dance.

"Can I get you something?" Michael said. "Glass of wine? Christmas cookies?"

"You have Christmas cookies?"

"Bake 'em every year. My mum's recipe."

"Well, then, I simply must try them."

Michael set out a plate of cookies cut in the shape of trees, and stars, and Santas, and reindeer, each one sprinkled with red and green sugar. He poured two glasses of wine, stoked the fire, and lit a candle. The moon shone through the window.

"So?" he said, when Cee Cee bit into the cookie.

"Perfect," she mumbled around the crumbles.

"How was your Christmas?" Michael asked.

Cee Cee's face dropped. An awkward silence chased romance from the room. "Can I see the horses?" she said.

"Of course. Let me just put on a coat."

He rummaged in his closet for his warmest coat, slung it over his shoulders, and turned to see Cee Cee standing in the doorway of his bedroom, holding the candle. In three strides, he reached her, put his hand on hers, and gently maneuvered the candle onto his dresser. Shrugging off his coat, he grasped the bottom of her sweater and slowly lifted it. Candlelight danced on her soft belly. Slowly, he lifted the sweater to her ribs. Her skin seemed to glow. He held her eyes with his. The faintest smile played on his lips as he raised the sweater up further to reveal the bottom of her breasts. His heart beat so fast he could barely breathe, but he went slowly still, revealing two perfect nipples, hard with desire. Cee Cee lifted her arms in the air. He pulled the sweater over her head, tossed it to the ground, and admired her in the candlelight.

"My God," he whispered and took her in his arms. He kissed her on the mouth, on the neck, on the shoulder, down her arm, to her belly-button, then let his tongue circle each nipple.

"Michael," she moaned.

Michael lifted Cee Cee in his arms and placed her gently on the bed. She pulled his shirt over his head and began working on his pants, but he pushed her down on her back, then stripped off her jeans, and explored her with his tongue.

Returning to her lips, he whispered in her ear, "Are you ready?" And even though he had never wanted a woman more in his life, if she had said no, he would have let her go.

Having only slept with Bucky, Cee Cee had never made love for longer than a few minutes. She had come close to orgasm by herself but had never felt a real one. Since nothing in her religion or experience told her different, she assumed sex was a matrimonial duty, moderately pleasant for the wife, but designed primarily for the husband. This made sense in her mind, and she accepted it. The husband was lured by the sensation, the wife by the chance to carry a child. It had never occurred to her that there were men who knew how to find the clitoris.

Having only slept with groupies, Michael assumed sex was a purely physical sensation. This made sense, and he accepted it. What could possibly feel better than an orgasm? Of love, he knew nothing. It had never occurred to him that pleasing a woman he loved could make time stop, could penetrate him down to his deepest core, could make him so vulnerable it seemed she held his entire life in her hands.

None of this was spoken or even thought. Each simply felt it with the holy power of a spiritual revelation. Her back arched. She bit her lip. A low moan rose to an almost inaudible squeak. Michael held on for dear life, needing to please her before he took his pleasure. And then she was quiet. She held her breath until she turned red from her face down to her chest. Michael had seen it happen a hundred times, but it had never looked so beautiful before. With a wild spasm and a panting cry, Cee Cee was rendered nearly insensible. Michael continued thrusting until the goosebumps on her body flattened, and then he let himself go. They lay intertwined, free of all thought. They were like people who, having lived their entire lives by lamplight, had suddenly stared directly at the sun.

The Colonel didn't sleep that night. After leaving Sam's mansion he sped to his storage unit in north Nashville, flung the door open, and began tearing the place apart, digging through decades of posters, stage costumes, and contracts, searching for something he hadn't thought of in twenty years. He found it crumpled at the bottom of a box of memorabilia from Sam's 1987 world tour. "Dear Sam," the letter read, "I am writing because my other attempts to contact you have failed. Even though you left without saying goodbye, I will always cherish the night we spent together. I have been trying to reach you. Are you okay? I just want you to know that you have a son. He's got brown curly hair like yours, and I think he has your nose. I don't expect you to leave Nashville, but I think you should be part of his life, if you want to be." The letter rambled on until the conclusion: "Love, Rosemary."

"Son of a bitch," the Colonel said to himself.

16

NOTRE DAME

TOURING WAS A PAUSE BUTTON on life. The Colonel didn't know how to burden Sam with the knowledge that Michael was his son, so he simply didn't. *Let him go to Europe and have a good time*, the Colonel thought, *while I figure out the angles.* Cee Cee didn't know what to do about Michael and Bucky. After returning home Christmas night, she felt so guilty she nearly vomited. While she showered to wash Michael off of her skin, she felt a kiss on her back and nearly screamed Michael's name before realizing Bucky had come home. He stood behind her, thankful that the steam and the scent of the shampoo covered all traces of what he had just done with Shelby. "Sorry I'm late," he said, as he kissed her neck.

Cee Cee knew she couldn't sleep with him ever again. But she also knew First Corinthians: "The wife is bound by law as long as her husband liveth." And she knew the first book of Peter: "Wives be in subjection to your own husbands." And she knew the Gospel of Mark: "What therefore God hath joined together, let not man put asunder."

Nothing in her life had prepared her for this moment. She felt sick with worry. But when Michael left for four months of shows, and she couldn't see him even if she wanted to, the worry faded. *He'll go to Europe*, she thought, *while I figure this out.*

The only people with nothing to figure out were Sam and Michael. They sat undisturbed in the eye of the storm they had created. Sam felt happier than he had in decades. He thought he'd never see Europe again and had resigned himself to it the way he resigned himself to the wrinkles on his forehead and the crow's feet at the corners of his eyes, the sagging jowls on his face and the graying hair on his head, the expanding paunch around his waist and the creakiness in his knees. It was simply the way of things. Your youth was your worth, and when you lost one, you lost the other.

But here he was, two months shy of his sixty-third birthday, in London, in Dublin, in Amsterdam, in Prague, in Berlin, in Vienna. *Full Moon* hit number two on the American and European country charts, second only to Michael's *Don't Change*. The tour sold out the instant it was announced. Fans wanted to fuck him again, young ones, beautiful ones, European ones, men and women. They lined up outside his dressing room after every show, supple and taut and eager. He swallowed a blue pill and became his old self again. They dug their nails into his soft back as he sweated over them, and moaned beneath the weight of his old body when he fell on them, sated.

If Sam felt happy, Michael walked on clouds. He had never been to Europe, so every country, every city, every experience was new. He marveled at the cathedrals: they didn't have those in Australia, or in America either. He sampled the girls like a box of chocolates: London girls were proper but eager to please; German girls liked it kinky; Czech girls fucked like a war might start any minute. In Budapest, where the Catholic church still dominated, Michael was caught in bed with twin sisters—he had handcuffed them both to the headboard—and the police threatened to jail him for breaking Hungary's incest laws. He called Martha, who had been sent on tour as a glorified babysitter to make sure the real world never infringed on Michael's good time. She put on her crucifix and her most chaste outfit and, with a mixture of piety and bribery, got him free.

"Thanks, love," Michael said as she led him out of the police station and back to the tour bus. Martha smiled her meek smile and recalled the Colonel's words to her before she left: "You're my eyes on Michael over there. If anything happens, I will hold you responsible." He needn't have worried. Watching Michael climb the stairs and disappear into the dimly lit bus, Martha knew she would do anything to protect Michael, even if he didn't notice it now. One day, she hoped, he would.

Each night Sam played an opening set, then Michael came on for the headlining slot, followed by an encore together, during which he and Michael made magic on stage for a few beautiful minutes, some nights playing one of Sam's songs, other nights one of Michael's, and on special occasions, letting the mood guide them, they played an entire extra set. After a quick celebration backstage, they'd retire to their respective tour buses to shoot through the night to the next city. *What a kid*, Sam thought. *What a kid to make this all possible again.* He felt honored that Michael knew his music so well. In every city, he bought a little trinket and gave it to Michael. Within a week, the two were inseparable, sauntering around the cities like tourists, ribbing each other during sound check, eating together at the same table before concerts. Within two weeks, Michael moved into Sam's bus.

One night in early April, driving to Munich, Michael sat at Sam's feet and strummed Sam's guitar and asked the breathless questions of a fan. Sam loved answering. He thought it was the best interview he ever gave. Michael wanted to know about making *Full Moon*, and Sam brought out his guitar and began to play. "See, this is a country waltz, this one," he said. "Everybody remembers the fast ones, but it's these old moaners I really like. I guess I was trying to give Kristofferson a run for his money. No one wrote 'em like him." Sam sang a few verses of Kris Kristofferson's "For the Good Times," then showed Michael how he simply inverted the chords for "Full Moon." Michael sat, stars in his eyes, as Sam sang:

> *I loved you but I left you*
> *Now my heart's out of tune,*
> *And no one sees my tears*
> *But the lonely full moon,*
> *Some say all good things, they must end too soon*
> *I loved you but I left you*
> *'Neath the lonely full moon.*

"It was a dark time," he said. "Twenty-three years old. Couldn't get out of bed without a fifth of whiskey, a line of coke, and three cups of coffee." He told Michael how the Colonel micromanaged every second of his schedule, becoming more and more controlling as he felt Sam slipping away. Sam went on his first world tour that year and learned what it meant to be famous. It shrunk the world. He recalled taking a few days off, disappearing to Nagaland, India, and hearing his voice coming through the tinny speakers in a local bazaar. He knew nothing would ever feel the same again. When the tour ended, Sam—or more precisely, one of the dozens of people handling his money—bought a house on Rosemary Beach in Florida, where he could hide out for weeks at a time to surf, get high, and have anonymous sex. He admitted to Michael what he had kept secret from the world: he preferred men, but, as he said, "If it walks and talks, I'll take it to bed."

Michael asked about the Colonel, and Sam swallowed hard and told the truth. "I always knew he loved me, but I could never love him back. Not the way he wanted." It was the first time Sam had ever said it, the first time he had even allowed himself to acknowledge it. He knew it killed the Colonel every time he had to pay the groupies to keep their mouths shut. The tension was terrible. After all those years looking after the business and cleaning up Sam's mistakes, the Colonel had settled into an uneasy acceptance. He took solace in his power. He took revenge in the relentless grind of stardom. Sam was on a treadmill—album, tour, album, tour. The faster he ran, the better for the Colonel. So he kept Sam on the treadmill, even when it was clearly killing him, and Sam kept running as a sort of masochistic penance.

Michael took the guitar, strummed Dolly Parton's "Jolene," and asked what she was like. "Sweeter'n cherry pie and tough as leather boots," Sam answered, and soon the whole gang was there with him, his old friends. As he talked about them, he began to cry. He didn't even realize it until the tears trickled into his beard. He saw them all again— Dolly, Loretta, Merle, Willie—so young, so full of piss and vinegar. And then came the hardening of their hearts, the crust of pain that turned to armor, which protected the real person from the glare of stardom until the real person was so far down inside, you sometimes couldn't see him, couldn't see her. That was the price of fame, of money, of success, of power. Not that those things were bad. Not that the price was too high. But, well, how could he explain that this life, this business wasn't what it seemed? He saw the stars in Michael's eyes and knew the kid couldn't hear him. Michael had to find out for himself, like everyone did.

"Just do me a favor," Sam said as the bus sped through the Bavarian Alps, which hulked on the horizon like silent giants in the dark. "Don't trust anyone in this business. Ever."

But he knew Michael couldn't hear him.

Slowly, the talk dwindled. Michael fell asleep on the floor. Sam sat there looking at him for a long time, feeling strangely moved by his beauty. Then he rustled Michael from the floor and led him to the bunks.

The next morning, Michael rubbed his eyes and yawned. He poked his head from the sleeping bunk and heard Sam snoring in the bunk opposite him. As quietly as he could, he swung his legs over the bed and dropped to the floor. The bus was a mess of beer bottles half empty and warm, bags of potato chips slumped over and spilling, clothes crumpled and musty. Dawn painted the window gold. Michael sat and watched the rising sun glint off the Eiffel Tower.

Paris.

The city was just as beautiful as he hoped it would be. He loved London with its quaint charm, and he admired Berlin with its geometric precision, but Paris was the first place in Europe he felt at home. Michael walked to the front of the bus and greeted the driver. "Where are we?"

"Almost at the hotel," the driver responded. He was a friend of Sam's, a chubby, pink-faced Southerner just past his prime who could stay up all night and sleep all day, which suited him for the job.

"Where's Notre Dame?"

It was Michael's dream to light a candle for his mother at the famous church. She had seen it once and spent his childhood filling his head with tales of its beauty. The driver tapped at his phone and handed it to Michael. "Five minute walk," he said, pointing in the direction of the Seine.

"Stop the bus."

Michael ran to the back and shook Sam.

"Come on old man," he said.

Sam grumbled and turned over. Michael shook him again. "Wake up, wake up, wake up," he called in a singsong, like a child. Sam let out a hacking cough and raised himself on an elbow. His face was pale and tight with pain. "Christ, you look horrible," Michael said.

"We hit it hard last night," Sam said in a frog croak. "Think I lost my voice."

"Time to repent," Michael answered, throwing open the curtain to Sam's bunk and tugging at his arm.

Sam dressed slowly, pretending to ignore Michael's pestering to hurry up, and the two stepped down from the bus into the Parisian morning. They walked through the Jardin des Plantes and along the Seine. The great river was lined with stalls—booksellers, tchotchke peddlers, art mongers. Michael smiled at all he saw, enchanted. He stopped in a stall and purchased a worn old copy of the Marquis de Sade's *The 120 Days of Sodom*. Sam trailed behind him, coughing and rubbing his sleepy eyes. "Keep up, old man," Michael called as they reached the Pont de l'Archevêché and crossed the Seine.

Then Notre Dame stood before them, its bell towers thrusting at the sky. Michael stood gaping beneath the Tympanum of the Last Judgment. He couldn't speak. It was just as magnificent as his mother always said. Michael floated into the cool, dark cathedral and felt her there with him. He gazed at the north rose window with its hypnotic fractal of stained glass. He ran his hand along a hard wooden pew and imagined the dust of centuries on his fingertips. He tiptoed like a nervous schoolboy around the back of the high altar and marveled at the tomb of Bishop Matifort. Every twist and turn of the great cathedral held a new treasure.

Michael separated from Sam and walked alone to find the Saint-Georges Chapel, his mother's favorite. She always told him the light coming through that particular stained glass window was proof of God. Michael stood there now and agreed. He dropped five Euro into a wooden slot, took a small wooden stick from a pile, held it over a flame until it began to burn, and picked out a candle with a good view of the window. He lit it and said a prayer for his mother. Then he lit another for Cee Cee.

Sam approached. "Let's get out of here," he said. "This place gives me the heebie jeebies." Michael smiled, and the sun coming through the stained glass glinted off his perfect white teeth. Sam was once again taken with his beauty.

"Gotta make one more stop, mate," Michael said. "Then let's get a croissant."

Leaving the cathedral, Michael and Sam squinted into the blazing sunlight. Michael texted Martha an address on the Rue de Ponthieu and said, *Meet me here in fifteen.* He and Sam hailed a taxi that sped them through small, winding avenues and deposited them on a commercial street lined with shops, where Michael led Sam into the Nina Ricci shop.

"What the hell are we doing here?" Sam said, taking a cocktail gown from a rack, looking at it uncertainly, and replacing it.

"Shopping," Michael said, and he walked with purpose to the women's lingerie.

"For yourself?"

"In a way. My bird is here for Paris fashion week. I'm seeing her tonight. I like to dress her up."

As Michael chose a lascivious black silk bra and panties to match, a saleswoman approached. *"Bonjour, monsieur,"* she called. *"Avez-vous besoin d'aide?"*

Michael stared at her dumbly.

"Do you need 'elp?" she said.

"Ah," Michael said, taking her slim hand and raising it to his lips. "*Non. Merci.* Just came for this." He held up the bra and panties.

The woman's cheeks blushed below sparkling blue eyes.

How does he do it? Sam thought.

Michael followed the woman to the register, admiring her as she walked before him. The bell on the door chimed, and Martha entered. "Just the woman I wanted to see," Michael said. He called her to the counter, where she paid with a credit card and took the bag. Outside, he stopped suddenly and said, "I forgot something."

With Martha in tow, Michael reentered the store and strode again to the lingerie. He rifled through a set of ivory bra-and-panty sets with pink embroidery, then returned to the register with one in his hand.

"Did you need something else?" the woman said, smiling.

"Yes. *Oui.* Do you have this in thirty-four B?"

The woman walked gracefully to the storeroom and returned with the item in hand.

"*Alors,*" she said, holding it up.

"Perfect," Michael said. "Can you gift wrap it and mail it for me?"

"*Bien entendu,*" she said. "'Oo is zee lucky lady?"

Michael whispered something to Martha and left her alone in the store. A slight flush rose to her cheeks. She didn't like the idea, but she knew better than to argue. She scrolled through her phone, found what she wanted, and wrote an address on a scrap of paper. Handing it to the saleswoman, she said, "Make it out to Cee Cee Porter."

17

PARIS

THE CLARITY CEE CEE HOPED to find during Michael's absence never came. Michael was simply too present, either in her thoughts or in the texts he sent every night as he prepared to go onstage: two pictures of himself in the dressing room and the question, *Which outfit?* While he performed in the one she picked, feeling her touch in the very clothes on his body, she agonized over every detail of every text, feeling like a teenager barely in control of her own emotions as she was yanked from the highs of gazing at Michael in his tight pants, to the lows of noticing a woman's arm in the background, zooming in on it until it filled her phone screen, and trying from such scant evidence to figure out who the woman was and what she meant to Michael. She wanted to scratch the woman's eyes out. She wanted to tell Michael he was allowed no lover but her. Instead, she composed and deleted passionate text after passionate text, sometimes sending a bland message instead, sometimes not responding for days.

She couldn't sleep anymore. The memory of her night with Michael tormented her. It almost seemed worse to have experienced such heaven only to wind up back in hell, back keeping house, back cooking dinner, back shopping at the grocery store, buying the trendy beer Bucky liked and the Kobe steaks he ate three times a week, and the paper towels, the soap, the toilet paper, and the garbage bags, each item feeling like another nail in her own coffin.

And then, one afternoon a FedEx truck pulled into the driveway. Cee Cee was running on her treadmill, wearing a black sports bra and yoga pants. A bead of sweat gleamed on her upper lip. Through the window, she saw the delivery man place a box on her doorstep, but she finished her workout and took a shower before going downstairs to retrieve it. Wrapped in a towel, with another towel in a turban covering her wet hair, she opened the door and grabbed the box in one fluid motion, shutting the door before the neighbors had a chance to see her. She took the box upstairs to her bedroom and placed it on the bed, letting the mystery deepen while she dried her hair. Finally, she opened it. Inside the box was another box, emblazoned with beautiful gold lettering that read "Nina Ricci, Paris."

Who do I know in Paris? she wondered, carefully opening the inner box to find a white silk and lace bra, 34 B, her exact size, matching panties, and a sealed card. Lifting the flap of the envelope with the edge of her thumbnail, Cee Cee remembered her honeymoon with Bucky in Paris, how they made love in the bathroom at the Louvre, nervous like naughty teenagers, and sat streetside at a Montmartre café eating *coq au vin*, laughing at the *garcon*'s pained face as Bucky mangled his French. This year was their tenth wedding anniversary. She was shocked Bucky remembered.

Cee Cee opened the card. She didn't recognize the handwriting. "Saw this and thought of you," it read. "Love, Michael." She dropped the box like it was on fire, then snatched it up again and nervously pressed the lingerie to her body. She had never felt anything so soft. How did he know the size? Then she realized with a pang of lust and a twinge of shame that he had been with so many women, he must have known her bra size just by looking at her. The towel had fallen from her body, and she sat naked on the bed, letting the lingerie caress her skin. She thought of Michael, and her nipples hardened.

She felt lovesick and wondered which was worse: wasting her life with a man she didn't love or twisting her guts into knots over a man she might never possess. She downed half a bottle of wine, took a picture of her cleavage, and sent it to Michael with the message: *Come home soon.*

The Shangri-La Paris hotel was built as a home for Napoleon's grand-nephew. Now it belonged to conquerors like Michael. He lay spread eagle on the bed. The double doors leading to the balcony were open, and a soft breeze rustled the curtains. In the middle distance, the Eiffel Tower glinted with the rays of the setting sun. It looked close enough to touch. The street traffic below murmured like ocean waves lapping at the shore.

At the edge of the bed sat Lily, wearing the Nina Ricci lingerie Michael had bought for her. She was so beautiful that it almost hurt to look at her, like staring at the sun. No wonder she was the star of Fashion Week. Lily was the answer to every woman who had ever taken a dress off the rack and complained, "Who do they make these clothes for?" Looking at the gentle curve of her breasts, the perfection of her thighs, the tantalizing thrust of her pubic bone, Michael became hard. He imagined her soft lips wrapped around him, her blue eyes, like two pools in the Mediterranean Sea, looking up at him.

But Lily played idly on her phone. She held it in both hands, her graceful neck bent to its hypnotic blue glow, her thumbs skittering across its screen like spider's legs. Michael patted the bed next to him. She looked up. He raised his index finger and made it say, *Come here.* She turned back to her phone. Michael's hand fumbled around on the bedside stand until he found his phone. He texted Martha, *Lily's doing it again. She's frozen.* Martha would know what he meant. He didn't expect her to do anything about it, though he knew she would if he asked. He just wanted to complain. And this was Michael's chief complaint. Sex was seduction for him. It was sight, touch, smell, lavishing attention on every part of a woman's body, memorizing her, concentrating on her reaction to his every kiss, and lick, and bite. But Lily did not react. Sex for her seemed like washing the dishes. It was a task to be completed. He often asked her to bring friends, and for a while that was enough. But now even the threesomes left him cold. Michael wanted warmth. When Lily finally came to him, he did everything in his power to awaken the carnal beast within her. He rattled the walls, tore the sheets, and pulled down the curtains, and for a few moments Michael bent her over the railing on the balcony while a crowd gathered to watch them below. She simply looked back at him and said, "Are you close?" Back on the bed, Michael pulled her lacy underwear to the side, closed his eyes, dreamed of Cee Cee, and finished.

Hours later, the bedside phone shattered the silence in the room. Night had fallen on Paris. "Um, excuse me," said a worried voice. "I'm supposed to drive you to the concert, sir." Michael rustled Lily awake, had sex with her in the shower, dressed, and left by the back entrance to the hotel, where a limo had been waiting for an hour to take him to L'Olympia, the oldest and most legendary music hall in Paris.

Backstage, Michael sat on a plush purple velvet couch and nursed a bottle of beer. Lily sat on his knee making polite small talk with the road crew. Michael felt the weight and the curve of her body on his knee. She wasn't wearing underwear. He was about to ask the road crew to give him a moment alone when Sam rambled in, followed closely by the Colonel, holding Dolly slobbering in one arm and Elvis on a leash. Dolly squirmed free and hit the floor with a thud, then began biting Elvis's back legs and snorting. Sam winced at the noise. He looked gaunt and pale. Beads of sweat stood out on his forehead. He fell heavily into a leather easy chair next to Michael, smiled politely at Lily, and whispered to the Colonel, "Tea."

The Colonel, his face lined with worry, yelled at the dogs to shut up, then rushed to a card table loaded with potato chips, a vegetable tray, beer, fried chicken, coffee, and tea. He took a paper cup from a stack, filled it, ripped open a bag of Egyptian licorice tea, and dunked it into the steaming water. Hands shaking, he placed it gently next to Sam.

"You okay, mate?" Michael said, playfully slapping Sam on the knee.

"It's the voice," Sam croaked. "Guess I'm not used to so much singing. I'll be fine come summer. Just gotta knock the rust off."

DOROTHY CARVELLO

The Colonel put his hand on Sam's shoulder and addressed the room. "Let's keep the talk to a minimum," he said. "Sam's having voice trouble."

"Poor Colonel flew all the way here to see our last show," Sam struggled to say, "and I can't give him a show." His voice sounded like gravel grinding on gravel. "He wants me to sit this one out. I told him I'd sit it out like hell. The Beatles played on this stage, and The Stones too. I'm getting out there if it kills me."

By showtime, Sam was a new man. With the roar of the crowd in his ears, his spine straightened, his eyes sparkled, and he found a way to sing. Toward the end of Sam's set, when his voice seemed too hoarse to finish, Michael strapped on his guitar and ran onstage to join him. The Colonel walked to the wings and watched as Michael backed up Sam for the rest of his set, playing every note perfect. He studied the way Michael held his guitar like a wild animal he was struggling to tame, and the way his lip curled when he sang, and the way his taut ass swung to the music. If he had any doubt about the letter, about Rosemary, about Sam's lost son, the performance was final proof.

The Colonel returned to the dressing room and sat tearing up napkins into tiny balls, his leg jogging uncontrollably. He wanted to tell Sam about Michael, but he didn't want to ruin the magic they had together just when it was starting to hit big. Eventually, Sam finished his set and joined the Colonel backstage, where he fell asleep while Michael performed. In the pale light of the dressing room, Sam looked like a cadaver. The Colonel shook him by the arm and said, "There's a car outside. I'm putting you on the first plane out of here." He hoisted Sam and walked him outside, the eternal crutch. The Colonel nearly had to lift his old friend into the car. He watched the taillights recede into the Parisian night, then, alone in the dressing room, feeling faint, listening to Michael's voice punctuated by the roar of the crowd, the Colonel poured himself a stiff drink, took out his phone, and called Dr. Robert.

"Good doctor, what have you got for me tonight?" he said.

"I think you're going to like what's on the menu," Robert replied.

The Colonel had always loved French men. They were more expensive than most, but then again, you got what you paid for. After receiving directions on where to go and who to look for, the Colonel said, "One more thing...something's wrong with Sam. I need you to make an appointment."

"Sam still into young men?"

"Not that," the Colonel said, grimacing. "I need a real doctor. And fast."

After the final encore, Michael and his band took their bows and stayed onstage, soaking up the crowd's love like flowers in the sun, blowing kisses to the women, throwing drumsticks and guitar picks to the men. The tour had started with medium sized rooms, two or three thousand seats, but as it went on and word spread the crowds got bigger and bigger, until now, on his final night in Europe, Michael waved goodbye to ten thousand fans, feeling invincible. He had left home a rising star; he would return home a king.

Home. Michael walked off stage like a boomerang about to turn back to the hand that flung it. He loved Europe, but now that home beckoned, he couldn't get there fast enough. His band followed him into the dressing room, where they drank a celebratory bottle of champagne. Then the band climbed in their hired limo and sped to the airport.

When they had gone, Michael crept to the backstage door and cracked it open. A feral cry went through the crowd of women assembled outside. Michael looked them over, selected two, and ushered them into his private limousine, leaving Martha in his wake to hand out T-shirts and stickers to the unchosen horde.

Michael and the girls had made a mess of the upholstery by the time the limo arrived on the tarmac, where a private jet had been commissioned to take Michael home. The baggage man opened the door just as Michael was pulling up his pants. He handed the man a pair of lacy underwear as a tip, then swaggered up the stairs and onto the plane, a girl on each arm. Up in the air they chased each other through the aisles naked, finding creative uses for every seat on the craft.

When it was over, they crawled into the sleeping bunk and slept naked. Michael usually loved the sound of two women sleeping next to him. It soothed him. But tonight he found no rest. Instead, the blue light of his phone shone in his eyes as he stared at the screen and replied to Cee Cee: *Coming.*

18

HOME SWEET HOME

DAWN CREPT OVER NASHVILLE AS the limo reached Michael's house. The driver grabbed Michael's suitcase and guitar followed him up the driveway, placing them gently on the front porch and waiting politely for a tip. Michael paid the man and entered his empty house, feeling a strange, hollow sadness, like a child after opening his presents on Christmas morning. The tour had only just ended and already he missed it terribly.

Having never performed to such huge crowds, with the glare of the spotlight in his eyes and the roar of the crowd in his ears, he did not recognize these—crowd, spotlight, roar—as drugs. As a seducer, he should have known when he was being seduced. And yet, he didn't feel it when he boarded the plane in Paris or when he landed in Nashville. Not until he returned to his empty house did it hit him.

He felt desperate to move.

He climbed in his brown Jeep and tooled around Nashville looking for a place to go. It was a slow Tuesday night. He found himself on Lower Broadway, where the neon lights made him feel warm. He parked and walked along the sidewalk. Heads turned as he passed, and soon he had amassed a cloud of satellites. They wanted his autograph. They wanted his picture. They shook his hand and patted his back.

Michael ducked into a bar called the Second Fiddle, where a honky-tonk band performed on a small wooden riser in the corner. His satellites stood outside like children at a Macy's Christmas display window, their noses nearly pressed to the glass. He took a seat at the bar. The bartender's eyes widened and quickly returned to normal, but in that fraction of a second, Michael understood that his old life, for better or worse, was over.

Before the bartender could bring his beer, Michael was gone. He nearly sprinted to his Jeep, drove home, and cracked open the beer in his refrigerator. It was half past nine. He sat in the dark and imagined himself on tour again. Sam would be taking the stage right about now. He felt the nervous excitement that electrified him every night in Europe. He couldn't stop his leg from jogging, so he got up and paced the floor, then grabbed his phone and texted Cee Cee: *Here I am. Come over.*

Michael, she replied, with a heart emoji. *I'm so sorry. My dad had surgery. I'm at their house now. Can't leave until tomorrow at the earliest.*

Tour starts again tomorrow, Michael replied.

Darn it. How long are you gone?

Six weeks, then a week off, then every day up to Thanksgiving.

We'll find a way, she wrote.

On a sweltering day in mid-May, in the bowels of Atlanta's Truist Park, Sam struggled to swallow a strand of spaghetti. He heard the sound of slobbering behind him, and he knew the Colonel had arrived. Dolly and Elvis made their introductions in the form of wet noses and slimy tongues. Then came the Colonel with a magazine in his hand. He slapped it on the table and said, "You're back, my boy." There on the cover of *Rolling Stone* Sam and Michael stood smiling, arms around each other, beneath the headline: "Country Music's Past, Present, and Future." That was what Cee Cee had said to Bucky the first time she saw Michael and Sam together.

Shelby sat alone at a table watching Sam and the Colonel. She hadn't even worked up the nerve to introduce herself. Bucky promised to be there, but he was late. In fact, she hadn't heard from him in weeks. It made her nervous. First, Dave Cobb backed out of producing her album. Then, she showed up to the *Rolling Stone* shoot on Bucky's command to be told they had never heard of her. It was humiliating. But at least he kept his word about her opening on the tour.

Bucky finally arrived with Cee Cee. He took a long time with Sam and the Colonel before even acknowledging Shelby. Then he approached, leaned in, and whispered in her ear, "I've been thinking about you."

"Really?" she said, trying to mask her excitement.

"Really."

Cee Cee stood awkwardly in the corner, watching. Then, all of a sudden, the energy in the room changed. Half a minute later, Michael walked in with Lily on his arm: like a powerful storm, it seemed his aura extended for miles around him, heralding his arrival, changing the weather in any room long before he appeared.

He smelled Cee Cee first, then saw her. She had resumed her place by Bucky's side. Taking Lily by the hand, he walked across the floor like he owned it, stopping to shake Bucky's hand with a casual, "All right, mate?" and leaning in to kiss Cee Cee on the cheek, a polite gesture held just a fraction of a second too long. But Bucky's eyes were busy undressing Lily, blind to everything but the supple curve of her breasts beneath her cotton sundress.

"Are you going to stay and watch?" Michael whispered to Cee Cee. She flushed red from her forehead to her shoulders.

"Of course," she said.

"Good. Maybe we can see each other after."

"Bucky's taking me to dinner," Cee Cee said. "Or so he says. Anyway, won't you be busy?" She glared at Lily.

Michael savored the jealousy painted on Cee Cee's face. He scanned the room and found Martha, who stood next to a table full of Zephyrhills bottled water, yelling into a walkie talkie, "The rider said sparkling water!" With a snap of his fingers, Michael called Martha to his side and said quietly, "Can you deal with Lily, please?" With the silent speed of a ninja, Martha crossed the room, took Lily by the arm, and led her away while cooing platitudes to smooth over Michael's graceless demand.

Before Michael could return his gaze to Cee Cee, Bucky cut in on the conversation. "Listen, Mike, baby," he said. "Do your thing out there tonight, okay? You let me worry about the numbers, which by the way, look very, very good." He yanked Shelby toward Michael. "And you watch this girl and give her some pointers, okay?"

Cee Cee felt she was being stabbed in the heart as Michael took Shelby's hand and introduced himself with that melting smile and those fathomless brown eyes. It was bad enough for Bucky to have Shelby, but now Michael would see her every night for the next six months. Cee Cee's face crumpled into a scowl.

Feeling her fury at his side, Michael surreptitiously grabbed Cee Cee's hand, gave it a quick squeeze, and turned that smile and those eyes on her. "Lovely to see you again, Mrs. Porter," he said. Then, addressing the group: "If you'll pardon me, it's time to prepare." He went to his dressing room and texted Cee Cee: *Find an excuse. We have five minutes.*

Cee Cee began to sweat. "Where's the bathroom?" she asked and walked off down the hall looking for Michael's dressing room. She knocked. He answered stripped to the waist, his hair falling around his shoulders in feminine curls, his sinewy, muscular arms resting on the door jamb. Cee Cee stared at him, speechless. He pulled her into the dressing room, shut the door, and kissed her with such passion it knocked all jealousy from her mind.

"Bucky's right out there," Cee Cee said as Michael began to unbutton her blouse.

"Do you want me to stop?"

She kissed him.

Cee Cee marveled at what a man could do in such a short time. Five minutes later, she stood in the hallway again, leaning against Michael's door for support. Her entire body seemed to vibrate. She fixed her hair and walked on wobbly legs to find Bucky.

During the concert, Michael kept shooting glances at Cee Cee, his eyebrow raised, his head cocked, his lip curled in a boyish grin, and in those moments, lasting no longer than the blink of an eye, the twenty thousand fans in Truist Park disappeared, and Bucky and the Colonel disappeared, and the band disappeared, and the only two people in the entire world were Michael and Cee Cee.

Then he was gone, driving up the East Coast, through Augusta, Charleston, Charlotte, Raleigh, Newport News, Washington, DC. The audiences swelled. The album sales soared. Michael and Sam broke every streaming record in existence—then broke them again. They hit New York City and turned west through Philadelphia, Pittsburgh, Akron, Dayton, Bloomington, Chicago.

After each concert, Michael took his guitar onto Sam's bus, and the two men sat strumming together until songs began to form. Michael recorded demos on his phone, and by the end of June, they had written half an album. Neither man spoke of it, for fear of scaring it away. Instead, they remained silent like hunters in a blind, until another song was in the bag.

Inwardly, Sam learned to trust Michael's instincts. It seemed every time a song got stuck, Michael's fingers knew exactly where to go on his fretboard to unloosen it with something unexpected, something Sam would never have thought of in a hundred years. For Michael, watching Sam work was like taking a master class. Sam's instincts for a hit had lost none of their sharpness. He just needed fresh ideas, which Michael knew he could provide. But when Sam made a suggestion—don't go to the chorus there, make 'em wait for it, build the tension, repeat the first verse at the end, put a guitar solo there, have the harmony come in beneath the melody—Michael listened as though the words had come from the mouth of the Buddha.

Neither Sam nor Michael had ever had a songwriting partner before, so the unique relationship—deeper than friendship, comparable to nothing except being in love—was new to each of them. Like young lovers, they believed themselves the first people in history to ever discover it.

All the while, Michael continued his ritual of texting Cee Cee before each show to pick his outfit. But now he noticed a change in her replies. Instead of long silences and formal responses, she seemed somehow free. One night she even sent a picture of herself in Christian

Louboutin black heels and black lace Agent Provocateur panties, her tresses carefully arranged to cover each breast. Michael called her immediately. "Now you have to finish what you started," he said.

Cee Cee had never had phone sex. It was yet another thing that set Michael apart from every man she had ever known. At first she struggled, it felt so silly. But Michael set the example. He made it seem so natural to describe everything they dreamed of doing to each other. When it was over, Cee Cee couldn't speak for panting. She felt high. Love, passion—these were drugs more powerful than anything she could have imagined.

19

DADDY'S HOME

THEN CAME MICHAEL'S WEEK OFF. Though the rest was badly needed, it took great effort to stop the momentum of such a huge production. Michael, Sam, and Martha each experienced a sort of emotional whiplash as the rhythm of the road turned into the confinement of a vacation.

The Colonel gave Martha one day off then called her into his office for a report.

"Well?" he said as she took a chair opposite him at his desk.

"He's fine," she said. "Typical rock star stuff."

"Are you keeping him out of trouble?"

"Not even close."

The Colonel let out a lewd laugh.

"At least it's the kind of trouble we can handle," Martha continued. "Although there is one thing."

The Colonel lit a cigar, puffed, and gave Martha a look that said, *Continue.*

"Something is going on between Michael and Bucky's wife."

The Colonel exhaled a cloud of smoke. His face struggled to grimace through the Botox. He jabbed a manicured finger at his phone, instructed Siri, "Call Doctor Robert," and growled, "Put a man on Michael this week. I want to know his every move." Then turning back to Martha, he laid ten crisp hundred-dollar bills on his desk and said, "Good girl. Go get yourself something nice."

Meanwhile, Michael retrieved his dogs from the animal spa where he had left them, drove home with a grumbling stomach, ransacked his house, and found nothing but a moldy block of cheese. *Goddamnit*, he texted Martha, *I told you to hire a housekeeper. What the fuck is going on?*

Sorry, I'm on it, Martha replied. She didn't tell him she couldn't just hire anyone to watch his house, or that vetting the candidates took time, or that she had other duties to attend to—like buying him horses, and dogs, and freeing him from his romantic entanglements. It was her job to make the impossible possible, and to do it so smoothly Michael would never feel the slightest discomfort.

Michael texted Cee Cee next: *I need groceries. Meet me at Whole Foods?*

Cee Cee climbed the stairs to her bedroom, stripped off her pajamas, pulled a cashmere sweater over her naked breasts and stepped into yoga pants. She put her hair up, then let it down, then put it up, then decided to let it fall nonchalantly around her shoulders. A touch of makeup, and she was downstairs writing a note to Bucky: "Going to get food for dinner. Be home soon."

Michael was waiting for her outside the store when she arrived. "You're early," she said.

"I told you I wouldn't be late again."

Michael had dressed in his normal disguise—thick glasses, a baseball hat pulled low over his eyes—but heads still turned in his direction as he led Cee Cee through the aisles. Neither cared. The world around them ceased to exist. They were lost in each other, on fire with the sudden realization that every cliché about love was true. And so neither noticed the sound of a camera clicking when Michael took Cee Cee's hand and intertwined his fingers with hers, then stuffed both hands in his jacket pocket.

In the parking lot, loading the paper bags into his trunk, Michael begged Cee Cee to follow him home. "I can't," Cee Cee said. "There's some sort of stupid event I have to attend. Another one of these industry soirées where they all pat themselves on the back."

"You can't get out of it?"

"I don't think so."

"You know I leave in a few days."

"I know," she said. "Be patient with me. You're not used to this, but the rest of us in the real world can't just do whatever we want at the drop of a hat."

"Why not?"

"Michael..."

"Do you love him?"

"Who?"

"Bucky."

Cee Cee looked up into Michael's eyes and took his hands in hers. Standing on tiptoes, she kissed him, letting her tongue dance across his bottom lip. Neither heard the camera click.

"What a fuckin' day," the Colonel muttered to himself as he steered his Cadillac into Sam's driveway, knowing the hardest part lay before him. He walked to the giant oak door, Elvis and Dolly slobbering in his wake. Betty greeted him and walked him through the mansion back to the pool, where Sam sat staring at nothing.

"You dead yet?" the Colonel said playfully.

"Almost," Sam replied. He was in no mood to play.

"How was the flight home?"

"Fine."

"What did the doctor say?"

"It ain't good," Sam said with a strange smile that the Colonel recognized as his attempt at a brave face.

"Oh?" the Colonel said, struggling to control his voice. Elvis lay panting at his feet. He fussed with the dog to hide his nerves.

"It's cancer, alright," Sam said. "My esophagus."

The Colonel felt faint. He sat down and ran his fingers through his elegantly coiffed hair. "Not now," he whispered to himself.

"I said the same damn thing," Sam said.

A dozen questions ran through the Colonel's mind. "How?" was all he could muster.

"Ever heard of something called HPV?" Sam said. "You get it from oral sex. Guess I blew a few too many boys. Or maybe it was the pussy. Presley once told me real men don't eat pussy. Should've listened."

The Colonel stared at Sam, his mouth opening and closing like a dying fish.

"You know, Colonel, I felt reborn these last few months," Sam said. Tears welled in his eyes. "Really did. Felt reborn."

The Colonel rested his hand on Sam's knee, and for a moment, they were boys again, sharing a ratty apartment, dreaming of fame and fortune. Sam was all the Colonel had, the only person he had ever loved except himself. The thought of losing him...no, the Colonel couldn't let himself go there. He pushed the fear down like he always did and returned to business like he always did. He had been waiting for the right moment to tell Sam about Michael, and it hadn't come. So he picked what he was sure was the wrong moment.

"Sam, there's something I have to tell you."

"Better be good news," Sam said with a smile that slowly faded as he saw the fear in the Colonel's eyes.

"Do you remember when you stopped drinking?" the Colonel said.

"January 25, 1987," Sam said. "Sick as a dog in a hospital in Sydney, Australia."

"Do you remember the nurse you fucked in that hospital?"

"Colonel, I barely remember what I ate for breakfast this morning."

The Colonel was silent for a full minute, working up his courage. Finally, he spoke. "Well, Sam, you slept with your nurse, and she got pregnant and had a son."

Sam nearly fell out of his chair. "You shittin' me, Colonel?" he said.

"The woman sent letters and made phone calls for about a year after the boy was born. I kept it from you because, well, that was my job, wasn't it? Keeping the parasites away."

Sam looked at the sky and said dreamily, "A son." Then, turning to the Colonel, he said, "Can I meet him?"

"Well, that's where it gets complicated," the Colonel said. "I just found one of the letters while I was looking in the old storage unit for...for something. Her name was Rosemary Jennings."

The dawning spread across Sam's face.

"Not Michael," he said.

The Colonel merely nodded. He handed Sam the crumpled letter, so he could see for himself. The paper shook in Sam's hands as he read.

"Why did you keep this from me?" he whispered when he had reached the end.

"Who knew if this chick was telling the truth? You know how many people tried to shake you down? I thought if she was for real, she would have a lawyer send a letter asking for a DNA test and child support."

"We gotta tell Michael."

"Not yet," the Colonel said. Sam flinched at the severity in his voice. "This can be the best thing for us. Give me some time to figure how to work it out."

Sam chewed it over, and it didn't feel right, but then again, he remembered the way he felt standing in front of a couple thousand screaming fans every night in Europe, and he thought of the American tour—stadiums—and he swallowed hard. That feeling, being wanted again, being famous again, being powerful again, was the only thing that made him want to live. Sam said, "Hey, ol' buddy, do what you gotta do." Then, pointing to his throat, "Just don't take too long to figure it out."

After the Colonel left, Betty came outside with a tray of lemonade to find Sam slumped in his chair staring desolately at the glimmering swimming pool.

"Everything okay Mister Sam?" she asked.

"Fix me a drink," he said. She placed the lemonade next to him. With a vicious swipe of his arm, he knocked the glass to the ground where it shattered, leaving the pool deck scattered with sharp little diamonds. "A real drink," he snarled.

"Mister Sam, we don't have that here anymore."

"Go to the fucking liquor store and make me a goddamn drink," he shouted.

Betty was a long time gone. When she returned, she threw a brown bag in his lap and, her voice trembling, said, "Make it yourself. I'm not going to help you do this."

"Get back inside, woman," Sam snarled. He eased the bottle of bourbon from the paper bag and tore at the seal. He tilted the bottle up, and the liquor caught the sunlight and turned a beautiful shade of amber. Sam had forgotten how good it tasted. His head began to swim. In the chaotic way of the mind, a long buried memory bubbled to the surface. It was 1987. During a concert at the Sydney Forum in Australia, he felt an intense pain in his side. He was able to eke out the show but collapsed in his dressing room. He was rushed to Sydney General and diagnosed with an inflamed liver. The rest of the tour was promptly canceled.

At the hospital he met a pretty young nurse. The next day, she brought in some of his records and asked him to sign them. Then she asked if there was anything she could do to make him feel better, and he said there was one thing and raised his eyebrow in that inimitable Sam Rogers way, and he slid his hand up her nurse's uniform and pulled her panties down, and a day later when the Colonel had put him on a plane to California with a ticket to the Betty Ford Center, he had forgotten the entire thing. "Haff to essplain to Michael," he slurred softly to himself as the booze stole his senses.

Driving home, the Colonel received a text from Dr. Robert and nearly crashed his car into the concrete median. "Son of a bitch," he muttered, staring at the photos of Michael and Cee Cee kissing. His mind hummed with plans. He never liked Bucky. Now he had what he needed to control him. But how? Some situations, the Colonel knew, called for the precision of a surgeon. Others called for a battering ram.

He decided on the battering ram.

He parked in a strip mall and texted the pictures to his burner phone, then sent them from the burner phone to a reporter he knew at *Country People*. Nothing like a little scandal to get things moving.

20

HIT THE ROAD

MICHAEL HATED PACKING. HE BELIEVED someone should do it for him, yet he knew it would take just as long to explain what he needed in his suitcase as it would to pack it himself. Socks, underwear, stage clothes, pants, shirts, belts. A toothbrush, a comb, nail clippers. Tylenol, vitamins, antacids. The dogs nuzzled at his hands and jumped on the bed to play in the open suitcase as Michael prepared his things in a pile. "Boys," he said sternly, "off." The dogs whimpered and obeyed.

Shaving cream, a razor, Q-tips. A bath towel, slippers, a robe. "Where are my boots?" he asked the dogs. They stared at him, panting. Like many performers, Michael had a touch of superstition. Grandma Pearl had given him a pair of black leather boots on his eighteenth birthday, and he never stepped on stage without them. He walked downstairs and ripped up the living room, upturning the couch and chairs, rummaging in the laundry, ransacking the garage. Back upstairs, he opened every cabinet in the bathroom, peered under the bed on hands and knees, and scoured the balcony. Tearing through his closet, he found the boots perched on a shelf in the corner. "When the hell did I put them here?" he muttered to himself, and as he snatched them from the shelf, he clumsily knocked over a cardboard box full of miscellaneous paperwork and possessions.

Cleaning his mess, he noticed a familiar sheet of yellowed paper and pulled it from the pile. "I just want you to know that you have a son," he read in his mother's voice. "I don't expect you to leave Nashville, but I think you should be part of his life."

The words didn't hurt him the way they usually did. They once had the power to propel him across the globe, to this very spot where he stood, but they now seemed so far away. In a strange way, Michael felt grateful for all these words had given him.

"Thanks, Mum," he said, kissing the paper, folding it, and placing it back in the box. He finished packing, zipped his suitcase, carried it down the stairs and sat it by the front door. Then he went back upstairs to pack what he referred to simply as "the bag." It went everywhere with him: sex toys, handcuffs, leg cuffs, condoms, a Polaroid camera, a stack of pictures of past conquests, and a copy of *The Kama Sutra*.

All finished, he texted Cee Cee: *Wanna come over?*

Cee Cee sat across the table from Bucky at Bourbon Steak, eating in silence while he conducted business on a phone call, pausing every now and again to stuff his mouth full of Kobe beef. "Hang on, getting a text," he said to the caller. He pulled the phone from his ear. His eyes narrowed. His mouth crumpled into a vicious sneer. He put the phone to his ear again. "I'm gonna have to call you back," he said in a strained voice and dropped the phone with a thud onto the table. He swallowed. He breathed hard. He grabbed his glass of bourbon and downed it in one gulp. He picked up his phone and stared again at the Colonel's text, a link to a photo on the *People* magazine website showing Michael and Cee Cee kissing, along with the message, *Get your house in order. I'll take care of the press.*

"Bitch," he said. He squeezed the phone in a trembling hand. "Jezebel. This is how you repay me for the life I gave you?"

"Keep your voice down," she said, her stomach sinking. "What are you even talking about?"

He showed her the phone. The blood drained from her face.

"What do you want me to say, Bucky?" she said, looking down at the table.

"How could you do this to me?"

Cee Cee snatched the phone from his hands, her eyes red and wild, and scrolled to his text thread with Shelby, then pulled up a picture of her wearing a see-through nightgown, her tits just visible through the black mesh, a cat emoji with heart eyes covering her vagina. She threw the phone on the table in front of Bucky.

"I don't love you anymore," Cee Cee whispered, her eyes brimming with tears.

"Cunt," Bucky screamed and slammed his hands on the table, spilling food and toppling Cee Cee's glass of wine.

"Don't make a scene, Bucky. It's not polite. Let's talk about it when we get home."

His voice became deadly quiet. "You don't have a fucking home anymore," he said.

Cee Cee rose from her chair and folded her napkin on the table. "I'm going to call a car," she said, her voice wavering.

"Where do you think you're going?"

"I'm sorry, Bucky, I tried to love you. I really did."

"You can't hide from me in this town," Bucky called after her as she walked away. "Bitch!" Heads turned in the restaurant. Bucky bellowed, "Get a good look at the whore of Babylon, everyone!"

Cee Cee took an Uber home and packed a small suitcase, checked into a penthouse at the Four Seasons, and called Michael. She could barely speak for sobbing. "He found out," she said. "He knows everything. Oh, God."

"Calm down," Michael said. "What happened?"

Cee Cee's crying subsided into small hiccoughs as she told Michael the story.

"Where are you now?" he said.

"I got a room at the Four Seasons."

"Can I come over?"

"I need to be alone tonight. Oh, God, what am I going to do?"

Michael thought for a moment. "Why don't you come on tour with me?"

"What? Michael..."

"Really, think about it. We can be together. He won't be able to reach us."

"He'll ruin you, Michael."

"I have a contract and a good lawyer. I'm not afraid of him."

"You mean it?"

"Don't you miss the open road?"

Cee Cee laughed through her tears. "What if you get sick of me?"

"Then they'll have to bury me, because that'll mean I'm dead."

21

A ROOM WITH A VIEW

THAT NIGHT, MICHAEL ENTERED THE Four Seasons in his best disguise. He carried a bouquet of peonies. The bellboy gave him a strange look, then immediately looked down at his own feet. At the front desk, Michael asked for Cee Cee Porter's room, and the concierge's eyes widened almost imperceptibly before her face resumed its mask of hospitality. Michael reminded himself that he belonged to a new world now, a secret world invisible to the unwashed masses, a world in which a man stayed in a luxury hotel because the staff there was trained to *not* recognize him. How strange, he thought, to work so hard for fame and then pay for anonymity.

The concierge handed Michael a slip of paper with a room number written on it. "Shall I call up?" she asked.

"No, thanks," Michael said. He rode the elevator to the thirty-fifth floor. The plush carpet absorbed his footfall as he searched for Cee Cee's room. He knocked at the door, unsure for the first time in his life what to say or do around a woman. But when she opened the door, and Michael saw her in the soft light, with the floor-to-ceiling picture windows showing the Nashville skyline behind her, a silk robe tied at her waist and the movement of her body beneath it, he acted on instinct, dropping the flowers on the carpet, taking her face in his hands and kissing her deeply.

"What are you doing here?" she said.

"This."

In one fluid motion, Michael lifted Cee Cee in his arms and carried her, legs wrapped around him, to the picture window. The glass shuddered with the impact of her body.

"Everyone can see us," Cee Cee said between moans.

"Does that bother you?" Michael said, untying her robe with one arm, while holding her with the other. She pulled down his pants and guided him inside her.

When they finished, they lay on the plush carpet, panting; Cee Cee had never felt so possessed. Bucky didn't matter anymore. Every part of her body, from the tips of her toenails to the follicles of her hair, belonged to Michael. She felt fully alive for the first time in years. "There's something I want to show you," she said, rising from the floor and tugging at Michael's hand. They stood and embraced, and in their nakedness there was no shame. Cee Cee pushed him onto the bed. "Wait here," she said, retreating to the small penthouse closet. As he waited, Michael took a peony from the ground, plucked its petals and scattered them over the bed. Meanwhile, Cee Cee slipped on the Nina Ricci lingerie, cued up Fleetwood Mac's "Gypsy" on her phone, and stepped into the moonlight streaming through her bedroom window.

"You liked the gift?" Michael said, surrounded by a halo of peony petals.

For an answer, she hit play. The sounds of guitars, flutes, and the insistent beat began. Cee Cee had taken ballet for years as a child and had classic dancer's legs. She began to move to the beat, her long hair flowing as she swung her head from side to side. Her arms moved gracefully around her body as Stevie Nicks sang "Gypsy" in her low voice.

Watching her dance, Michael became hard again. As the song neared its end, he jumped off the bed and knelt at Cee Cee's feet. He kissed up her leg, removed her panties with his teeth and explored her with his tongue. As he moved up to her stomach, planting slow kisses like flags in virgin soil, the music stopped. In the still of night, she moaned, "Michael, I love you."

His answer was a kiss on the lips by the light of the moon. He steered her to the bed, and at the height of pleasure whispered in her ear, "I love you too."

After it was over, Michael stroked Cee Cee's back, carefully plucking off the mashed peony petals stuck to her sweat. She cooed with each brush of his fingers.

"So what happened?" he said.

Cee Cee was silent for a long time. She tried to find the pictures on *People* magazine, not knowing the Colonel had ordered Martha to threaten the magazine into killing the story. "Funny," she muttered. "They were just here." Then, turning to face Michael, she said, "I told Bucky I don't love him anymore."

"What did he say?"

"I can't repeat it."

"What did you ever see in him, anyway?"

"He was my first real boyfriend. We were in college. He was older. I was only a freshman, and he was a grad student. It seemed like he knew everything. He fooled around, but I guess I thought if we got married and had a baby…"

"He'd change."

"Funny, right?"

"And then you were stuck."

"In my world, you don't even say the word 'divorce.'"

"Why do people make these prisons for themselves?"

"You're free, Michael. That's why I love you. I don't think you can understand it."

"I guess not. Is it over?"

"Basically."

"Good. Tour starts in three days."

"I have to figure out so many things," she said.

"Does that mean you're not coming?"

She went silent again. She thought of her mother, her grandmother, her great-grandmother, all of whom stayed faithful to unfaithful men, dutifully cooking, and cleaning, and hosting bridge club, and weaning children, and joining the PTA, and 4-H, and the Daughters of the American Revolution, until the lack of love desiccated them, shriveled them, sapped them of all sweetness, leaving them lemons for hearts and faces drawn in a perpetual pucker. To renounce that life was freedom, but it was also a kind of death. She turned and looked at Michael, his hair wild against the backdrop of the city skyline, and knew her choice had been made but didn't yet know what it meant.

"You got room for me on the bus?" she said, kissing him.

"Of course. You'll sleep on top of me."

Cee Cee swatted Michael with a pillow, laughing.

"Maybe we can write a few songs together," she said.

"I wish I didn't have to go out at all. I just want to stay here."

"Yeah, right. There's a lot of girls out there that need to see the great Michael Jennings."

"Too bad for them. I got a girl."

Slowly the talk subsided until they fell asleep in each other's arms.

22

AMERICAN DREAMS

THE TOUR RESUMED ON THE Fourth of July in Washington, DC. Michael began his evening singing the national anthem at Nationals Park before the All-Star Game. Cee Cee stood by the third-base dugout, feeling naked under the eyes of forty-odd thousand baseball fans. It was the first time since college she had not been Bucky's girlfriend, fiancé, or wife. Scarier still, it was the first time she had appeared in public as Michael's girlfriend.

She didn't know how to feel. Martha stood beside her, casting awkward glances in her direction. Michael finished to a standing ovation. Martha pulled out her walkie talkie and said, "I've got eyes on Michael; we're coming to the limo...three of us," and it seemed Martha said the word "three" with a touch of disdain and a sour glance at Cee Cee.

Cee Cee knew how a professional tour worked, its rhythms and necessities, its nightly triumphs and daily crises. She also knew the demands placed on the star. It hadn't been so long since the entire machine was spinning around her. Though Martha made her feel out of place, Martha could not make her feel she didn't belong. More than that, Martha couldn't stop the idea from dawning in Cee Cee's mind that she could help Michael. She knew this end of the business better than Martha. She also knew how hard Martha had to work for the crumbs that fell from the men's table, and she didn't want to take Martha's job. But she did want to protect Michael, grow his brand, and take his career even further, even higher.

Inside Capital One Arena the limo parked behind Bucky's car. Cee Cee's stomach tensed. He had come. Of course he had come. Walking to the dressing rooms, her heels echoing off the concrete halls, Cee Cee barely felt Michael's arm around her shoulder. In her mind's eye, she saw Bucky attacking Michael like a chest-thumping gorilla. She saw the two men brawling on the floor. She saw herself being asked to leave the tour, leave Michael, return to Bucky rather than ruin Sam's comeback and Michael's career.

As they turned the corner, she smelled Bucky's cheap cologne and felt Michael tense at her side for a fight. But Bucky pretended not to notice them. Cee Cee wasn't sure if it was cowardice or the tactics of a brilliant general who knows never to fight unless he has the advantage.

Bucky had his arm slung around Shelby's waist, and he led her into her private dressing room.

"I'm so sorry Bucky," Shelby said, as he shut the door. "I heard about Cee Cee. Don't worry, baby. We don't have to hide anymore." She shoved her hand down his pants and stroked his penis.

Bucky ripped her hand away.

"What about your husband?" he sneered.

"I'd leave him for you. I told you that. He doesn't understand this world anyway." She gestured at the arena around them.

"So you want me because I can help your career, is that it? You think you can fuck your way to the top?"

"Bucky, come on, you know that's not—"

"I can't believe you'd even bring this up," he said. "Unbelievable."

Shelby slunk back, chastened. "You're right," she said. "I'm sorry. I shouldn't have said it." Bucky turned to walk away, but she grabbed his arm. "Bucky, wait. I wanted to ask about my album."

"I'm working on it," Bucky said sharply. "'In due season we shall reap, if we faint not.' Galatians 6:9. If you do well out there tonight, maybe it'll move things along."

But while Shelby prepared in her dressing room for another performance to a stadium of mostly empty seats, Bucky held a hushed conversation with the Colonel outside her door. "I don't think she's going to make it," he said. "She just hasn't developed the way I hoped she would. I think we should terminate her contract."

"We sold out the whole tour already," the Colonel said. "It would be a pain in the nuts to get a new opener. Let's give her one last hurrah."

When Michael saw Sam backstage, all thoughts of Bucky disappeared. Most of Sam's hair had fallen out, but that was easily covered with a ten-gallon cowboy hat. Harder to hide was the gauntness in his face, the sunken cheekbones, the hollow eyes. Sitting next to the old man, Michael took off his sunglasses and baseball cap and ran his hand through his hair. "Christ almighty, Sam," he said. "You okay?"

"Nothing to worry about, young buck," Sam said, forcing a laugh. "Doctors say I'll be all patched up by the time we hit Houston. Ain't that right, Colonel?"

The Colonel stepped into the conversation, but Michael ignored him. His eyes were fixed on Sam with an intensity that smothered the energy in the room. In Sam's face, Michael saw the ghost of his mother as she wasted away, silent in her agony. Sam averted his eyes sheepishly. Michael walked to his dressing room without a word and slammed the door.

Why had no one told him? Not Sam, not the Colonel, not Martha. Hot tears welled in his eyes. He texted Martha, *What the fuck?*

Did I miss something? she replied.

Was anyone going to tell me Sam has cancer?

Oh. That. Sorry, Michael. They didn't want you to know. Who told you?

I know what it looks like. I watched my mother die.

When the time came for their encore together, Michael could barely bring himself to look at Sam. Sam had lied to him. The voice trouble—just knocking off the rust of age. The hacking cough—just allergies. The inability to eat—just an old man's finicky stomach. Sam hid it from him, just like his mother did, and Michael found out too late to stop it, too late to prepare himself, again. But when Sam began strumming "American Dreams," the gorgeous opening ballad from

Bicentennial, Michael remembered his mother singing it to him as she put him to sleep, and his heart softened:

> *Close your eyes darlin'*
>
> *Hope springs perennial*
>
> *From July the fourth to the bicentennial*
>
> *The flag still waves, the torch still gleams*
>
> *So dream your sweet American dreams.*

Sam removed his in-ear monitor, leaned close to Michael, and said, "I didn't want you to worry, but I shoulda told you. I'm sorry." Michael looked at Sam—the great Sam Rogers, the man he had revered since childhood—and he saw him old, frail, and frightened, but still alive because of the music. His heart flooded with love. He wanted to protect Sam. He wanted to save him.

After the concert, Michael took Sam aside and said, "Come on, old man, we're going to get you something to eat." He, Cee Cee, and Sam disappeared in an Uber and went to Ben's Chili Bowl, where Michael forced Sam to finish a large chili half smoke.

When Sam excused himself to the bathroom, Cee Cee took Michael's hand and said, "He doesn't feel comfortable around me."

"What are you talking about?"

"He doesn't know how to act. He can't even look at me. He's not used to…you know…*us*."

As soon as Sam returned, Michael said, "I know things are a little tense right now, but Cee Cee's going to be with me from now on."

"Michael, don't," Cee Cee said.

"You don't have to be scared of her or anything," Michael barreled on. "She's got great ideas."

"Is that right?" Sam said. "Well, little missy, let's hear 'em."

All eyes turned to Cee Cee. It was an audition for Sam's acceptance. She cleared her throat. "Um," she said. "Okay. Sam, I notice you never play anything off *Old Dog, Old Tricks*."

"No one wants to hear that, darlin'," Sam said. "It was a bad attempt at a comeback. Didn't work in '95. Won't work now."

"I disagree. I always thought it was one of your best albums. I used to play one of the songs, 'A Guy Like Me,' back when I was touring." Cee Cee began to sing in a clear, sweet voice:

> *I'm just a boy with holes in my jeans*
>
> *And you are a girl of money and means*
>
> *But someday I'll sweep you right off of your feet*
>
> *And you'll fall in love with a guy like me.*

"Of course, I changed it to 'a girl like me,'" Cee Cee said, "but people went crazy for it."

Sam grinned. "Maybe you're right," he said, chuckling. "What else you got?"

23

BIG TIME

AUGUST AND SEPTEMBER ROLLED BY, along with Sioux City, Denver, Las Vegas, San Francisco. Cee Cee marveled at Michael's innocence. Fame and money protected him the way a parent protects a small child from the ugliness of the world. Every problem came with someone whose job it was to solve it. Every care came with someone paid to cater to it. When he wanted wine, a glass full of rich red Madeira appeared in his hand. When he wanted a cigarette, a lit Marlboro was thrust between his fingers. Michael had only to knock, and the door was opened.

Cee Cee loved seeing America through Michael's eyes. He demanded to visit all the famous landmarks and attractions he had read about as a child. He stood for an hour under the Gateway Arch, saying, "How did they do it?" He toured a ghost town just outside Denver and had a pretend gunfight with Cee Cee in the middle of the road, standing back to back, counting ten paces, making gunfire with his mouth, then reeling like a silent film actor and falling in the dust. He traipsed through Disneyland like a ten-year-old boy and rode Space Mountain until he got sick. He sat in front of a slot machine at the Sahara in Vegas until three in the morning, holding out every quarter for Cee Cee to kiss for luck before he placed it in the machine, pulled the lever, and yelled at the top of his lungs for the jackpot.

Everywhere he went, a parade of women followed, but he would not even look them in the eye. Though they clamored for his attention, he saw only Cee Cee. And this was the better part of his charm: the entire world seemed made just for him, and everyone in it seemed to exist only to fulfill his desires, and from this bounty, this limitless offering, he had chosen her, Cee Cee.

She did not know he did this with every woman. And she didn't allow herself to imagine what would happen if she left him alone for the night because somewhere deep inside she knew he would not sit and pine for her. She knew his passion, his lust, must find an outlet. Had she asked, Michael would have told her this was true. He would have also told her it did not change his love for her, which had grown more powerful than he imagined possible. This too was true.

Cee Cee didn't care. She didn't want to think. She wanted only to feel. The tour protected her as much as it did Michael. She no longer thought of Bucky. Home was just a word. Whatever trouble awaited her there, it could not touch her here, hidden in the bosom of the great American West, barreling down the unspooling ribbon of highway.

But in her sober moments, Cee Cee knew Michael needed help, and he wouldn't get it from anyone around him, not even Martha. Like all the others, Martha was trained to say yes, to make the impossible possible. In the end, this would only lead Michael to his own destruction. Cee Cee had spent long enough with Bucky to know the music business would feed on Michael until it sucked every last dime out of him, then it would throw his carcass to the vultures and keep on churning.

She began reading his contracts and checking his riders against what the venue had actually provided. After each concert, before she and Michael went dancing or retired to the bus to make love, she tallied the numbers—tickets sold, gross revenue, merchandise, overhead—to make sure they added up. Martha bristled at this encroachment on her territory, and Cee Cee let her bristle. Martha's ego was not her priority; Michael was.

She felt justified when, on a day off in Los Angeles, sitting by the pool at the Waldorf Astoria Beverly Hills, a bell man brought Michael a phone and said, "Mister Jennings, it's Blake Shelton on the line." Michael took the call, laughed a bit, and said, "Yes, I'd love to."

"What was that about?" Cee Cee said when he hung up.

"Blake asked me to open for him on his tour. He's gonna pay me a fortune."

Cee Cee called the bellman and ordered him to redial the number.

"Hi, Blake," she said, when the call went through. "This is Michael's manager, Cee Cee. Sorry to disappoint you, but he's a headliner, not an opener." She hung up.

"Why did you do that?" Michael said.

"Don't you know who you are?" Cee Cee said with a smile. "You don't open for anyone. They open for you."

As they turned back east, Cee Cee came to know Sam better, too. She liked him. She liked the way Michael revered him, cleaned up for him, forced him to eat, and helped him administer the chemo drip, just as he had for his mother. By the time the tour hit Dallas for a concert on Halloween night, Sam's round of chemo had come to an end and he regained some of his energy. That night, he added "A Guy Like Me" to his set and called Cee Cee out onstage to sing it with him. She refused, but Michael gave her a little push in the back and sent her skittering out in front of the crowd, where she received a standing ovation. She couldn't believe so many people remembered her.

Singing in a stadium with a full band behind her hit Cee Cee like a shot of adrenaline to the heart. When time came for the guitar solo, she picked up a Gibson Les Paul sitting on a guitar stand by the drum riser and traded riffs with Sam's guitarist back and forth until the entire stadium lit up with cell phone lights like ten thousand fireflies. When the song ended, the crowd roared and held their lights higher, begging for more. "That's it for me," Cee Cee said into Sam's microphone. "Sam's got a few more things he's gonna do for you. Thank you all."

When Sam finished his set, he bounded backstage and wrapped Cee Cee in a bear hug. "Goddamn, girl, I didn't know you could do that," he said, lifting her off the ground and twirling her around. Setting her down again, he got a wicked twinkle in his eye and said, "Hey, I got an idea." With Cee Cee's help, he stole some of Michael's stage clothes—the lascivious black leather pants, the billowing shirt unbuttoned to the navel—and he donned a wig of long, curly hair, and came out for the encore in costume, dressed like Michael. The crowd roared so loud, it drowned out the band for half the song. Michael looked over to Cee Cee standing in the wings, doubled over with laughter. Then he looked up to the arena ceiling and laughed until tears rolled down his cheeks.

On Sam's bus after the concert, Michael pretended to be angry. "Who the hell did that?" he said, grabbing Cee Cee in a playful head-lock. "Who would have access to my clothes? I wonder."

Sam handed him the wig, laughing, and said, "In case you ever need it." They sat together, Sam on the couch and Michael and Cee Cee on the floor at his feet, dissecting the performance.

"We took 'American Dreams' too fast tonight," Michael said. "You want to tell the drummer or should I?"

"I'll do it. Easier to hear coming from an old legend." Sam winked.

Michael cracked a beer, and Sam asked for one, but Michael refused. "I got too much riding on you, old man," he said with his boyish grin. Then, looking around the bus, he let out a grunt of exasperated dis-gust. The floor was a heap of dirty clothes, empty bags of medicine, used syringes, bottles of beer. "We can't live like this," he said. As he began cleaning, he muttered, "Never thought I'd be Sam Rogers's maid." Michael shook out a plastic trash bag and filled it to the brim, then tied it off and put it near the front of the bus to take out at the next stop. When he began to fold Sam's clothes, Sam protested: "Now wait just a minute. I'm a grown man. I can do for myself." Michael ignored Sam's wounded pride, hoisted a pile of folded clothes in his arms, and walked through the narrow hallway past the bunks to where the lug-gage was stored.

"We only got a couple more weeks anyway until break," Sam called after him. "Might as well stop cleaning and have a good time."

Michael heard Sam and Cee Cee giggling together and returned to find Sam with three unlit joints in his mouth. "Someone gave 'em to me," he mumbled. "Come on, let's light 'em up."

"You're in no condition for that," Michael said.

"He thinks he's my daddy," Sam muttered to Cee Cee.

"Just one won't hurt," Cee Cee said.

"You're supposed to be on my side," Michael laughed, and before he knew it, he was stuck to the floor of the bus, stoned.

"Hey driver," Sam called. "You got any Willie?"

They lay transfixed in the smoky dimness as Willie Nelson's "I'd Have to Be Crazy" poured from the speakers. Michael felt Cee Cee crawl to him and lay her head in the crook of his arm, her nose nuzzling his neck. Sam stretched out on the couch above them. As Willie sang, "I'd Have to Be Crazy," Michael experienced a stoner's epiphany: he had never really had a family. His mother and Grandma Pearl did the best they could, but from the time he could remember, he always felt somehow hollow. After his mother died, the hole inside him became a chasm. Since then, although he still called Grandma Pearl every week and wrote her letters a few times a year, he felt truly alone in the world. Until now. With Cee Cee next to him and Sam above him, Michael realized there are different types of families. Some are given. Some are made.

Cee Cee felt a tear drop on her cheek. "What's wrong, Michael?" she asked.

"Nothing," he said. "Just happy."

24

TRUTH

THEY WOUND THEIR WAY BACK home via Shreveport, Little Rock, and Jackson. By the time they hit Memphis, winter had crept into the air. For so long Cee Cee had ignored Bucky's calls, his profanity-laced voicemails, his threatening texts, but as Nashville came closer, mile by mile, a knot seemed to tighten in her stomach. She found it harder to concentrate on Michael as he strutted onstage. She couldn't follow the thread of conversation on Sam's bus. The full weight of real life fell on her at once. She had so much to do. She had no home, no job, no money, no clothes except what she packed in her suitcase. She'd have to go home—but it wasn't home, she reminded herself; it was Bucky's house—and gather her belongings. Where would she put them? And what about the Thanksgiving charity meal, which was less than three weeks away? She knew Bucky would attend, just as she knew Michael would insist on going with her. And what would she do when Bucky came after her with the best lawyers in Nashville, as she knew he would?

She kept her worry from Michael, wanting to live inside the bubble a little longer before it burst. She kept it from Sam, too, for a bond had grown between them. He reminded her of her uncles, her mother's brothers, who had fucked up their lives beyond recognition but were still the life of every party. She hoped to save Michael from the excesses that ruined Sam, but she also valued the wisdom and experience Sam brought to Michael.

For the first time since she gave up her singing career, Cee Cee felt part of a team. No longer was she a lone woman bending her back in toil for which she'd earn no recognition. Michael listened to her. He valued her input and her guts. He recognized her industry savvy and began to trust her with more and more of his day-to-day life. Sam recognized it too and sometimes asked her for little favors, which she was only too happy to oblige. And when they all sat on the bus together after another sold-out concert, singing along at the top of their lungs to Loretta, or Willie, or Dolly, Cee Cee shared Michael's feeling of family. For years she had lied to herself about Bucky, but deep down she knew they were never a team. She knew their house would never become a home. She knew, in fact, that a baby would be the worst thing to happen to them. She wondered if she had subconsciously made herself infertile with Bucky.

She also noticed Sam growing quieter as the tour wound down, but she attributed it to the natural sadness of saying goodbye. She could not know that with each passing night, Sam came closer and closer to telling Michael the truth, but the Colonel's voice echoed in his head: *Wait, wait, wait.* Wait until I figure it out. Wait until I can see the angles. Wait until I can squeeze every last bit of money, and power, and control out of this news.

On their way back to Nashville, where they'd have a day off, then perform at the Grand Ole Opry, then break for Thanksgiving, Sam said, "Come on, let's get a picture of the Three Musketeers." Cee Cee set the timer on her phone—Sam and Michael were hopeless with technology—and snapped the picture. As Michael slept beside her that night, she gazed at the picture and thought of how often she stood next to Bucky and wore a wooden smile for the cameras. But not this time. Every smile in this picture was genuine. Whatever Bucky did, he couldn't take that away from her.

She kissed Michael on the cheek and curled up against him, smiling still. Yes, whatever Bucky did, she'd be ready for him.

Back in Nashville, Cee Cee had the limo drop her off at her old house. Michael begged her not to go, then he begged her to let him come. "I'll only be an hour," she said. "Go home, get ready for the Opry."

"You promise you'll just pack up your things and then bring them over to my house?" he said.

Cee Cee detected the hint of jealousy and the undertone of neediness in his voice, and it filled her with butterflies. The great Michael Jennings belonged to her. She called the house phone first to make sure Bucky wasn't home—called it seven times and let it ring until the answering machine picked up, because she knew Bucky was lazy enough to let it go two or three times, but even he would get up off his ass if the phone kept ringing.

Exiting the limo, she crept around to the back door and peered in the windows until she felt satisfied no one stirred inside. Then she let herself in quietly and stood transfixed in the doorway as a flood of memories washed through her mind. She seemed to be watching a movie of her own life. It was the smell that did it, the house's aural signature. Every house had one, and it was always invisible to the people who lived there. You could only smell it in someone else's house. Cee Cee understood and accepted that this was now someone else's house.

She walked through the living room and saw herself and Bucky making love on the leather couch the day they moved in, whispering promises to each other, dreaming of everything they would do together, dreaming of themselves withered and gray and happy with their children—two girls, two boys—sitting happily around them while the grandchildren played in the yard.

She climbed the stairs, trailing a finger along the balustrade, and lingered in the nursery, or what should have been the nursery, feeling the pain of that day as though it was new. Five months. Everything was going so well. And then the baby just...died. Bucky had left town on business. Cee Cee drove herself to the hospital and sat in the examining room, sobbing. The doctor told her she had chlamydia, which can cause a miscarriage. He asked her questions about her sexual history, but Cee Cee barely listened. How she drove herself home, she never knew. And she never told Bucky the real reason she lost the baby. She had often suspected him, but that was the first time she knew he was cheating. After that, a veil seemed to fall over her eyes. The world looked gray.

She locked a part of herself away from the pain and created a numb shell around the rest of her. She didn't even know she was doing it. Something inside her simply sensed she could not handle the full brunt of such agony. On the outside she was the smiling, supportive wife; but buried deep within, so deep it lived below her consciousness, was a fathomless pool of sadness, anger, and bitter disappointment.

She felt tears rolling down her cheeks. She hadn't felt present in her own life for so long. Her love, her joy, her passion had been stunted, blunted, deadened like a lame limb. Then came Michael with the key to unlock her. He reached through her flesh and bone and touched her in the invisible dungeon where she had hidden herself. He extended his hand and said, *Come out now, it's safe.*

Cee Cee dried her eyes and got down to work packing her things in a cardboard box—a few books, a few photos and keepsakes, her favorite clothes. Working in the master closet, she heard the front door open and Bucky enter. She considered telling Bucky she was home, but then she heard another voice: the Colonel. Cee Cee crept to the bedroom door, and listened.

"I don't want to talk about it, okay?" Bucky said. "It's my business, and I'll handle it."

"What are you going to do?"

"I'm going to fuck her every way I know how."

"Except the one way."

Bucky laughed. "Exactly," he said. "This will not be a pleasant fucking. She's got no money. I control the royalties for her so-called hit song. I'm going to leave her begging on the streets."

"What about Michael?" the Colonel said.

"I want him out of the picture."

"He's the goose that laid the golden egg."

"More like a fox in a henhouse. I want him gone."

"Why, because he put his hands on your wife? Who are you kidding? No woman is worth that. This is real money we're talking about."

Bucky spent a moment in silent thought. He didn't care about Cee Cee. Their relationship had been a sham for years, maybe forever. But a public display of weakness he could not allow. Not in Nashville, where his enemies pretended to be friends while they sharpened their daggers with scripture and sized him up for the perfect place to stab.

"I can't have this hanging over me, Colonel," he said.

"Let me show you something," the Colonel said with a heavy sigh.

Cee Cee heard the rustling of paper, then silence. She peeked her head around the bedroom door and looked down on Bucky and the Colonel sitting in the living room. Bucky was reading from a crumpled page.

"What the hell is this?" Bucky said when he finished.

"I'll tell you what it is," the Colonel said. "Sam has a son."

"What exactly are you telling me, Colonel?" Bucky said.

"What I am telling you, Bucky, is that almost thirty years ago, Sam was laid up in a hospital in Australia, and he knocked up his nurse, and she had a boy." The Colonel sat silently, rubbing his diamond-studded cufflinks between his thumb and forefinger, while Bucky digested the news.

"Impossible," Bucky said.

"I thought so too."

"Do they know?"

"Sam does."

"So it's just dumb luck Michael came here looking for Sam?"

"Not exactly. His mother filled his head with Sam's music. Practically sent him on a quest." The Colonel paused. A smile creased his face beneath the plastic surgery and spray tan. "Now here comes the fun part," he said. "We have Michael announce it to the world. He changes his name to Michael Rogers, records a full album with Sam, and you become the owner of the biggest label in the history of recorded music. We're going to be legends, my friend."

"What if Michael won't do it?" Bucky said after some thought.

"He's got no choice," the Colonel answered.

"What if Sam dies?"

The Colonel chuckled. "That old bastard is too mean to die. But if it comes to that, at least the old records will start selling again. Shit, he's worth more to us dead than alive."

"Worth more dead than alive," Bucky said dreamily. "I like the sound of that. Fine. We'll do the album. Then I want Michael gone. "

Bucky opened a bottle of champagne, and Cee Cee waited patiently upstairs while he and the Colonel got drunk. "Come on," the Colonel slurred. "I'll have Doctor Robert scare us up some tail. Do you good."

As they walked to the door, Bucky slapped the Colonel on the back and said, "You know she couldn't even have a baby? What kind of woman can't have a baby?"

Cee Cee watched through the bedroom window as the Colonel drove crookedly down the road, then she rushed downstairs, her mind unwilling to understand what she had just heard. She found the letter and read it with shaking hands. "No," she said to herself. "This can't be." She read it again and felt sick. She texted Michael: *I need to see you.*

25

GRAND OLE OPRY

MICHAEL WAS OUT WITH THE horses. He returned to see Cee Cee's text and a missed call from Sam and a voicemail: "Grand Ole Opry tonight, Mike. You nervous? I'm nervous as hell. It's all because of you, boy. All because of you. Can't wait for it. See you around, partner."

Michael replied to Cee Cee: *Come over. Bring your stuff.*

An hour later, Michael lifted Cee Cee's boxes and bags from the trunk of her car and escorted her into the house.

"So what did you *need* to see me about?" he said, kissing her neck, trying to unclasp her bra through her shirt.

"Stop it, Michael," Cee Cee said.

Michael backed away as though he had been slapped. "Are you okay?" he said. "What did he do to you?"

"It's not that," Cee Cee said. "There's something you need to see." She handed him the letter. As he read it, his face dropped. He reached the end and with his forefinger traced the lines of the signature he knew by heart: *Love, Rosemary.*

"What is this?" he said, his voice trembling. "Where did you get this?"

"The Colonel brought it to my house."

"What?" Michael stared dumbly at her, his mind unable to process the information.

"Sit down, Michael," Cee Cee said, leading him to the couch. "I was up in my closet packing my clothes when I heard Bucky and the Colonel come in, and I heard their whole conversation."

"Did you say anything?"

"I didn't want them to know I was there. I went downstairs after they left and found this letter."

"I don't understand," Michael said.

"Sam is your father."

"What?"

Cee Cee took Michael's hand and held it firmly. "Sam is your father," she said.

"What?"

Cee Cee went to the kitchen and poured Michael a glass of whiskey. "Drink this," she said. "I should have waited until after the performance tonight. I just couldn't keep this from you."

"The Colonel knew?"

"Yes."

"Sam?"

"He knows."

Michael's face went white. He wanted to cry but some deep-held masculine pride kept the tears inside.

"Are you okay?" Cee Cee said.

Michael looked past her, staring out the window, his eyes wide and unblinking. "Why didn't he say anything?" he asked, finally.

"I think he just found out, himself."

Michael poured another drink. The liquor lessened the shock. "What am I supposed to do now?" he said.

Before she could answer, Michael's phone went off again. He stared at it, the blue light illuminating his face. From Martha: *Meet-and-greet before the show tonight. Be there early. I'm sending a car in an hour.*

"Shit," Michael said. "I forgot I gotta be there early tonight. Martha's sending a car. Get ready."

"You want me to come with you?"

"Of course. Don't you want to?"

"Won't Bucky be there?"

"Fuck him. You're mine."

Cee Cee spent half an hour in the bathroom mirror looking at the clothes she had brought to wear, shame and excitement fighting inside her. She hardly recognized herself: the thick black eyeliner, the rouged cheeks and glossed lips, the rock 'n' roll tousled hair, the bangles jangling on her wrists, the black leather vest pulled tight over a white bustier that pushed her tits front and center, the short denim skirt, the rhinestone studded cowboy boots. She wanted to look like she belonged on Michael's arm, but when she finally worked up the nerve to let him see her like this, all he said was, "Look at you."

Michael made the limo wait outside in his driveway as he got drunk, then he drank more on the ride. By the time they arrived at the Opry, the meet-and-greet had long since ended and his band was already on stage playing a rollicking instrumental to appease the crowd while they waited for him. Cee Cee had to help him out of his seat and hold him as he staggered through the backstage doors. Everyone stood still. Bucky's face turned white, then red. He looked like a bull about to charge. "Your tits are out," Bucky hissed in her ear as she passed by him.

Michael pulled Cee Cee close. "I don't want to leave you alone with him," he whispered. She squeezed his arm and pushed him toward the stage doors. "Go," she said. He walked to the stage without acknowledging anyone. The Colonel held Bucky back as Michael passed him.

A hail of boos greeted Michael on stage. He squinted in the spotlight, then stumbled and mumbled through his set, forgetting lyrics, struggling to hit the high notes. Finally, he walked in a crooked line offstage into a roomful of angry faces. Bucky wouldn't even look at him. The Colonel tried to scowl. Sam grabbed Michael's arm and said, "What's gotten into you? Get yourself together."

"Good advice, Dad," Michael slurred. Sam's face tightened. Taking the letter out of his back pocket, Michael began to shout the words: "I just want you to know that you have a son. I don't expect you to leave Nashville, but I think you should be part of his life." Swaying drunkenly, he sneered at Sam: "How long did you know?"

Bucky stepped forward. Michael reflexively put his arm across Cee Cee to protect her. "Alright, you piece of shit," Bucky said, "let's get something straight. If you ever embarrass us like this again, I'll bury you so deep they'll have to dig to fucking China to find your ass. Now get your goddamn hands off my wife."

"She ain't your wife, mate," Michael said.

Bucky swung at Michael and missed.

"You're making it worse, Bucky," Cee Cee cried.

"Shut up, whore," Bucky said and swung at Michael again, drawing blood from his bottom lip.

Michael countered with a jab to Bucky's nose, sending Bucky reeling like a stooge to the floor. He scrambled to his knees, then fell back against the wall, legs out, hair disheveled, eyes wild. Blood dripped onto his pink Ferragamo tie and spread in red Rorschach blots on his white Hugo Boss shirt. A few drops stained his blue Brioni suit. He screamed: "I'll fucking sue you! I'll fucking sue both of you!"

Now Sam stepped forward. "Whoa, whoa," he bellowed like a man trying to calm cattle. "Pull yourselves together. This is pathetic."

Michael turned on him and said: "You know about being pathetic, old man."

Everyone froze.

"Can we speak alone?" Sam asked.

"Depends on what you have to say."

"Please, Michael. Let me explain."

Michael grabbed Cee Cee's arm and walked toward the dressing rooms.

"Get your fucking hands off my wife," Bucky shouted after him.

Sam followed Michael and closed the door behind him. "Cee Cee, I'd prefer to be alone with Michael," he said.

"Anything you have to say to me, you can say to her," Michael said. "She's my manager."

"Really?" Cee Cee said under her breath to Michael, her eyes glowing.

"You're the only one I trust," Michael said. Then, turning to Sam: "Talk."

"I swear I only just learned," Sam said. "I didn't know how to bring it up. I barely remember what happened. I met your mom in the hospital, and the next day, the Colonel had me on a plane back to Nashville. He intercepted her letters and phone calls. I never even knew."

"When were you going to tell me?"

"I wanted to tell you right away. Believe me, I did. But the Colonel, he told me to wait. I've been listening to him my whole life. Too old to change now."

"Do you even want to be my father?" Michael said with a catch in his voice.

"God, Michael, I—"

The Colonel burst into the room. "Hope I'm not interrupting," he said, ignoring the daggers in Michael's eyes. He sat on the couch and crossed one leg primly over the other, making sure to keep the crease in his pants. "Sit," he said. "All of you."

Sam sat on the couch next to the Colonel. Michael stayed standing.

"Fine," the Colonel said. "Have it your way." He took a dramatic pause and tried to purse his lips. Then he said, "Michael, once you're in a better frame of mind, you're going to see what good news this is. For all of us."

Michael looked at the Colonel and saw the greed glowing in his eyes.

"And what do you think, Sam?" Michael said. "*Is* this good news?"

"You know how great it is when we sing together," Sam said. "Imagine how much better it will be now."

Sam's eyes glowed now too. The Colonel's greed was contagious.

Michael felt utterly alone. "I need some time," he said. Then he took Cee Cee's hand. "We're going home." He led her out of the dressing room and out the backstage door, where snowflakes fell lazily on their shoulders as they bent into the limo.

26

ROPE 'EM IN

MONDAY MORNING FOUND BUCKY, SAM, Martha, and the
Colonel in the Colonel's office, trying to solve the problem of Michael.
They got nowhere. They sent texts and placed calls to Michael Tuesday,
Wednesday, and Thursday, all of which he ignored. Michael was with
Cee Cee. In the afternoons, they rode his motorcycle, going nowhere,
smiling in the gleaming sunlight, riding until their faces were numb
and red with cold. Evenings, they ordered takeout and made love until
they could no longer move.

Thursday night, she said, "You know they're angry at you."

"Who?"

"Bucky, the Colonel, all of them."

"How do you know?"

"Bucky called me, begging. You know how hard that was for him?
They really mean it."

"Tough shit."

"The Country Music Awards are Saturday. You're supposed to
present an award with Sam and perform together. They're worried
you won't be there."

"Let them worry."

"You should give Sam a break. He didn't know."

"He knew."

"He didn't. The Colonel kept it from him. Try to see it from Sam's
viewpoint. Imagine learning you have a son at his age, and the son is
you. What would you do? You always wanted a father. This is your

chance. I know it isn't perfect, but nothing is. Forgive him. 'For if ye forgive men their trespasses, your heavenly Father will also forgive you.'"

"What's that?"

"Book of Matthew."

Michael sighed heavily. "You think I should?" he said.

"Yes."

"I trust you."

She kissed him on the forehead, rested her head on his chest and fell asleep. But Michael didn't sleep that night. He thought of his mother and wondered what it must have been like to be ignored all those years. He saw himself as a child in school, hating his classmates when they taunted each other, *My daddy can beat up your daddy*. He recalled being a teenager in church, choking on the Lord's Prayer, refusing to say the words "our father." Worst of all, he remembered staring at his mother's records, wishing Sam was his father. But Cee Cee's words stayed with him. *Sam didn't know*. It was the Colonel's fault. The Colonel was the one who must pay.

Michael fell asleep after daybreak. When he awoke in the afternoon, he called Sam. "I'll be there tomorrow," he said. "On one condition. I don't ever want to see the Colonel again."

Saturday afternoon, a gaggle of reporters waited outside the stage entrance at the Bridgestone Arena. Michael sped in on his motorcycle, Cee Cee perched on the back. Their faces were raw and red from the cold. He parked and pulled a hat over his face, the brim nearly touching his thick-rimmed spectacles, then tried to slip by the reporters unnoticed. A black bear would have had a better chance at hiding in the snow.

Something was different though. He noticed the stares weren't just for him anymore. Not even the Colonel could stop the news of Michael and Cee Cee from spreading. Everyone in Nashville still saw her as Bucky's wife and couldn't help but look at her and Michael together with the morbid curiosity of drivers passing a car crash on the highway.

"ABC News," said a pretty blonde woman with a microphone, as she grabbed Michael's arm and pulled him toward her. Turning to the camera, she flashed a billboard smile and said, "The hottest star in country music has just arrived, along with Cee Cee Porter, wife of Bucky Porter, head of DMG Records. Michael, rumor has it you've got a big surprise for us tonight. Can you tell us anything about it?"

"Hang on a sec," Michael said. He tore off his hat and glasses and turned to Cee Cee. She ran her fingers through his hair and straightened his shirt. "Can we start again?" Michael said. "Since the disguise clearly didn't work, I might as well look good."

"Ready, Jim?" the reporter said to the cameraman. "Three, two, one. Michael, rumor has it you've got a big surprise for us tonight. Can you tell us anything about it?"

"That's news to me," Michael said.

"Come on, now, don't be coy," the reporter said.

"I'd tell you if I knew myself."

"Not even the tiniest hint?"

"Sorry."

"Playing it close to the chest," she said with a jocular grin. "Well, you heard it here first, country fans. We'll just have to wait."

"What the hell was that?" Michael said to Cee Cee as they pushed their way into the building. Backstage was an embarrassment of country music riches. Brad Paisley stood against a wall in pleasant conversation with Trisha Yearwood. Rascal Flatts sat around a coffee table playing poker. Like a vision, Dolly Parton turned the corner, dispensing smiles like gumdrops.

A skinny kid with a lanyard around his mop-handle neck, an earpiece in his floppy ear, and a clipboard in his bony hands, stopped Michael. He pulled a walkie-talkie from his pocket and spoke into it. "We've got Michael Rogers."

"Jennings," Michael corrected him, but the kid was listening to a voice in his ear.

"I'll show you to your dressing room," he said.

Taped to the door of Michael's dressing room was a sheet of foolscap paper with the words "Michael Rogers" printed in bold font. The kid made a note on his clipboard and turned to leave, but Michael grabbed him by the arm and spun him around. "Oi, mate," Michael said, struggling to control his voice. "The name is Jennings. J-E-N-N-I-N-G-S. Get someone to fix this."

"Right away," the kid said. Michael watched him walk away and knew he wouldn't see him again. He ripped the paper from the door and didn't even bother to go inside.

Michael felt a hand on his shoulder. "Aren't you a sight for sore eyes," said a voice behind him. He turned and was caught in Sam's embrace. Struggling free, he took a step back from Sam and said, "Where's the Colonel?"

"I told him to sit this one out," Sam said.

The tension in Michael's chest relaxed. He gave Sam a once over. The old man was still hollow about the eyes, still wearing a wig, still fifteen pounds too light, but the twinkle in his eye had returned. He wore a tuxedo.

"You look good," Michael said.

"Doctor says it's going my way."

"I'm glad."

Sam handed Michael a garment bag. "I bought you a tux," he said. "Figured we might as well look good together."

Michael took it and slung it over his shoulder. "We'll see," he said.

Sam turned to Cee Cee. "Pleased to see you," he said.

Cee Cee wrapped him in a hug and planted a kiss on his cheek, trying desperately to cool the chill between him and Michael with her own warm cheer. She stepped away and gave Michael a little push in the back toward Sam. Sam cleared his throat. "Michael, I know why you're angry at me. Believe me, I get it. It's been eating at me this whole time, wanting to apologize, wanting to make things right. You and I are good together. You know it. I know it. Hell, everyone knows it. Can't we see our way clear of this? Can't we start over?"

Michael looked at Cee Cee for strength, then said, "You might be my father, but I'm not sure yet if I'm your son. Do you understand that?"

"All we can do is try," Sam said, holding out his hand. Michael shook it.

Waiting for his segment, Michael daydreamed about his mother. A lump rose in his throat as pieces of his past locked together. He understood, finally, why his mother played Sam's music so much in the house. It must have torn at her heart, but it was her way of giving her son a relationship with his father. It was, perhaps, the best she could do. He wondered if she knew when she bought him his first guitar that it would bring him here. Impossible. How could she have? But it didn't matter. It no longer seemed strange to him. Life was always leading him here, to Nashville, guitar in hand, looking for his hero. The only surprising part, the only miracle of it all, was that instead of ending up like the legions of talented musicians who struggled in obscurity until reality crushed their dreams to dust, Michael made it.

27

THE PRODIGAL SON

A KNOCK ON THE DRESSING room door startled Michael awake. "You're on in thirty minutes," the voice said. Michael dressed hurriedly in his normal stage clothes—the leather pants, the billowing shirt, the black boots. Then he ripped them off and donned Sam's tuxedo, feeling out of place, trapped, itchy, like a child in church clothes.

In the hallway, he nearly ran into Bucky in conversation with Sam and Martha. Martha acted quickly, leading Bucky away into an adjoining room. Then she returned with a young man with shaggy brown hair and a neatly trimmed beard wearing a flannel shirt and holding a white acoustic guitar. "Michael," she said, "this is Thomas Rhett. Keep your eye on him. He's going to be bigger than you some day."

Michael glared at Martha as he shook hands. "Best of luck, mate," he said, his eyes still on Martha. As the two men stood trapped in a strange handshake, Martha whispered in Michael's ear, "Be nice. I'm trying to poach him from his management."

"Thomas was it?" Michael said with a smile, looking at him for the first time.

"Rhett. Thomas Rhett. I'm a huge fan. It's just such an honor to meet you."

"Can't wait to hear you sing, mate."

"Oh, well, I already did. It's okay."

"I'll catch it on the telly. Cheers."

Martha waved goodbye to Thomas and mouthed, "We'll talk later."

Michael turned to her. "Well, well, well," he said, "young Martha Moran making moves."

"Maybe this guy will have half a brain in his head," Martha said with a wry smile.

"Is that about me?" Michael said.

"No, of course not," Martha said sarcastically.

"I only hope I was of some help in your eventual rise to world domination," Michael said.

"Well, you already have a manager, so forgive me if I try to move on with my life."

The young man with the clipboard appeared at Michael's elbow. "Sorry to interrupt, but it's time," he said. He walked Michael, Cee Cee, and Sam to the side of the stage.

"Nervous?" Sam said.

"Never," Michael replied.

Host Carrie Underwood began her introduction: "Not long ago, our next guests were strangers." Michael looked out across the stage and saw Bucky standing in the wings opposite. The whites of his eyes glowed in the darkness. "But miracles do happen," Underwood continued, "because tonight, for the first time ever, we can announce them as father and son. Presenting the award for Best New Artist, please give a warm welcome to Sam and Michael Rogers."

Michael couldn't move. He shot a wounded look at Cee Cee, but she was as shocked as he was. Sam prodded him in the back, and all of a sudden, the lights were in his eyes, and the roar of the crowd was in his ears. The ovation went on so long, it cut into advertising time. Michael didn't hear anything else. He didn't even know if he spoke, or who won the award, or how he walked off stage and back to the press room, where someone stood him next to Sam beneath the biggest poster he had ever seen. "Father and Son," it read, "The new album from Sam and Michael Rogers, coming next year." And there stood Bucky, grinning like a villain. A crowd pressed in on Michael, severing him from Cee Cee. Amidst a frenzy of flashing bulbs, a hundred questions were shouted at once. Michael looked at Sam, his mouth gaping. "Ain't it grand?" Sam said, laughing. "Ain't it just too goddamn grand?"

Bucky called for quiet. "You'll all get to ask your questions in just a moment," he said. "First off, however, I want to say a few words. It isn't often in this business that you get a chance to make history. Well, tonight we are making history. Not only does DMG have the two best-selling country artists of the year on its roster, not only are they father and son," here he gestured to the poster, "but to cap it all off, after the New Year, we're going to get them in the studio together for an album that will be unique not only in the history of country music, but in the history of all recorded music." Bucky paused for effect, then pointed to a reporter with her hand raised. "You there, start us off."

"A question for Michael," she said. "How does it feel?"

"Um," Michael said.

"Tell us about the name change," a man shouted from the crowd. "Will you ever go by Jennings again?"

"I...um," Michael stammered. He was a little boy thrown to the wolves. Searching the room for a kind face, his gaze landed on Cee Cee. She stood just outside the scrum of reporters, her blue eyes welling with tears. *I'm sorry*, she mouthed. Michael felt raw, naked. Fear became anger. "Jennings always was my name and always will be my name," he spat. "I never agreed to any of this."

The room went silent. Sam, trying to salvage the situation, said with a forced chuckle, "I guess his momma never taught him manners."

Michael leaned away from the reporters and said, "Don't you ever say a fucking word about my mother." He grabbed Sam by the shirt. He cocked his fist. A gasp spread through the crowd. Michael regained command of himself and pushed his way through the room. Flashes popped in his face. He swung his arms wildly, not caring who he hit, only caring about escaping.

Cee Cee tried to chase after him but the scrum of reporters beat her to the door and blocked her path. "Michael," she shouted, but her voice was lost in the mayhem. She heard Michael's Harley roar to life and his wheels peel out of the parking lot. Then she smelled Bucky's cheap cologne behind her.

"'If, while her husband liveth, she be married to another man, she shall be called an adulteress,'" Bucky whispered.

Cee Cee spun to face him. "I don't have time for you right now, Bucky," she said. "I have to find Michael."

"Like hell you do," Bucky said.

"We don't have to make this hard on each other," Cee Cee said.

"You don't even know the meaning of the word," Bucky said. "Just wait until I'm through with you. And don't even think of trying to come crawling back once you see what your new life looks like."

"I don't want to come back."

"You know how many women he fucks? What makes you think you satisfy him? Your pussy ain't that good, baby."

"Stop acting like a child," Cee Cee said.

"I hope Michael doesn't get tired of you taking his money, because you won't get a fucking dime from me."

"As a matter of fact, I'm his manager now."

Bucky snorted.

"I mean it," Cee Cee said.

"You? A manager?"

"Every good idea you ever had was mine," Cee Cee said. "Who told you to send Michael and Sam to Europe? Who told you to get Dave Cobb?"

"You can't manage him. He's already under contract."

"About that," Cee Cee said. "We're going to make a new contract. Matter of fact, we're going to make two new contracts: one for Michael, and one for me. I want the money from 'A Good Man Is Hard to Find.'"

"You're something else," Bucky chuckled. "You really are. I mean, I knew you were no genius, but if you think for a second I'm going to agree to any of this, you're dumber than I thought. Come on, Cee Cee, what's gotten into you?"

"I have to go find him," Cee Cee said, turning toward the door. "I'll have my lawyer contact your lawyer. Two new contracts. That's what I want."

Bucky grabbed her by the arm and squeezed until her skin turned blood red. "You think because you used to be my wife I'm going to take it easy on you? If you start this war, you will not survive to see the end of it. Do you understand? You know who I am. You know what I can do. You know better than anyone. I will show you no mercy."

Cee Cee removed his hand from her arm. "How many people know where you got the money to start the label?" she asked in an even voice.

Bucky's face flushed.

"You wouldn't dare," he said.

"Embezzling from church...in a town like this?"

"You can't prove it."

"As a matter of fact, I can. Remember when you said I should stop performing? You told me I'd be more effective behind the scenes. Well, that's when I started keeping our books. I have the receipts, darling. You're lucky I'm not asking for more. But then again I'm not like you. Neither is Michael. We're going to build our empire on love."

Bucky bit his lip. He started half a dozen sentences but couldn't finish one. As Cee Cee pushed past him on the way to her car to chase Michael, he yelled, "This isn't over."

The wind ripped at Michael's hair as he tore down Demonbreun Street. He merged onto Route 65, then headed up Hickory Lake, pushing the bike until it shook from the speed. He swerved off the highway and climbed the winding lake roads, doing eighty, ninety, ninety-five. He couldn't get the reporters' voices out of his head: *How does it feel to be Sam's son?* As he hurtled around a bend, he saw something brown and white in the shadows near the edge of the road. The deer jumped in front of the bike so fast he didn't have time to slow down. He yanked the handlebars and felt the motorcycle fishtail. Time slowed. He flew over the handlebars and landed headfirst on a boulder.

Everything went black.

28

CHANGES

MICHAEL'S EYES OPENED. THE ROOM came into focus. He felt the scratchy hospital bed sheets. He heard the beeping of the machines keeping him alive. Standing over him, smiling like an angel with a halo of fluorescent white hospital light, was Cee Cee. He tried to ask what happened, but there was a tube in his throat. She bent over to kiss him on the forehead. He inhaled deeply, but he couldn't smell her. He panicked. He blacked out.

Days passed into weeks. Michael slipped in and out of consciousness, while Cee Cee stood over his bed, directing the nurses and dealing with the doctors. She texted Sam over and over again but got no response. No one came to visit except the Colonel, once, smiling his wolf's smile. The bouquet of flowers he brought did nothing to hide the reason he had come. He was like a property owner surveying his investments after a hurricane, wondering how much the damage would cost him. He spent thirty seconds inside the room looking at Michael sleeping, then fifteen minutes in the hallway on the phone. Cee Cee cringed at the sound of his muffled voice, wheedling: "No, no, no, there's no reason to cancel the article. He's alive. The album is still on, it's just postponed."

You can't seriously think of going through with this album, she texted Sam.

He didn't respond.

When Michael could finally breathe on his own, a nurse came in and said, "Today is graduation day," as she wheeled him out of the ICU and into an isolated room.

"Can you speak?" she said.

"I don't know," Michael croaked.

The nurse and Cee Cee glanced at each other, misty eyed. "You don't know how close you were," the nurse said. "It's a miracle."

Michael's eyes stayed open long enough now to see the cast on his right arm, and the one on his left leg in traction. With his left hand, he carefully explored the bandages on his head. They covered most of his face. He passed out.

Slowly and slowly he regained his strength. With it came pain. His nurse returned holding a magic wand. "When the pain becomes too great," she said, "press this button. It's morphine. Be careful." Days went by again, days and nights filled with morphine. How long? No time, or all the time that had ever been. Cee Cee was always there at his side. Or was she in a dream? And then the wand was taken from him, and the pain returned, the pain of healing bone and screaming withdrawal.

Then he could sit up. He tried to eat the grubby hospital food, but it had no taste. A doctor, his white coat neatly ironed, his stethoscope hanging neatly around his neck, entered brusquely, and began prodding and poking.

"Ouch," Michael said, but the doctor was not interested in his critique.

"Do you remember anything?" the doctor said, removing the bandage on Michael's head halfway, poking painfully at a row of stitches, and wrapping it up again.

"No."

"You were in a terrible accident. Five broken ribs," a painful poke in the side, "a broken arm, broken leg, and serious trauma to the brain. Comatose for seventy-four days. A miracle you're up and talking."

Flashes of memories flitted through Michael's head: the dark road, the wind ripping through his hair, the deer, the crunch of bones on rock. Then he remembered what came before—the press conference, his father, the poster that called him Michael *Rogers*.

"What day is today?"

The doctor checked his watch. "January the thirteenth." Then, rising to continue his rounds, he said, "Happy New Year," and was gone.

As soon as he could stand under his own power, Michael walked to the nurse's desk and demanded to be set free. The nurse warned him against it, but Michael didn't listen. He texted Cee Cee: *Where are you?*

Just popped out to grab lunch, she replied.

Take me home.

You need to stay in the hospital.

Please.

What did the doctor say?

"Goddamnit," Michael muttered. Then he texted Martha: *Come drive me home. My head is killing me. Can you get morphine?*

Martha didn't reply.

Cee Cee returned from lunch to find Michael sitting in the outpatient waiting room in a wheelchair. His face was gaunt and bruised, his arm and leg in a cast. With his good leg, he pulled himself toward her. A nurse rushed after him with a bag of pill bottles, gauze, medical tape, and alcohol wipes. "Change the bandage around his head once a day," she said, hanging the bag on Cee Cee's outstretched hand. "If he's in pain, he can take one of these." She rattled a bottle of OxyContin. "But be careful with them. No more than two per day." Handing Cee Cee a pair of crutches, she said, "The doctor wants to see him in two weeks to go over the CAT scan and remove the cast on his arm. Then he can start using these."

"Anything else?" Cee Cee asked.

"This isn't a good idea," the nurse said.

Cee Cee gave her an exasperated shrug as Michael fidgeted in his seat and grumbled, "Okay, okay, let's go."

Getting Michael into the hired car took fifteen minutes of pushing and pulling and jamming and stuffing. Cee Cee shut the door on him, folded the wheelchair, and threw it in the trunk. Beads of sweat dripped down her back. She took a seat next to Michael.

"What happened?" Michael said.

"You were in a crash—" Cee Cee began.

"I know that," Michael cut her off. "What happened since I've been out."

"Nothing," Cee Cee said. "We've all just been worrying about you."

"Did Sam come?"

Cee Cee didn't want to lie, but she didn't want to tell the truth either. "No," she said after a silence.

Michael bit his lip and gazed out the window. "What about *Father and Son?*" he said, putting a withering emphasis on the words.

"It's, um, it's moving forward," Cee Cee said.

Michael scoffed and shook his head sadly. "What do they want from me?"

"I don't know yet."

"Well you're my manager. Figure it out, darling."

"You want to do it?"

"Fuck no. Get me out of it. I don't want to see those animals ever again."

When they reached the house, Cee Cee repeated the ordeal in reverse, yanking Michael out of the car, struggling under his heft to plop him in the wheelchair and bring him inside.

"I'll go fix up our room," Cee Cee said, wheeling him in front of the television and clicking it on.

"*Our* room?"

"I moved my things in. Is that okay?"

Michael took her hand and kissed it.

"Where's Isabel?" he asked.

"Gone for the day. Do you need anything?"

"A glass of wine."

"Yeah right. That'll go real good with the medication." She opened the refrigerator to see row upon row of every kind of soft drink, mineral water, and fruit juice. In the pantry was every kind of cereal, bread, and brand of potato chip. "What do you like?" Cee Cee said.

"I don't know. I didn't buy it."

She found bread, jelly, and peanut butter. "You need to eat," she said, making him a sandwich and bringing it to him. Michael took the plate and felt ashamed of the tears in his eyes. His good leg jogged nervously. With a breaking voice, he said, "Are you doing this for your career or because you care about me?"

Cee Cee sighed. "I hope you don't actually need me to answer that question. Eat the sandwich, Michael. I'll go turn down the bed."

He heard her heels clicking up the stairs. His stomach grumbled. Salivating, he tore at the bread like a starving man. Half the sandwich was gone before he realized he couldn't taste it. Strange. Just like the hospital food. Panic welled in his chest. He fought to master it, dragged himself with his good leg to the refrigerator, tore open the door with his working arm, and ripped out everything inside. He shoved it all in his mouth, not caring what it was, only hoping he would taste it. But his tongue was a numb slug. It would not speak to his brain. His heart pounded like the roll of a snare drum. His vision tunneled. "Help," he tried to shout, but his voice failed him.

29

STUDIO A

SAM STOOD IN THE CONTROL room of RCA Studio A, listening to a playback of the take he had just recorded. While Dave Cobb added Autotune to his vocals to erase the creaks of age and cancer, Sam turned to Bucky and whispered, "It just doesn't sound like *me*."

"Dave is a magician," Bucky replied, his eyes glowing. "This is how it's done these days."

Sam looked to the Colonel for help. Sitting in a plush easy chair, Dolly and Elvis at his feet, the Colonel said, "Bucky's right. It ain't the seventies anymore. You're not competing with Willie and Merle. This has to sound good on the radio next to Luke Combs and Dierks Bentley."

"But this ain't the way me and Michael wrote the song. We wanted to take country back to its roots."

Bucky pulled Sam aside. "Trust me," he said. "You never sounded better. This is Sam Rogers in the twenty-first century, baby."

Sam looked around the room and saw that he was alone. "You sure Michael is okay with this?" he said. "It don't feel right taking these songs we wrote together and recording them without him. You said he'd be here."

Bucky's eyes darkened. The Colonel stepped in and cooed, "You just worry about singing. We'll handle Michael."

Sam returned to the mixing board and asked to hear the song again. Dave Cobb clicked a button and leaned back in his chair as the song filled the room. Sam winced at the sound of his computer-tuned voice. But then he imagined himself sitting in the audience at the Grammys as his name was called. He imagined giving his speech, hearing the wild applause, standing in the press room afterward answering questions, then flitting from party to party, a king rethroned. Maybe Bucky and the Colonel were right. New music always sounds strange to old ears. Maybe it was time to join the future. Once Michael put his parts on it, the song would come together. As the last notes faded, Sam surrendered.

Every inch of Michael's body hurt.

"Don't go," he begged from his bed, as Cee Cee sprayed perfume on her wrists and gave herself one last look in the mirror.

Cee Cee looked at him and frowned. "I have to go pick up your prescriptions and run a few errands," she said. "I'll just be gone an hour or two."

"Please."

"Michael, stop it. You'll be fine. Take a nap."

"I can't be alone. Call Martha."

"Michael, I don't think she's going to come."

"Just call."

Cee Cee sighed and dialed the number. Martha didn't answer.

Dusk had fallen, and with it a gloomy rain. As soon as Cee Cee left, Michael made a phone call of his own. "Come over," he said to the voice on the other end and hung up.

As she drove to the drug store on rain-slick roads, Cee Cee felt a lonely silence hanging about the city. She passed an abandoned lot, grown high with weeds, and felt sorry for it. A lone pigeon perched on a telephone wire, its head huddled down into its feathers. Cee Cee wondered what birds thought when it rained. An old woman took shelter beneath a dirty plastic bus stop overhang. A grimy shopping bag sat on either side of her, and she pulled them close to her body. Cee Cee wondered if the woman had ever been in love, wondered if anyone alive still loved her, wondered what chain of tragedies had led her here. She ran her errands and lingered in a coffee shop, wondering what to do about Michael.

An hour and a half later, she returned to a cacophony of dogs barking. A woman sat on the front step and shielded her face from the headlights. Cee Cee cut the engine and approached cautiously. It was Lily, crying, a deep red mark turning to a bruise on her arm.

"Lily," Cee Cee said, unable to conceal her shock. "Are you okay?" But her heart was full of murder. She couldn't believe Michael would cheat on her. The word stopped her short. Was it possible to cheat on someone you were cheating with?

"Don't bother with that asshole," Lily said, gathering her things and rising to leave. "He's sick."

"What happened?"

"He calls me over, then starts screaming that he can't taste me. Look what he did to my arm. Nearly threw me off the bed. Then he tells me he doesn't want to see me again and gives me a wad of cash to leave him alone." Lily showed Cee Cee a crumpled mess of bills in her hand. "Never in my life. I'm leaving. You should too."

Cee Cee watched Lily drive away, then put the bags in the kitchen and slowly climbed the stairs, unsure of what she would say to Michael. She knew she had no right to be jealous, and yet, the sight of Lily had pierced her heart. Having never been in love like this before, Cee Cee was a stranger to love's agony. But when she crept into Michael's room and saw him sleeping on the bed, his body bruised and broken, she forgot everything. She wanted only to heal him.

"Michael," she whispered, sitting on the bed next to him.

He stirred. "Is it you?" he said sleepily.

"It's me."

"I'm sorry," he said and closed his eyes again.

"For what?"

Half asleep, Michael tried to roll over. The pain shocked him awake. Cee Cee helped him onto his back and rearranged his pillows behind him.

"Lay with me," Michael said.

She crawled under the covers and curled up next to Michael, her arm around his chest, her head nuzzled in the crook of his neck. He kissed the top of her head, burying his nose in her hair and breathing in deep. Cee Cee felt hot tears drop from his face.

"I keep waking up and thinking it was all a nightmare," he said, stifling a sob. "And then it comes back."

"What's wrong, sweetheart?"

"Can't smell. Can't taste. My head hurts all the time. My leg itches, and I can't reach it to scratch."

"The cast comes off tomorrow," Cee Cee said, kissing him on the chin.

"Will you take me to see the doctor?"

Michael had drifted to sleep before Cee Cee could answer. She slipped from the bed, trying not to wake him, but as she reached the bedroom door, she was stopped by a whimper and a voice thick with sleep and drugs: "Don't leave me."

30

MOVING ON

THE ALARM WAS AN UNWELCOME intruder, cleaving the warm, intertwined bodies on the soft bed. Bucky reached for his phone, turned off the alarm, rolled over, and kissed Shelby on the forehead. "Good morning, beautiful," he said. With Cee Cee gone, he decided to wait a few months to tell Shelby she was off the label. He needed her companionship now.

"Coffee," she said, pulling a pillow over her head.

"Where's the French press I bought you?"

"In the cabinet to the right of the stove."

Before Bucky could get out of bed, Shelby turned to him, the white bedsheet just covering her breasts, and ran her hand up his leg. "We got distracted last night," she said. "You didn't get to hear the song I wrote for Michael and Sam." She wrapped her hand around him and squeezed. "You're still going to get it on the album, aren't you?"

"Ask and it shall be given you," Bucky answered, sliding his hands beneath the sheets and rubbing her nipples. Five minutes later, he padded downstairs in a cuckold's bathrobe and started the coffee. He heard the shower hiss and patter upstairs. "You coming?" he shouted.

"Leave the coffee," she yelled. "I'm washing your cum off. Again. I'll see you later."

Bucky checked his phone and saw three texts from his ex-wife:

> *Your lawyer has not responded.*
>
> *I'll give you to the end of the week.*
>
> *Do the right thing, Bucky.*

He clicked off his phone and muttered, "Bitch."

The alarm buzzed. Cee Cee stretched and yawned and reached for it, not caring to cover her nakedness.

"Leave it," Michael said. "Stay here with me."

"It's almost noon," she said. "I can't keep hitting snooze. I have to get you to the doctor."

She helped Michael dress and held his arm while he negotiated his way downstairs, then she scrambled the eggs in Michael's refrigerator and brewed coffee. She set the plates on the table and sat down to eat. Michael sat motionless.

"Are the eggs okay?" Cee Cee asked.

"I'm not hungry," he said.

"You gotta eat if you want to take your Oxy," she said.

Michael lifted his fork like an obstinate child and stuffed the eggs into his mouth, then lifted the plate and threw it against the wall. Cee Cee let out a scream as it shattered. His ribs seared in pain. Terror shivered through him. He saw in Cee Cee's eyes that she was terrified too—of him. He snatched the bottle of Oxy from the table, poured a pill into his hand, and swallowed it with a gulp of coffee, then broke down sobbing. Anger, fear, sadness: they were strings on a guitar someone else was playing, and every time the player strummed a new chord, Michael had no choice but to dance along.

"I'm sorry," he said. "I don't know what's wrong with me. Cee Cee, don't do that. I'll clean it up."

"How?" she said, sweeping up the broken shards. "You can barely walk."

Cee Cee helped Michael dress in his disguise—baggy clothes, baseball hat pulled down low—and called the car to take them to Vanderbilt Hospital. In the VIP waiting room she checked in with the nurse at the front desk, then took a seat next to Michael in a plush chair and waited. An hour passed. "Why does it always take so long?" Michael said. "Every minute lasts a fucking day in here."

Finally, his name was called. Cee Cee helped him into the examining room, where they waited again. "I'm thirsty," Michael said.

"What do you want?"

"Doesn't matter. Can't taste it. Something wet."

Cee Cee left the room to find a drink and got lost in the maze of hospital halls. Turning a corner, she nearly ran into Sam, who was whistling a jaunty tune. "'Scuse me, Miss," Sam said, not recognizing her.

"Sam, it's me."

"Cee Cee? Well, I'll be damned. What are you doing in the hospital?"

"I came here with Michael."

Sam frowned and took a deep breath. "By God, I wanted to visit," he said. "Bucky and the Colonel didn't think it was a good idea. Didn't want to upset him."

Cee Cee glared at him.

"Walk with me a minute," Sam said, taking Cee Cee by the hand. "Just got a clean bill of health. Gonna hightail it out of this place and celebrate."

As they walked to the exit, Sam asked about Michael's accident. Cee Cee explained the broken bones, the concussion, the loss of taste and smell, the wild mood swings. "We're getting the cast off today," she said. "And we'll get the results of the CAT scan. Hopefully the doctor can fix whatever is wrong."

"They can work miracles these days," Sam said. "Just look at me."

The automatic sliding doors *whooshed* open, and Sam took a step outside. He turned to Cee Cee, who stood just inside the threshold, and took his hat in his hand. "Tell Michael I asked about him," he said. "Tell him I'm recording our songs. He can come finish them when he's ready."

"So you're really going to do it?" Cee Cee said.

"Hell, I just do what I'm told. Never was much good at anything but singing and playing guitar."

"Take some responsibility, Sam," Cee Cee said. "For once in your life."

Sam looked at the ground and scratched his chin and placed his hat on his head.

"Tell Michael I asked about him," he said and walked away.

With help from the front desk, Cee Cee navigated her way back to Michael. Inside the examining room, a power drill whirred. "Stick your fingers out straight," said the nurse as she cut into the cast on Michael's arm.

"No drink?" Michael yelled to Cee Cee over the noise.

"I got lost," she said.

When the cast was off, the nurse took Michael's arm and gently twisted it this way and that. "Any pain?" she said.

"Nothing," Michael answered.

"Good. Looks like the arm is all better. Doctor says he wants to keep the cast on the leg for another week or so. He'll be right with you."

"Where did you go?" Michael said when he and Cee Cee were alone again.

"Oh, I just took a wrong turn and couldn't find my way back. You know how hospitals are. So what did the nurse say? Good news?"

The door opened. With a flap of his white coat, the doctor sat on his stool and rolled it up to Michael. "Your body is healing nicely, Mister Jennings," he said, pressing his stethoscope to Michael's chest. "Breathe. And out. Good. How does the arm feel?"

"Fine. But why can't I smell or taste anything?"

The doctor pulled a small flashlight from his coat pocket and shined it in Michael's eyes, then rolled to the computer and clicked on a black-and-white image of Michael's brain. "You've had what we call a traumatic brain injury, or TBI. If you look here," he pointed at a dark black splotch on the picture, "that's a contusion—bleeding in the brain tissue. With this type of injury, anosmia, the loss of taste and smell, is common. It's most likely temporary. Permanent loss happens in very few people. If it's not back in a few weeks, we'll have another look. Have you been experiencing anxiety or depression?"

"No."

Cee Cee caught the doctor's eye and silently nodded yes.

"Sudden or violent changes of mood?"

"No."

Another silent nod from Cee Cee.

The doctor scribbled on a pad. "Well, just to be safe," the doctor said with a knowing look at Cee Cee, "I'd like to start you on Zoloft, fifty milligrams. If you tolerate it, after two weeks, go up to one hundred. Before you leave, the nurse will schedule you for cognitive therapy. It's impossible to predict the outcome of these injuries, but you still have a chance for a happy, healthy life, if you take this seriously. No drugs or alcohol. After the leg heals, mild exercise. Watch the blood pressure. Get as much rest as you can. Avoid stress as much as possible. If you experience any sudden changes in mood or thoughts of self-harm, call us immediately. Otherwise, in a few months we'll repeat the tests."

The doctor left. Michael turned to Cee Cee and said, "A few months?"

"It'll be over before you know it," she said. "Come on, let's get you home."

Back in the chauffeured car, holding Michael's hand, Cee Cee fought to push away the fears: What would happen to Michael? What would happen to her? Had she left Bucky for this? She remembered the old cliché her mother always used to say: Out of the frying pan, into the fire. But she had come too far to turn back. She'd just have to make Michael better through force of will. At home, she helped him upstairs, where he took another Oxy and fell asleep. Then she called Martha. No answer. She called again. And a third time.

"What is it?" Martha said.

"You must be busy," Cee Cee said. "You haven't answered your phone in months."

"What do you want?"

"I saw Sam today. I guess they're still trying to do that father and son album."

"They are."

"You can't let them do this, Martha. Please. It will kill him."

"I don't think they care."

"But *you* care. You love him."

Martha began to object but Cee Cee cut her off: "I know you do. It's okay. I love him too. We don't have to be enemies. You and I are in the same predicament. We don't have a chance against these men unless we stick together."

Martha went silent, thinking of all the things she'd like to say: that Cee Cee couldn't possibly understand her predicament, that they came from different worlds, that being the wife of a rich and famous record executive gave Cee Cee every advantage, allowed her to swoop in and steal Michael away, and everyone let her do it because they feared Bucky even though none of them took her seriously.

"Can't you talk to Bucky?" Martha said, and her mind flashed with a memory of Bucky, his sweaty face contorted in pleasure as she took him in her mouth.

"He'd never listen to me. Please, Martha. For Michael's sake."

"I'll see what I can do," Martha said before she hung up.

31

GOOD TIMES/
BAD TIMES

THREE MONTHS PASSED WITHOUT A word from Martha, Sam, Bucky, or the Colonel. At first the silence was a sanctuary, letting Cee Cee focus all her energy on Michael. Despite occasional mood swings, Michael acted the model patient. He didn't complain when she threw out all the wine bottles and kept a strict ration on his pain pills. He laid still while she tore off his old bandages and dressed his wounds. The worst he did was run his hand up her skirt as she bent over him, barely waiting until she had finished putting on new bandages to pull her into bed. Cee Cee had to climb on top and do most of the work, but even so, Michael found ways to show her pleasures she had never felt before.

When his body healed, he got the itch to move. He took Cee Cee into every store in the Mall at Green Hills, buying anything that caught her eye. Then he took her to dinner at Kayne Prime or Yolan, and she felt so bad for him when he couldn't taste the food, she looked the other way as he downed two or three beers with dinner and then a few more afterward at Santa's Pub.

Michael's fame reflected off of her. She felt surprised at how quickly she reacclimated to the constant crowds of people elbowing each other for a look, the widening of the eyes whenever they walked into a room, the weekly appearances in the tabloids. Then came the night sitting beneath the glittering chandeliers at Drusie & Darr, eating ahi tuna tartare and Maine lobster, when two women in their late twenties nervously approached the table, and Michael flashed his megawatt smile and prepared for a picture and an autograph and was left smiling as the girls took Cee Cee's hand and said breathlessly, "Our mom used to play your album all the time. We grew up on you. It's such an honor to meet you." One of the girls shoved her phone into Michael's hand. "Do you mind?" she said, joining her friend behind Cee Cee for a photo. Michael snapped the picture, handed the phone back, and smiled at Cee Cee as the girls retreated to their table.

"Dinner with a rock star," he said with a sly grin.

And a few weeks later at Lonnie's Western Room, after a girl sang to a karaoke track of "A Good Man Is Hard to Find," then asked for Cee Cee's autograph, Michael said, "So this is what it's like to be famous."

For Cee Cee, it was like finding an old beloved jacket and putting it on to realize it still fit perfectly. She had reclaimed something she thought she'd lost forever. Each time she was recognized, her stride gained more purpose, her words carried more force, and her dress became more daring and provocative.

But with each passing week, the silence from the Colonel's camp grew louder, and with it Cee Cee's sense of impending danger. Nothing good could happen in that silence, she knew. Maybe they were trying to freeze her out. Maybe they were trying to neutralize Michael and take away any power she might wield through him. Plus, she noticed his eyes looked glassy now every night after dinner, and when she counted his pain pills, one or two always came up missing. She felt stuck in a trap she couldn't see but could only feel as it tightened around her.

She texted Martha: *Any word?*

Martha didn't reply.

The next day, Cee Cee texted again, then called and left a voicemail, then texted one more time: *I have a proposition for you. Meet me for dinner tonight.*

Cee Cee sat frowning at a plate of fried chicken and biscuits at the Loveless Cafe, wondering if Martha would come.

"Is everything okay?" said the server in a chipper voice. "Doesn't look like you're enjoying your meal."

"No, it's fine, thanks," Cee Cee said, struggling to smile. "I'm just waiting for someone."

Cee Cee waited some more, then sent the food away uneaten. She ordered a piece of peach pie and stared at it—anything to purchase a little more time at the table. Slowly the restaurant emptied until Cee Cee sat alone in front of a balled up napkin and an uneaten slice of pie. She poked idly at the congealed peach preserves with a fork and turned to call for the check when the door opened and Martha walked in.

Martha sat opposite Cee Cee. The silence at the table was as thick as gravy.

"I don't have much time," Martha said.

"Did you talk to Bucky or the Colonel about the album?"

"Not really."

Cee Cee seemed to deflate in her chair.

"You know Michael won't do it," she said.

"Bucky already has the entire DMG promotional machine running at full speed," Martha answered too quickly, as though she had come prepared for this exact speech. "The album Michael and Sam are recording together is going to come out whether you want it to or not."

"But they're not recording an album together," Cee Cee said.

"Doesn't matter. They wrote a bunch of songs together on tour. Bucky already has half a million orders for the album. If Michael isn't in the studio by the end of this month, they'll take his voice from the demos, work their magic, and release it like that."

"I'm his manager now," Cee Cee said, banging her fist on the table.

"Not according to his contract."

"We'll sue."

"Cee Cee," Martha answered, "you know as well as anyone, there are maybe half a dozen men who run this town. Bucky is one of them. I know he seems like an idiot, but if this were the Mafia—and it's not far off—then he'd be Don Bucky. If you come at him with lawyers, he will ruin Michael's career, and that will be the best thing that happens to both of you. Michael won't even be able to get a cup of coffee in this town. You, on the other hand, will disappear."

"So you're saying we should just let them win? I know you hate them as much as I do."

"What I'm saying is, Michael hasn't released an album in almost eighteen months. The cycle is every twelve at most. This business is a meat grinder. You know that. It consumes you and spits you out and moves on to one of the thousands of hungry artists waiting behind you, clawing for your space."

"Michael's fans are loyal," Cee Cee said. "Besides, he broke every record on the books. They'll be waiting for him."

"Do you know who held the Spotify streaming record before he broke it?" Martha said.

"No."

"Exactly."

Cee Cee stared at her uneaten pie. "I have a plan," she said. "I'm going to start my own agency. I'm going to manage Michael. I want you to join me."

Martha sighed. "Just let this one go, Cee Cee. They won. They always win."

"I knew about you and Bucky," Cee Cee said. She took a bite of the pie to let the moment land. Then she continued, "I never held it against you, but I always knew. And I know what he did to you. You have gone as far as they will let you go. You must know that. Don't you want more?"

Martha's phone buzzed with a text from Thomas Rhett: *Appreciate everything u did for me but gonna go a different direction. Best of luck!*

"Fuck," Martha muttered to herself. Tears glistened in her eyes as she met Cee Cee's compassionate gaze. "What do you want me to do?" she said.

"Schedule a meeting with the Colonel."

"When?"

"Later this week. I have to take Michael to the Mayo Clinic tomorrow. Make sure Bucky isn't there. Make sure he doesn't even know about it."

"And what do I get?"

"Vice president."

"I'm keeping my job until this is real," Martha said. "Okay?"

Cee Cee nodded. "Deal," she said.

32

NIGHTMARES

THE MAYO CLINIC LOOKED MORE like a concert hall than a hospital. Everything was sleek and new and done with an artist's touch. The doctor was young and athletic. She bounded into the room with the easy arrogance of a woman who has held the mysteries of the human body in her hands. Instead of a medical chart, she held a tablet, which she poked at with a stylus.

"Is it okay if she stays?" Michael asked, gesturing to Cee Cee.

"If you don't mind, I don't mind," the doctor said. "So, Mister Jennings, I have examined your case carefully. Bones heal, as you know. But with brain trauma, it's impossible to know for sure how a person will respond over time. There are good signs in your case. I see no blood on your brain. You haven't lost motor function. Your speech is normal. Stand up for me. Close your eyes and tilt your head back. Raise one foot. Good. Your balance seems fine. All of this is positive. Many people aren't so lucky."

"But I can't smell or taste anything," Michael said.

"This is where it gets tricky." She grabbed a model of a human head, split in half to show the inner workings. "As air enters the nose," she said, pointing at the nasal passages, which were painted blue, "it triggers nerves that bring information to a part of the brain called the olfactory bulb." She pointed to the brain, which was painted bright red. "That information then goes to the part of the brain that creates our sense of smell. With brain trauma, these nerves often become damaged. Most people recover their senses within six weeks or so. The bad news is, if the senses don't come back after that, the loss is usually permanent."

"But I had my accident in November," Michael said. "That was five months ago."

"There are options out there," the doctor said. "Different kinds of holistic therapies, unproven but worth checking into. Don't lose hope."

"Wait, wait," Michael said. "You told me most people recover their senses after six weeks."

"Yes."

"But my accident was five months ago, and I still can't smell or taste."

"As I said, Michael, unfortunately in rare cases the loss is permanent. Have you had any other trouble? Any mood disorders? Anger, sadness, confusion, difficulty controlling outbursts?"

Michael could not hear her. His mind was stuck, unable to process his loss. The doctor looked at Cee Cee, who frowned and silently nodded her head.

"Michael," the doctor said, "emotional and behavioral changes are also common with brain injuries. Your doctor gave you Zoloft, which was good. Are you still taking OxyContin?"

Again, Michael said nothing. His eyes were far away. Again, Cee Cee frowned and nodded.

"I want you to stop that. Wean yourself. Don't just stop cold. But the sooner the better. I'm going to prescribe Klonopin, which will help even your moods and alleviate depression. Take only as needed. It isn't as dangerous as the Oxy, but it's still habit-forming."

The doctor led Michael and Cee Cee out of the examining room. Michael walked in a daze. He hardly noticed as Cee Cee checked him out of the hospital and the driver pulled up and opened the door.

"So it's not coming back," Michael said.

"Michael, we're going to—" Cee Cee said, helping him into the car, but she couldn't think of a way to finish the sentence. "Let's go to the hotel and rest," she said.

"I want to go home."

"We have a flight first thing tomorrow morning," Cee Cee said.

"Take me to the airport. Buy a new ticket. Now."

"Michael, dear," Cee Cee said.

"Now," Michael shouted.

Wheels down, a private car, and Michael was home. Cee Cee ran a bubble bath. She lit candles and dimmed the lights. "Get in," she said. Michael obeyed. In one motion, Cee Cee pulled her dress over her head and was naked. She climbed in the warm bath behind Michael and pulled him toward her. He sunk down, his body covered in bubbles, the back of his head resting on her breasts.

"I can't live like this," he said. "My head hurts all the time. Can't smell.

Can't taste. What am I going to do?"

"It's going to be okay," she said, running her hands over his shoulders and down his chest. "We're going to find a way out. I promise."

Michael turned and pinned her to the tub. "Michael," she said through his forceful kisses. "You're on my arm, Michael. It hurts." He lifted his body to free her arm and was right back on top of her. Cee Cee's neck bent at an awkward angle against the tub wall beneath his thrusting heft. She tried to steady herself, but her feet and legs slipped on the porcelain. "Michael," she said, but he put a soap-bubbled hand across her mouth. "Stop," she tried to say, but it came out *stphhhh*, and her mouth filled with bubbles. Cee Cee scratched at his hand until she pried it from her mouth.

"Stop," she shouted.

The surging, swirling bathwater calmed. Michael slid to the opposite side of the bath and began to cry. "I'm sorry," he said. "Jesus Christ, I'm so sorry. I don't know what's happening to me. It's like I'm watching someone else in my body, and I can't control him."

They lay in silence until the bath water went tepid. Cee Cee got out without a word, dried herself, then went to the bedroom to dress for dinner. Waiting for her on her phone was a message from Martha: *Meeting tomorrow. Be there at noon.*

33

DEAL WITH
THE DEVIL

CEE CEE STOOD OUTSIDE THE Colonel's office uncertain of whether Martha had scheduled a meeting or an ambush. She took a deep breath and entered the room to find the Colonel sitting behind his desk. He gestured her into a chair opposite him without a word, then lit a cigar, puffed it twice, and said, "You have thirty seconds to tell me why you're here and why I'm keeping this meeting a secret from my current business partner, your ex-husband." He leaned back in his chair, put his boots on his desk, and looked at his gold Rolex. "Starting now."

"I want you to rip up Michael's contract," Cee Cee said.

"He ain't gettin' out of the album," the Colonel said. "Twenty seconds."

"You can have the album. I want to manage him from now on."

"Ten seconds."

"I can give you the power to control Bucky."

The Colonel took his feet from his desk and leaned forward.

"Say that again, sweetheart?"

"I have information that will ruin him if it gets out. You give me Michael, I give you Bucky."

"What kind of information?"

Cee Cee handed the Colonel a manila envelope full of old bank statements and Xeroxed checks.

"Bucky embezzled half a million dollars from the church to start his label," she said. "There's the proof."

The Colonel whistled through his teeth.

"Well, little lady, you now have my attention."

"Do we have a deal?"

"What's Michael's status?" the Colonel asked.

"He's got a serious brain injury, that's his status. He can't smell or taste. Seems to have no control over his emotions. Doctors can't figure it out. The Mayo Clinic said it might be permanent."

"Then why do you want him so bad?"

"Because I can protect him. I can make him better."

The Colonel nodded his head as though confirming an inner suspicion.

"See, that's what I figured," he said. "Let's talk straight. Sam is my meal ticket. Always was, always will be. At first, we thought Michael was the Lord and Savior. Best thing that ever happened to Sam. But then, well...let's just say things haven't gone the way we hoped they would. You see, Michael has become a liability. And we just got word from the Country Music Hall of Fame—this is between us, sweetheart—that they're inducting Sam right after the Grammys. They want him and Michael to perform at the ceremony."

"What's your point?"

The Colonel chuckled.

"My point is there's a little less than six months from now until then. A lot can go wrong in that time. If you guarantee Michael will not do anything to hurt this album, and if you get him through the awards season in one piece, you got yourself a deal. He'll be your mess from then on."

"That's it?" Cee Cee said.

"That's it," the Colonel replied, sitting back in his chair, a grin of satisfaction struggling to his face.

34

FATHER AND SON

BY THE END OF OCTOBER, Michael's face was everywhere. A billboard in downtown Nashville touted the hit new album from Sam and Michael Rogers. Every magazine on the rack featured a cover article about it. The songs filled the radio. The eponymous first single set new streaming records. Shane McAnally and Dave Cobb had taken the chorus of a haunting song Michael had begun writing for his mother, but didn't have the heart to finish; they sped up the tempo, changed the key, changed one lyric—substituting the word "father" for "mother"—and added Sam's voice in counterpoint harmony:

My eyes still cry your tears, my heart still beats your blood

If I live a thousand years, I won't forget your love

And when the dark day comes, my final race is run

I'll come back to your loving arms, my father, I'm your son.

Meanwhile, Sam appeared alone on the cover of *Billboard* under the headline, "Old Dog, New Tricks," and he smiled from the front page of the *New York Times* music section. BuzzFeed spat out a flurry of listicles with titles like "Every Sam Rogers Song, Ranked," and "The Beginner's Guide to Sam Rogers."

Despite tepid reviews, *Father and Son* debuted at the top of the country and pop charts and was certified platinum within a week of its release. Michael and Sam were each nominated for the Country Music Awards Entertainer of the Year, Male Vocalist of the Year, Vocal Duo of the Year, and Album of the Year, and the smart money was on a sweep. The album also received several Grammy nods, and *Rolling*

Stone announced Sam's induction at next year's Country Hall of Fame ceremony, where he was to appear onstage with his son, young country phenomenon Michael Rogers.

The only thing missing from this circus was Michael. The Colonel bought time, claiming Michael was sick and would only do email interviews. The emails went to Bucky's assistant, who had been coached on what to say. In print, Michael had never been so happy, so pleased with his work, so nurtured and protected in the crook of his father's arm. In reality, Michael only had the slightest awareness any of this was happening.

One night, watching television, Michael perked up when he heard his name. It was a commercial for the Country Music Awards. He was being used to sell the show.

"Can I get out of that?" he muttered to Cee Cee and fell back into his trance.

"Michael, you need to be seen. It's the only way you're going to get leverage over Bucky and the Colonel."

"Are you saying this as my girlfriend or my manager?"

"Both."

Michael heaved himself upright. "Just make it easy on me, okay?"

As the day neared, Cee Cee called Martha and said, "He'll be there, but I want you to make sure we control the press. Limited engagement. No one can ask about the way he looks. No questions about Sam or the album."

"I don't see how we're going to get them to agree to all that."

"They either agree, or they don't talk to him."

On a cold night in early November, Cee Cee and Michael arrived at the Bridgestone Arena. The press swarmed Michael. Flashes popped in his eyes, leaving him dizzy and disoriented. He hung on Cee Cee's shoulder, his face a strange combination of gaunt from pain and puffy from drugs.

Cee Cee sat in a row with Bucky, Sam, Martha, and the Colonel, all smiling for the cameras while they schemed to betray each other. Then came the award: "Album of the Year goes to Sam and Michael Rogers,

Father and Son." And a standing ovation. And Bucky's eyes drilling holes in Michael and Cee Cee from behind as they climbed onstage to accept the trophy. And Sam throwing his arm around Michael's shoulders and making a mawkish speech. And Michael, his eyes hidden behind black sunglasses, mumbling a few words and almost keeling over. And behind them, the Colonel putting his hand on Cee Cee's shoulder in a gesture of camaraderie, and squeezing until she winced.

"Sweetheart, I've been doing this a long time," he said, "and I know when a man is about to crumble. Michael looks like shit. Maybe you ain't giving him enough pussy, but whatever it is, you better get it fixed."

"Get your hands off me," Cee Cee hissed.

"Little lady, do you know why they call me the Colonel?" He squeezed tighter. She refused to look at him. "I thought not," he said. "Lots of people have found out over the years, but the strange thing is the word never seems to get around. You know why? Because once you're in a position to find out, that's the end for you. You don't stick around and talk. You're as good as dead."

Cee Cee had once taken a self-defense class at the Young Women's Christians Association, and she used her knowledge to break the Colonel's grasp. In one fluid motion, she had him pinned in a bear hug and was squeezing the air from his lungs. As far as the audience knew, she was simply giving him a celebratory hug. She sold it to the cameras, smiling so big it seemed all her teeth were showing, as she leaned in and put her lips against the Colonel's ear. "Did you ever wonder," she said, loud enough to hurt him, "since I have all that dirt on Bucky, what I might have on you? Do your job, let me do mine, and maybe I'll let you off easy."

On their way back to their seats, Martha caught up to Cee Cee, her eyes huge, and whispered, "I've never seen anyone talk to him that way. You're my hero."

35

HOLY NIGHT

AS CHRISTMAS APPROACHED, CEE CEE spent more time with Michael but enjoyed it less. He was drunk. He was aggressive. He was high on pills and God knew what else. The sex got better but somehow meant less. Michael was once so tender with her. That was the man she fell in love with, not this walking erection who needed more and more, more than Cee Cee could give, so much more that he began to invite other women into their bedroom. When Cee Cee refused, he simply waited until she left the house on an errand to call them. Sometimes they were waiting like buzzards in the driveway as she left.

Michael rarely wanted to leave the house anymore, and when he did take her out, he complained about her clothing, wanting to know why she dressed like a whore and who she dressed that way for. One night at Pinewood they bowled next to a group of teenagers whose eyes became as big as dinner plates every time Cee Cee bent over to pick up her ball, and Michael almost came to blows with a tall one. The boy had the wisp of a mustache on his lip and the fake arrogance of untested manhood. He was about as old as Cee Cee's baby would have been, the one she lost, and she felt ashamed of Michael.

And then there were times when the clouds broke, and he was himself again, though Cee Cee never knew how long it would last. Two days before Christmas, he took her for a date. He was shampooed and shaved and trim and neat, dressed in a white shirt and blue blazer with a peony in the lapel. His charm seemed to fill the entire restaurant, and in his every gesture was the promise of hair-raising sensual power. He was insatiable all night, touching her under the dinner table, going down on her in the hired car, tying her to the bedpost at home and moving inside her until she screamed. As soon as he finished, he wanted more. Three hours she lay tied up, until her body ached and the ropes cut into her wrists, and still he wouldn't set her free until he was certain she had nothing left to give.

Untying her, he kissed the marks on her wrists and pulled her to his side. The dogs came sniffing, and he shouted them out of the room. Outside, lazy snowflakes fell like powdered sugar.

"I still love Christmas," Michael said, his eyes glinting.

"I still love you," Cee Cee said, kissing his lips.

"Do you want your present?"

"I thought I was supposed to wait for Santa," Cee Cee said.

"It's a good one," Michael said. And there he was again, the Michael Cee Cee loved, all boyish enthusiasm and uncomplicated sweetness.

"The waiting makes it better," she said, running her hand through his long hair.

"Okay," he said. "Christmas morning it is, then."

"But I can't stay that night, remember."

"What?"

"I have to go see my parents. I told you this weeks ago."

"What does that mean?"

"I can be with you Christmas Day, but I have to go see them for dinner that night."

"I don't understand," Michael said tensely.

"It'll just be one evening."

"You're leaving me alone on Christmas?"

"Come on, Michael. You can survive a few hours alone."

"Like hell I can," Michael said, struggling to control his anger.

"Michael—"

"No. Goddamnit, Cee Cee, I can't take this anymore. What do I need to do? You want me to get on my knees?" He crawled out of bed, went down on his knees, and took her hand. "Marry me. Is that what you want?"

"Don't put me in this position," Cee Cee said. "I have done everything for you. I will do anything for you. But I have my life too."

"You're ashamed of me, aren't you? You don't want them to know you're a cheater."

"Cheater?" Cee Cee sat up and moved away from Michael to the edge of the bed. "You think I don't know how many women you fuck?"

"They don't mean anything to me. I think of you every time."

Cee Cee felt like she had been punched in the stomach. She found her clothes, took them into the bathroom, and locked the door. Michael stood outside, pounding on the door. When she finally opened it, she was dressed, her purse on her arm, her car keys in hand.

"Fine," Michael shouted at her back as she walked downstairs. "Get the fuck out of here."

Cee Cee turned and looked up at Michael standing naked behind the balustrade. "If you love me, stop acting like this," she said, tears smudging her mascara. "Think of what *I* need. Just once."

"Don't bother coming back," Michael said. He retreated to his bedroom and slammed the door.

36

CHRISTMAS
IS BUSINESS

CHRISTMAS FOUND THE COLONEL ON Sam's couch, his feet up on the coffee table, Dolly and Elvis snoring beneath him, the television murmuring in the background. Papers lay scattered around him. Through half-moon glasses, he scoured Country Aircheck and compared it to an open copy of *Billboard* magazine. "Can you believe it?" he called to Sam, who stood in the kitchen dodging whacks from Betty's wooden spoon as he stole bites of Christmas dinner. "If I told you this two years ago," the Colonel yelled, "you'd'a called me a liar." He let out a rumbling laugh and pulled from his cigar.

Sam stuck out his head from the kitchen.

"Working on Christmas, Colonel?" he said.

"Listen," the Colonel said, rummaging through his papers. "'Father and Son,' number one. 'Happy Christmas,' back up to number two. Now here's the kicker: 'American Dreams,' number three! Between you and Michael, there's six singles and three albums in the top ten. Plus a sweep at the CMAs, and I guarantee you're going to win a Grammy, and then the other kicker: in a little more than one month, you enter hallowed ground. The Hall of Fame. You're back on top, old man."

During dinner, the Colonel drank a whole bottle of wine, then moved on to whiskey. When Betty carried the dirty dishes into the kitchen, the Colonel turned to Sam, his eyes swimming, and said, "I knew you had it in you." His hand searched across the table and found Sam's. "I always knew," he said, pressing Sam's hand.

"What are you doing, Colonel?" Sam said stiffly, jerking his hand away and hiding it under the table.

"Don't you know? Haven't you always known?"

"Known what?"

"Come on, Sam. After everything we been through. All these years looking for something that wasn't there."

"You feeling alright, ol' buddy?"

The Colonel had worked so hard all his life to lose his backwater drawl, to pass in the hip, urbane world of New York and Los Angeles as an equal, not just some country bumpkin. But now, with the wine flowing through his veins and his heart on fire, he felt like the boy from Kentucky again. "Lookie here," he drawled. "Every damn good thing we ever done, we done together. Tell me it ain't so."

Sam quailed under the Colonel's passionate gaze. He didn't want to hurt his old friend, not now, not like this. But he wasn't up to riding down this road with the Colonel, either. He stood and tried to escape to the kitchen, but the Colonel reached across the table and grabbed his hand.

"Set," he drawled. "Set down and look at me, goddamnit."

Sam sat, chastened.

"What do you want from me?" Sam murmured.

"I want you to look me in the eye and tell me you ever found anything better'n me out there in all those years tom-cattin' around. Tell me you ever found anything better'n me."

"Colonel, I think you better let me call you a cab."

Suddenly the Colonel's plastic facade seemed too big, as if the man inside had deflated and withered. "No," he said. "No. I'll be just fine. Tell Betty the meal was wonderful, as always." The Colonel stood and tottered crookedly to the door.

Idling in Sam's driveway, the Colonel called Dr. Robert and said, "Get me a suite at the Four Seasons, and a pretty little present to unwrap. I want him hung. Make sure there's plenty of booze in the room. I been a good boy this year, Doctor." Then, swerving on ice slick roads he made his way to the Four Seasons, left his car two wheels up on the sidewalk, threw his keys to the valet, staggered to the front desk, retrieved his room key, nearly vomited in the elevator, found his suite, and opened the door to find a statue of a man, not tall but chiseled, da Vinci's David in the flesh. The man wore a fluffy white towel around his waist and nothing else. The Colonel weaved his way to the man without a word, ran his hands down the man's bare chest and stomach, and under the towel. "By God, where'd you get that thing?" he said. "Tear the sheets and tie me up."

After their fight Cee Cee accepted Michael's apology, pushed all second thoughts from her mind, and ignored the disturbed feeling in the pit of her stomach. She loved the Christmas gifts he gave her: a first edition of her favorite book, *To Kill a Mockingbird*, a tan Birkin bag from Hermes, and a copy of *The Kama Sutra* with the inscription, "Let's go through the whole book together." She gave him a snakeskin belt from Australia. Then, in bathrobes and slippers, they lay stretched on the couch in sugarplum sweet bliss, sipping from a bottle of red wine, the dogs snuggling into their every warm crack and crevice. The house was as silent as falling snow. Frank Sinatra sang "It Came Upon a Midnight Clear" on the stereo.

She didn't want to leave, but she had to see her parents. The second she shut the door, Michael called Amber. "Bring a friend," he said.

Amber arrived thirty minutes later with a skinny blonde, her lips plump and Botoxed. Michael looked her up and down and said, "Strip."

The friend gave him a wicked smile, stuck her hand down his pants, and began stroking. "In due time," she said, pulling down his pants, kneeling down before him, and admiring his erection. From her bag, she produced a baggie of white powder and tapped out a line on his penis, then snorted it off. "Your turn," she said, laying back and pouring a line that ran from her bellybutton to her pubic hair.

"What is it?" Michael said.

"China White. Primo shit. It's not like coke. This'll make you float. Feels like the universe is sucking your dick."

He snorted it and ended with his nose on her clitoris, while Amber ran her warm mouth up his leg to his testicles. In an instant, the whole world was as warm as a mother's lap. His body pulsed with pleasure. The sun poured in the windows like honey. Birds sang in euphony. There was no pain, only the repeated explosion of bliss as the girls took from him all he could give.

When he came to his senses, Michael wanted more. "Sorry, she's gotta go," Amber said, gesturing to her friend, who was half naked and rummaging around on the floor for her drugs. "But she works out of the Thompson Hotel if you want to meet us there later."

"Why wait?" Michael said. "Come on, I'll drive."

Swerving wildly on the icy roads, he dialed Martha. "Book me a room at the Thompson, love," he said. "A suite."

Martha heard the girls giggle in the background. "Where's Cee Cee?" she said.

"No questions."

"Michael—"

"Stay out of this, Martha. It's none of your business. Or hers."

Martha tried to talk sense into Michael but realized she was speaking into a dead phone. She sighed and called the Thompson. "I'd like to book a suite," she said. Then, lowering her voice, "You'll know what to do when he arrives. No press. No cameras. If a single word leaks, you'll be so buried under lawsuits you'll need a shovel to find your ass."

Michael swerved to a stop in front of the hotel and staggered inside, leaning on the girls for support. Heads turned. Voices whispered. Cell phones came out of pockets and pointed at him until hotel staff approached the patrons and made sure all photos were deleted. Michael signed in as Johnny Rivers, grabbed the key to the penthouse, and stepped in the elevator, oblivious to everything but the girls at his side. Up in the room, he drew the curtains and did not see the sun rise until New Year's Day.

37

AUSTRALIA CALLS

NEW YEAR'S DAY DAWNED BLUE and beautiful. The whole world looked scrubbed and shiny and new. Birds chirped outside the window, but Cee Cee could barely hear them. She blew the steam off her coffee, her hands trembling, her eyes bloodshot, her mind jerking like a fish on a line. She looked at her phone and sighed. *What's the point?* she thought. Then she set her jaw, picked up the phone and dialed again. She nearly dropped her mug when a voice came through on the other end.

"Where the hell have you been?" Cee Cee yelled into the phone.

"Sorry," came Martha's reply.

"Sorry? That's all you have to say? You haven't answered the phone in six days. What the hell is going on?"

"He told me not to talk to you."

"And you do everything he tells you?"

"I'm just trying to keep my job."

"By letting him disappear?"

"Look, Cee Cee, it's none of my business what he does in his personal life."

"You don't mean that, Martha. We just have to keep Michael under control until we can figure out what's wrong with him."

Martha snorted. "No one controls him. Come on, you've been around this world long enough. You know what this is. He does what he wants, and we clean up the mess."

"Where is he, Martha? I've been calling him night and day. Both of you. If I hear another answering machine, I'm going to scream."

"You don't want to know."

"I haven't slept. I'm exhausted. I'm scared. I'm angry. For the love of God, just tell me."

"He's going to drag you down with him."

"I just want to know where Michael is."

Thirty minutes later, Cee Cee rode the elevator at the Thompson hotel up to Michael's penthouse. His door stood cracked open, and she pushed through it and into the room. The cold blue day peeked through the cracks in the curtains; otherwise, the room was dark. On the bed, Cee Cee could just make out a jumble of shapes—bodies intertwined, asleep. She tore open the curtains with a violent *whoosh.*

Michael rolled over and blinked his eyes in the sudden brightness. "No room service," he mumbled.

Cee Cee ripped the sheets off the sleeping bodies to reveal Michael, naked, half erect, his hands resting between two naked women's legs. Slowly he recognized Cee Cee. "Fuck," he shouted, and fell out of bed, pushing Amber along with him to the floor. He shot up, grabbed the sheet from Cee Cee's hand, and wrapped it around his waist. "What are you doing here?" he slurred.

Amber's friend stirred awake. "Who is this bitch?" she said.

Cee Cee took Amber and her friend by the hair and threw them out of the room into the hallway, naked. Darting around the room, she collected their clothes, opened the door, and threw them in the hall. Then she turned to Michael. The blood was in her cheeks. Her hair was wild. Her eyes burned with the fire of a lover scorned. She breathed heavily, unable to speak but communicating perfectly.

But before she could give voice to her wrath and devastation, Michael began to cry. "I'm sorry," he said. "I need help." Cee Cee threw him in the shower and ordered black coffee and a pitcher of water to the room. She packed his bag, scowling at the sex toys, made him drink the coffee and the water, then took him down to the lobby, paid the valet to keep his car safe, walked Michael to her car, and drove him home.

Halfway home, Michael couldn't stand Cee Cee's silence any longer. It was worse than the worst tongue lashing he had ever received. "Let's go to Australia," he said. "Get away from all this. Give me a chance to clear my head." She didn't so much as look at him. "It's summer there," he continued. "Everything's the reverse. We can go surfing. Have you ever been?" No response. "It's the most incredible feeling. We can get a place on the Gold Coast. That's in Sydney. The kangaroos hang out on your front lawn. It's paradise."

Michael kept at it all evening, begging, pleading, apologizing, crying, singing, laughing, begging again. She still wouldn't speak to him. The best he could do was convince Cee Cee not to sleep on the couch. As they lay together in bed, he pressed himself against her back, and despite her resolve to reject him, Cee Cee melted into him once, twice, and one more time. Then, her head on his shoulder, her hand trailing across his chest, she heard him whisper, "You'll go to Australia with me, won't you?"

"Yes," Cee Cee said.

But Michael had fallen asleep.

She crept out of bed, found her phone, and texted Martha: *Well, I found him. Very long story short, he's home.*

I tried to warn you, Martha replied.

I know.

Is it worth it? I mean, all these women...is he really that good?

Unfortunately.

Cee Cee went back to bed but couldn't sleep. Near dawn, she went downstairs and stretched out on the couch with the dogs, watching television until she dozed off. Just after dawn, she awoke with a strange feeling in her stomach that rose up her chest and into her throat. She ran to the bathroom, knelt down, and threw up.

38

A DEVIL INSIDE

THERE WAS NO MORE TALK of Australia. Michael could barely get out of bed. He wore his bathrobe and slippers all day, only to sleep in them all night. Cee Cee kept him sober, but she wondered if that made him worse. The doctor prescribed Prozac—start with ten milligrams, he said, and wean off the Zoloft, then go up to twenty on the Prozac and call again.

Michael's funk only deepened, so Cee Cee tried to get him to work. She'd put his guitar in his lap and say, "Play for me," or she'd leave it on his chair with a pad and pencil and a little note: "Just in case lightning strikes." When that didn't work, she offered to help. "I used to write," she said. "Let's make something together."

The Grammy Awards were in two days, then came the hall of fame induction. Cee Cee knew she had to get Michael to the ceremony for her plan to succeed, but he could barely stand under his own power. Worst of all, her period was a week late, and every morning found her crouched over the toilet, throwing up. She had always wanted a baby, but not like this. *Please, not now*, she prayed.

Then Michael disappeared again.

Cee Cee had barely left the house all month for fear of leaving him alone, but the second of February was her mother's seventy-fifth birthday dinner. She begged Michael to come, but he said his head hurt too much, and amidst much yelling, Cee Cee finally left. By the time she got home, he was gone.

She went to the Thompson and asked for Johnny Rivers's suite, but the girl said there was no Johnny Rivers there. Cee Cee pulled her aside and said, "I'm looking for Michael Jennings. I know you know who he is. Just tell me if he's here. I'm his...his wife." Still the girl wouldn't budge, so Cee Cee rode the elevator to the penthouses and began searching for Michael's room.

She had her ear to the second door in the hallway when she saw two girls she recognized slipping out of a room further up the hall. She had kicked them out of Michael's room last time. But now their faces were red with fear. They whispered hurriedly together. Cee Cee ran to them, grabbed the shorter one by the arms, and shook her. "Is he in there?" she shouted. The girl ripped herself free, and she and her friend ran to the elevator on bare tiptoes, carrying their shoes and bags and coats in a heap in their arms.

Cee Cee pushed open the door. The messy bed sat before her, a silent witness to the depravity it had seen. "Michael," she called. No answer. Searching the room, she found his clothes in a pile on the floor. "Michael," she called again. She turned to the bathroom and stood with her nose pressed against the closed door. "Michael," she called a third time and slowly turned the handle.

Her eyes grazed over the black tile, silver mirrors, and marble countertop, gazed through the floor-to-ceiling window, then came back inside to the titanium tub. She followed the puddle of water on the floor up to the hand dangling over the side of the tub, and the hand up the arm, and the arm to the face, deathly blue, eyes closed, mouth drooping.

He wasn't breathing.

"Michael." Cee Cee patted him on the face. "Michael, wake up." His head lolled to the side. She climbed in the tub, sending water pouring over the rim, soaking her clothes to the chest. "Come on, come on, come on," she said, shaking him, beginning to hyperventilate. With a store of strength she didn't know she possessed, Cee Cee lifted Michael bodily from the tub and laid him on the cold tile. She snatched a towel from the rack and placed it under his head, then began beating on his chest with both hands. "Wake up," she shouted. "Wake up." Tears streamed down her face. The veins in his neck bulged. How long? How long had they left him here without breathing? She opened his mouth and blew the air from her lungs into it, again and again, until she saw black spots, then pounded on his chest again. "Michael," she screamed. His face was bloated and blue. His hair clung to it in wet strands. His lips were blue and white. "Please," she said, draping herself over his naked body. "Please."

Michael coughed.

His eyes fluttered.

"Yes," Cee Cee breathed. "Yes, Michael, yes. Come on. I'm here. I'm here. Come back to me." She cradled his head in her arms. "You're okay," she said. "Just wake up."

He opened his eyes and looked up at her. "Hello, love," he said. "What are you doing here?"

Cee Cee collapsed.

39

KINKY BOOTS

THE MORNING OF THE FLIGHT to Los Angeles, no amount of prodding, pleading, or threatening would make Michael get out of bed. Cee Cee called Martha. "Come over and help me. We're going to have to fly commercial at this point."

Martha took a car to the house and gasped when she saw Michael. He was bloated from too much alcohol, his eyes bloodshot from lack of sleep, his hair disheveled and dirty and smelling of heroin. Martha had been in music long enough to know the smell. His fingers were burned from holding his cigarettes while he fell asleep. The middle finger on his right hand was infected from the burn. His forehead was lined. She couldn't believe this was the same man she met in the coffee shop all those years ago.

"Michael, you're a mess," she whispered while Cee Cee was up in the bedroom packing. "How many of these are you taking?" she said, grabbing an empty bottle from the sofa and reading the label: Prozac, twenty milligrams.

"As many as it takes."

Martha wondered if she had made a mistake siding with Cee Cee. On the way to the airport, she studied Cee Cee's face in the rearview mirror and saw the fear, the exhaustion, the love written on it. The cheeks were fuller, the chin heavier. *She must be eating her feelings,* Martha thought. Michael dozed in the backseat, awaking with a start when they arrived at the airport and complaining like a child who lost his toy at having to fly commercial. On the plane, he drank half a bottle of champagne and passed out while Cee Cee watched helplessly.

"I can't trust him alone," Cee Cee said to Martha as the plane began its descent. "I need you to help me. I have a lot of work to do today and tomorrow, and I need you to promise that if he's not with me, you won't let him out of your sight."

Martha breathed heavily. "Cee Cee, you know I'll do my best. But you also know who he is."

Upon landing in Los Angeles, Cee Cee shook Michael awake, then held a coat over him to shelter him from the flashing cameras, and poured him into a private car with instructions to go straight to the Chateau Marmont hotel. At the hotel, she tipped a bellboy, who walked her and Michael to their bungalow, set back amidst the areca palms, the clusia, and the birds of paradise. She ran a bath, but the warm water did not relax her. She felt sick. Getting dressed, she instructed Michael, "I have to go pick up the credentials for tomorrow. Martha is going to take you to dinner. Please behave."

But when Martha arrived at the bungalow, it was empty. A pool of panic heated her guts. She sprinted to the hotel restaurant, where she saw Michael seated at a table with two empty bottles of French red wine. Catching her breath, she watched him and saw him as he used to be. He sat making jokes with the wait staff, with all the women fawning over him, the center of attention, irresistible as always.

But when she sat next to Michael, Martha was shocked again at his appearance. His eyes were puffy and red. His cheer was the pancake makeup of an aging actor, drawing attention to the very weakness it sought to conceal. He was a lonely little boy, pathetic in every sense of the word. He snapped his fingers, and a liveried waiter brought a new bottle of wine. As the waiter fumbled with the cork, Michael snatched the bottle from his hands, pulled out the cork with his teeth, put the bottle to his lips, and turned it to the ceiling. When he slammed the bottle down on the table, half the wine was gone. He lit a cigarette and smoked it in four deep breaths. Then he returned to the bottle.

"Michael," Martha whispered, "you're drunk. Eat something."

Michael smiled at her. "Yes, I am drunk, darling. And seeing as how I can't taste anything, I am going to continue to drink until I pass the fuck out."

"I won't sit here while you do this to yourself," Martha said.

"The world is your oyster, darling," Michael said. "You can come and go as you please."

"You know what your problem is?" Martha said, trembling. Michael's look of shock nearly made her lose her nerve, but she remembered the way Cee Cee talked to the Colonel, and she forced herself to continue: "People let you get away with everything. I'm tired of it. Stop acting like this."

Michael pulled a wad of hundred-dollar bills from his pocket. "How much will it take to make you leave me alone?" he said thickly. He licked his thumb and began counting bills onto the table. "One? Two? Three?"

"Put it away," Martha said tensely.

"Here," Michael said, pushing the entire roll of money toward her. "Take it all. Half is to leave me alone, and half is to stop blaming me because you're not good enough to make it in this business without me."

"I don't know what to do with you anymore," Martha said quietly. She rose from the table. "Tell Cee Cee I'm sorry."

"Sorry for what?" Michael said, but she didn't answer.

On her way out of the restaurant, Martha nearly knocked over Bucky. They looked at each other for an awkward moment. "Michael doesn't look so good," Bucky said, breaking the silence.

"Just stay out of it," Martha said.

"He's on my label. I have a right to know what's going on."

"Leave him alone, Bucky. Give him a chance to heal."

Martha pushed past Bucky, who turned to his dates and said, "You see that man over there? That's Michael Jennings. You recognize him?"

The girls giggled.

"How'd you like to meet him?"

"Yeah right," the younger one said.

"No, really. He's one of my best friends. And you're just his type. Both of you. Tell you what, why don't you take this"—Bucky handed the girl a wad of bills—"and have a good time. It's on me. Give him anything he wants." Bucky gave the girls a meaningful look. "*Anything.*"

The girls giggled again.

"Oh, one last thing…we never had this conversation," Bucky said, holding the girl's hand before she could take the money. "Understood?"

She nodded.

Michael was near the bottom of the bottle when he noticed two girls approaching. *Hookers,* he thought. *Finally something interesting.* The one on the left was a tiny young blonde, her gigantic green eyes rimmed with too much mascara. A mischievous smile played on her pink lips. She was dressed like a Catholic schoolgirl, but the skirt was cut, so Michael could see her creamy thighs, and the shirt was unbuttoned just enough to imply the heave and sway of her exquisite breasts. The older one was taller, a brunette with massive fake breasts. She wore six-inch stiletto heels and a turquoise dress that fit like second skin. The maître d' tried to stop their advance, but Michael shouted across the room, "They're with me, my good man." With the slightest arch of his eyebrow, he brought the girls to the table. As he rose to pull out their chairs, he nearly collapsed. Once the women were seated, Michael ordered three more bottles of wine—one for each of them.

"You're Michael Jennings, aren't you?" the younger woman asked.

Michael grinned drunkenly.

"Can we come to the Grammys?" she said.

"The tickets are expensive," he answered.

"How much?" asked the older one.

"Make me an offer," Michael said.

The women drew their chairs closer to him and began kissing him on either side of his neck. Then they kissed each other. Heads turned in the restaurant, but Michael didn't care.

"I think there's something wrong with the television in my room," he said. "I wonder if you kind ladies could help me fix it." Leaving the wad of cash on the table, he put his arms around the women and used them like crutches on the way out.

At the door to his room, the older woman started unbuckling his belt. "Want me to blow you right here?" she whispered in his ear.

"No, I wanna see what one of these rooms look like on the inside," said the younger one.

They stumbled into the bungalow, and both women hit the mini bar. The younger one popped a small bottle of champagne. The older one fished in her purse and produced three joints and a baggie of cocaine. She lit the joints and passed them around, then laid out the cocaine in neat rows.

"I'm not paying for this," Michael slurred, and the women giggled.

"This is off the clock," the younger one said as she began undressing her friend.

Michael watched, as high as he'd ever been in his life. He began shouting commands at them like a film director: "You, take off your bra and panties. You, go down on her. Now switch."

Naked, the women crawled to Michael and began undressing him. Off came his shirt, down went his pants and underwear. The older one said, "I see we're in for a long night." The women took turns fellating him, until he grabbed the younger one, pushed her on her back, and climbed on top of her. An hour later, the women lay in a sweaty heap, panting and glassy-eyed. Michael left them and jumped in the shower. Minutes later, they joined him.

"He's hard again," said the older one. "Why don't you take care of that?"

As the younger one went down on him, the older one whispered in his ear, "Want to learn a new game?" The women led him out of the shower and back to the bed, dripping wet. The younger one ripped Michael's belt from his pants lying on the floor, while the older one said, "Candy is going to put this around your neck. Any time you want to stop, just say the safe word."

"What's that?" Michael asked as Candy tightened the belt.

"How about 'Grammy'?" Candy said, while the older one—Michael never did catch her name—ran her tongue down his body. Candy tightened the belt further, until the veins in Michael's neck bulged, as the older one swirled her tongue around his penis. He gasped. Gone was his usual stamina. In its place was an explosion of pure euphoria. For those few seconds, he received a blessed release from the constant pain. When he finally returned to earth, the older woman handed him a glass of champagne. Candy loosened the belt and raised her eyebrow to say, *Well?*

"Holy shit," Michael panted. "I've never…what *was* that?"

"Auto-erotic asphyxiation," said the older one. "Like seeing the face of God."

"I want to do it again," Michael said.

"Once a night is enough," said Candy, laughing. "We're not trying to kill you."

40

MUSIC IS POWER

CEE CEE STOOD IN FRONT of the Staples Center and breathed deeply. This was it. When she walked through those doors, it was not as a wife or girlfriend but as a manager.

Inside, the lobby was full to bursting with music business heavies. Bucky was right about one thing: true power lived behind the scenes. Look at all these managers and publicists—none of them could write a song that connected with the hearts of millions or step on a stage and bring the house down, but they could count, and they could keep books, and they could read contracts. Singers were a dime a dozen. The real talent was knowing how to make money.

Walking through the crowd, she felt like she had a bullseye on her forehead. No one talked to her, but their eyes did the talking. These were people she knew. How many years had she spent at events just like this, squired on Bucky's arm? But now the context was changed. She was trying to become one of them, and whether or not she succeeded depended largely on how afraid they were of Bucky. She waved to Dale Cunningham of Big Smoke Records, but he ignored her. Then, wondering if Bucky was in the room, she took refuge behind a column near the bathrooms and steeled herself to go out among the crowd again.

"Cee Cee, what a surprise," said a voice behind her.

Cee Cee turned to see Bobby Jones, who had begun her career working with Britney Spears and now managed Reba McEntire, Florida Georgia Line, and Steven Tyler. She always liked Bobby. In a world of smug men, Bobby had the biggest balls in any room she entered. But she was also a sweet, kind woman. Cee Cee wondered if she called herself Bobby, rather than her full name Barbara, to fool the men into thinking she was one of them on paper. Cee Cee wondered if she should do the same. *C.C. Porter*, she thought. *Not bad.*

"Hi, Bobby," she said. "Glad to see you."

"I heard what happened with Bucky. Are you okay?"

"Yeah. I'm going to be."

"What brings you here?"

"Michael."

Bobby raised her eyebrows and nodded knowingly. "Lucky girl," she said.

"You don't know the half of it. Listen, can I ask you a question? I'm sort of managing him now. I want to set up a company, but I don't know how.

"Here's my card," Bobby said, digging in her purse and handing Cee Cee a business card. "When this is over, call me. I can walk you through it. You're going to need a lawyer."

"I got one," Cee Cee said, with a shrug. "The divorce...you know how it is."

"Don't let that bastard get away with anything."

"I'm entitled to half of DMG. And I'm gonna get it."

"Good for you. Call me. Seriously. There's a lot to it—office space, accountants, legal bullshit—but it's not impossible. And you've got a good client at the top of your roster."

"Thanks, Bobby," Cee Cee said. She felt tears rising in her eyes and blinked them away. "It means a lot."

41

TOGETHER FOREVER

BACK AT THE BUNGALOW, THE door handle turned, and Cee Cee's stomach turned with it. The door cracked open, and Cee Cee recoiled at what she saw. It wasn't the women—she was used to that by now, although it still hurt. It was Michael. His eyes were bloodshot and red-ringed and distant. His hair was matted and dirty. His face was bloated and ashen. His neck was bruised.

"Alright, out you go," she said to the prostitutes. She had become adept at kicking women out of a bedroom. Then she sat down next to Michael on the bed and searched his face for the man she loved. He was slipping away. She didn't realize how bad it was until now. She felt powerless to stop it and guilty for not helping him more.

For Michael, looking into Cee Cee's eyes was like looking in a mirror. He saw what he had become, and it frightened him.

"I need you," he said.

"I need you too," she replied and desperately believed it. She took his face in her hands. "It's going to be okay."

Michael turned away from her, ashamed. "I'm going to change," he said. "I promise."

"I know you will," she said, not knowing whether or not she believed it.

"I think I'm going to take a shower."

She looked around the filthy room and said, "You'd better."

While Michael stood under the warm water, Cee Cee called for room service and ordered coffee and scrambled eggs. Then she cleaned up the room, throwing out empty pill bottles, wine bottles, beer bottles, and spent roaches. She scooped up a handful of pills from the table and washed them down the sink. She tipped the bellhop when the food arrived and sat on the bed listening to Michael sing softly to himself as he shaved in the bathroom. He came out wearing only a towel and leaned in to kiss her again. "Eat," she commanded.

For the first time since the accident, Michael felt hungry. He couldn't taste the eggs or smell the coffee, but he wanted them. He cleaned the plate, dropped the towel, and began to undress her. "They don't mean anything," he said, unclasping her bra and resting his face in the cleft of her breasts. They were firmer and rounder than he remembered. "You know they don't. You know I love you only."

He playfully took her hand and rubbed it over his entire body, kissed her neck, and sang Willie Nelson's "You Were Always on My Mind," in her ear. The tiny hairs on her neck and arms stood on end. He climbed on top of her and let his hair fall around her. Cee Cee touched his neck where it was raw and bruised. "What did you do?" she asked.

"Don't remember," Michael said and forestalled further questioning with his fingers and tongue. Then Cee Cee felt the marvelous mixture of tenderness and power, the giving and the taking away, the gentle agony. He seemed to know the exact moment when to let up and when to surge ahead until she was so full she nearly screamed for mercy. But like a beautiful song slowly going out of tune, the feeling changed. The thrusts became jagged and violent. The moaning turned to snarling. Without thinking, Michael wrapped his hands around her throat and squeezed. "Michael," she gasped. "Michael, stop." She slapped at his hands. A tear rolled down her cheek.

Michael opened his eyes to see the terror in hers. He jumped off of her and slumped to the floor, crying. "Cee Cee, what is wrong with me?" he said. "I don't know how to fix it."

She climbed off the bed and joined him on the floor, fear, love, and pity mixing within her.

"Leave me," he said. "I don't deserve you."

Cee Cee thought about Bucky and the divorce. She thought about Bobby Jones and the business she was going to start. She thought about the Colonel and his promise: *Get Michael to the Grammys in one piece, and he's yours.* She had come too far to turn back now. "This isn't you," she said. "It's the accident. We're going to get you the help you need."

Slowly, his breathing calmed. He looked at Cee Cee, and the sincerity in his eyes nearly broke her heart. "I can't make it through this without you," he said.

"Me neither."

42

IN THE KEY OF LIFE

THE NEXT AFTERNOON, THE COLONEL paced side-stage at the Staples Center, yelling at no one and everyone. Bucky stalked the shadows, secretly hoping Michael wouldn't show. Only Sam felt at peace.

"Hey, Colonel, you believe this?" Sam said triumphantly, standing stage center, guitar slung around his shoulder, gazing in wonder at the pageantry as sound technicians swarmed around him, laying down cables, taping down cables, plugging in cables, while a ragtag team of roadies constructed the lighting rig above the stage. "Hey, Colonel," he said again, "check this out." He tapped the microphone and squealed with delight as the sound, amplified through an eighty-thousand-watt speaker stack, reverberated like thunder.

It wasn't that the sound or the pageantry was new to him, nor was it the thrill of winning an award. As a young man, he had ridden this same wave. It had dashed him against the rocks and sucked him in the undertow, and he was left for dead, but so what? Most people never caught the wave to begin with. Hell, most people never set foot in the ocean. Only a few short years ago, Sam had been content to sink to the bottom and lay with the carcasses of all the other wrecked dreamers. But against all odds the wave came again, towering and shimmering and beautiful, and it lifted Sam from the abyss and carried him on its crest, and now, cancer free, surging once more in the surf of fortune, Sam felt like a boy again.

Back at the Chateau Marmont, Cee Cee cradled Michael's head in her arms and let him sleep. He needed it more than anything, she knew. But she had forgotten to silence her phone, and its piercing ring caused

Michael to shoot awake. She freed one arm and grabbed the phone off the bedside table. It was Martha. Before she could answer, Michael snatched it out of her hands.

"Hello, darling," he said.

"Michael?" Martha shouted over the noise of Sam's soundcheck. "Everyone's freaking out. You need to get here now."

Like flicking a switch, Michael turned on the charisma that could fill an arena. Cee Cee didn't know what to make of the transformation. He stood up, his naked body long and muscular, and said, "Darling, how many times have I told you? The show can't start without me."

"Are you sure you're up for this?" Cee Cee said as Michael dressed himself.

"No. But I trust you."

"I promise we're almost free."

Michael seemed to float on stage, wearing dark sunglasses, a shirt open to the chest, and black jeans threaded with Cee Cee's belt. His hair was up in a bun atop his head, exposing the bruises on his neck. He was oblivious to the faces that gaped at him. "Hey, mates," he said casually to the band.

"Michael, son, are you all right?" said Sam.

Michael didn't even look at him. He saw Bucky and the Colonel hiding in the shadows and said, "I don't want them here."

"Well, that's too goddamn bad," Bucky spat.

"Say one more word to me," Michael said. "Go ahead. I dare you."

The tension on stage was like a guitar string tuned higher and higher until it seemed bound to snap. Sam unplugged his guitar and approached the Colonel and Bucky. "Listen," he said, "why don't you guys take tonight off? We're okay here. You go have a nice dinner, come back, and sit out in the crowd. I'll make sure they save you a good seat. You'll enjoy it more out there, anyway. Get to hear everyone clapping and shouting for us. Won't that be somethin'?"

A scowl struggled through the layers of the Colonel's face. He wasn't bothered by being asked to leave—he had already decided to do whatever it took to survive this night. It was looking in Sam's eyes and realizing the man he loved all these years, the man he sacrificed everything for, had never deserved it.

"You still don't get it, do you, ol' buddy?" the Colonel said. "You're nothing without me. Never were, never will be." Sam stared at him dumbly.

On stage, Michael tuned his guitar, strummed a chord to check it, and said, "Alright, what are we doing? One of yours or one you stole from me?"

"Well," Sam said, "we were gonna do a kind of medley. Some of mine, some of yours, and then end with 'Father and Son.' You know, make the crowd go wild."

"Count it off," Michael said.

As they worked through the medley, everyone in the building stopped and watched. Michael was as sharp and magnetic as ever. His voice was pure emotion. When the song ended, the tech crew and roadies burst into spontaneous applause.

"Let's do it just like that tonight," Sam said.

Michael grabbed Cee Cee's hand and walked backstage without a word to anyone.

The time came to perform. Sam walked onstage, guitar in hand. The crowd came to its feet. Michael was supposed to follow him, but he wasn't there. In an instant of sweaty silence, Sam saw the whole show sink into an abyss of shame. Michael was going to stand him up. Of course he was. But then the ovation returned more raucous than ever, and Sam saw Michael appear next to him out of the corner of his eye. "If it ain't the prodigal son," Sam said into the microphone, and the crowd laughed. Then, *one, two, three, four*, and they began.

Now it was Sam's turn to be magnetic. He performed with the finesse of a master, slower maybe for the passing of time but more natural, more in command, more powerful than ever. Michael, meanwhile, mumbled his way through his verses. He was unfocused and unconvincing, and the crowd noticed. The song ended to polite applause. Michael dropped his guitar and ambled off stage to the sound of screeching feedback. He seemed not to know where he was.

Bucky watched from the crowd, the embodiment of vengeance. His plan was going to be easier than he had imagined. Michael was doing all the work. The next step was to bury him. Send him on tour and let his momentum take him down in one epic, fiery crash. Imagine the sympathy that would pour out for Bucky, for Sam. Imagine the reissues and special editions that would go Platinum as soon as they were announced. And there would always be another Michael. There were hundreds of Michaels. Bucky would find the next one and continue to write his story in the book of country music history while Michael would remain forever a footnote. He turned to Dr. Robert, who was seated next to him, and said, "Do you have anything you can give him?"

"Like what?"

"I heard he likes the white powder."

"Cocaine's easy to come by in this town."

"Not cocaine."

Dr. Robert silently nodded and pulled out his phone.

Backstage, Cee Cee and Martha bent their heads together in heated discussion.

"We need to get him home tonight," Cee Cee said.

Martha got on her phone and booked a redeye flight back to Nashville, then called for a limo to take them to the airport. Michael didn't want to leave. His eyes were hateful and red. But by the time the limo arrived, the fight had gone out of him. They drove in silence to the airport, then flew through the black pit of night and landed in Nashville at four in the morning, where, mercifully, another limo waited to take them home. Martha marveled at what money could do.

Michael collapsed in a heap on the side seat. "My head hurts," he moaned. Cee Cee had to shake him awake when the limo reached his house, and she and Martha nearly carried him to the door and up the stairs, where Cee Cee put him to bed.

43

NASHVILLE RAIN

A HARD RAIN POUNDED THE roof and walls. Michael awoke and couldn't tell what time it was or where he was. He fell out of bed and struggled to his feet, knocking everything from his dresser. "Cee Cee," he called. She was sleeping on the couch downstairs and didn't hear him. The rain fell harder. His stomach ached with hunger, but instead of eating, he rummaged in his suitcase for a bottle of pain pills, and then it came to him in flashes: the hookers, the hotel, Cee Cee. She had thrown out all the good pills. The only thing left was the Prozac. His head pounded. Fear quickened his breathing. Fumbling in the suitcase, tearing out shirts and pants and throwing them haphazardly on the floor, his hand came upon the snakeskin belt. He sat with it for a while, staring into the darkness, then made a noose of it, took it to the bathroom and spent what felt like hours figuring out how to make it work. Finally, his drug-numbed fingers tied the other end around the bathroom doorknob. The belt dug into his flesh as he touched himself. He pushed as far as he could. Black spots danced before his eyes. For a few sublime moments, he felt no pain.

Empty, he loosened the belt from his neck and fell to the bathroom floor, where he slept.

Cee Cee found Michael shivering on the cold tile. Fearing the worst, she shook him awake. "Michael, what are you doing?" she said. "Why didn't you call for me?"

"I tried," he moaned, head full of thunder.

"Why do you do this Michael? I don't understand it."

"It's the only thing stronger than the pain." He rolled over and wretched.

"You could kill yourself," Cee Cee said, rubbing his back. She was crying.

"I'm in complete control, love."

Brushing his dirty hair from his eyes, he struggled to his feet, staggered to the bedroom, tore every sweater he owned from its hanger in the closet, and pulled them one by one over his body. A pair of thick socks and soft sweatpants, a wool-knit cap and gloves, and the shivering ceased. He padded downstairs, looking like a child who was allowed to dress himself. The dogs whined at the door.

"Just a minute, boys," he said. Searching for his slippers, Michael's thin patience snapped. "Can't find anything in this fucking house," he shouted, kicking the coffee table over on its side. "Where the fuck is Isabel?" He saw the slippers peeking from under the couch, but bending down to grab them only made his head hurt worse. He fell to his knees and nearly vomited. The dogs whined.

"Okay," he gasped. "I'm coming."

Cee Cee followed in his wake, trying to calm him. She heard the doctor's voice in her head: *Erratic behavior, violent mood swings, self-harm.* "Michael, stop," she said, but he either didn't hear or wasn't listening. Heaving himself upright, he found the leashes hung up by the kitchen door. He wanted a glass of wine. Rummaging through the cabinets, he searched for his bottle of Oxy, only to remember again that Cee Cee had thrown it all away. The dogs whined.

"Fucking hell," he said, clipping their leashes to their collars and opening the door. The cold air smacked him in the face. The shock cleared his head.

"Michael," Cee Cee shouted, grabbing his arm. "Where are you going?"

Michael turned and flashed his megawatt smile. "Gotta walk the dogs, love," he said. It was as though he had become himself again. The transition was frightening.

"Hang on," Cee Cee said. "Let me throw on a jacket."

Cee Cee reappeared, swaddled in her parka. Michael gazed at her face and said, "You're so beautiful." He kissed her on the red apple of her cheek, then shut the door behind him and fumbled to fit the key in the lock, all the while yelling at the dogs, "Don't pull. Don't pull. We're going to go slow today." Turning around, he saw three men with cameras skulking like buzzards behind the bushes at the edge of the property.

These were not the Colonel's spies. After Michael's strange, disastrous performance at the Grammys, every magazine and two-bit blog was jammed full of speculation. Where was he? Who was he with? What was wrong with him? The paparazzi had come to Michael's house to answer these questions, sucking sustenance from the scandal like ticks feeding on a hog. Their eyes gleamed greedily as they snapped away at him. He was clearly in distress, which meant the pictures would fetch a higher price.

Michael tried to ignore them, but they followed him and Cee Cee down the road. Turning a corner, they were joined by two of their brethren. "Michael," they called. "Michael, over here."

"No pictures," Cee Cee commanded. "Come on, guys, have a little respect."

"Sweetheart," the man said, "this is bigger than when Narvel left Reba. My kids gotta eat too."

Cee Cee's face reddened with fury, but Michael knew there was no reasoning with them. He pretended not to hear them as he doubled back toward his house. They became more brazen, closing in on him, their cameras thrusting ever closer. Michael broke into a jog. The dogs, obliviously happy, ran ahead, tongues lolling from their panting jaws. Cee Cee followed. The cameramen ran along. The two in front of him ran backwards, snapping all the time. Michael raised his free arm to shield his face. The cameras kept snapping as Michael and Cee Cee hurried to the door and inside.

He was too hot now. He tore off his sweaters and sunk to the floor, his heart pounding. The dogs slopped noisily at their water bowls. Michael crawled to the window and looked outside, where the cameramen had screwed on telephoto lenses and pointed them at the house. Shirtless, he ran to the back windows and peeked out, careful to show as little of himself as possible. They were there too, cameras pointed like rifles.

"We gotta get out of here," he said to Cee Cee.

"Where will we go?"

"The Thompson. You take the Jeep. They'll follow you. Drive them the opposite direction. Once they realize I'm not with you they'll leave you alone. As soon as they're gone, I'll take the Harley and go to the hotel. Meet me there later tonight."

"Are you sure that's a good idea? The motorcycle. It's just—"

"It's the only way. I'll be fine."

Cee Cee climbed the stairs and packed her suitcase. "Michael," she called, "I'm ready to go." No answer. "Michael?" she called. She rushed downstairs and found him still sitting on the floor beneath the window, crying.

"It's too much," he said.

Cee Cee sat next to him. "I know, my love," she said. "We're going to make it through this. Just be strong a little longer. For me. And for... well, for..." She put Michael's hand on her belly and looked him deep in the eyes. His eyes widened.

"Really?"

She nodded. "We're going to have a baby," she said, smiling, tears trickling from her eyes.

"A baby!" Michael shouted so loud it made Cee Cee's ears ring. He wrapped her in a bear hug, then loosened his grip. "Sorry, love," he said. "Mustn't hurt the baby."

"It's okay," Cee Cee laughed. "Just get ready and let's go."

"I'm going to be a father," Michael said to himself. "A father."

44

THE MUSIC MAN

MICHAEL TEXTED MARTHA: *ISABEL NEEDS to stay here for a while to take care of the house and the dogs.* Upstairs, he zipped his suitcase, which was still packed from the Grammy trip, and dressed himself. He carried his and Cee Cee's bags to the garage and threw them in the back of the Jeep. Embracing her again, kissing her full on the lips, he said, "Be careful."

Cee Cee backed out of the driveway, luring the paparazzi. Five minutes later, Michael gunned the Harley—a new one bought after the accident, against Cee Cee's protests—in the opposite direction. At the Thompson, he asked for a room under his pseudonym, but it was no use. The girl at the front desk knew him. Of course she did. She'd tell her friends, he could see it in her eyes. She wouldn't do it out of malice like the paparazzi, but the result would be the same. By sundown, everyone in Nashville would know where he was. He took out his bankroll and peeled off a crisp hundred dollar bill. She looked at it, puzzled. Michael pressed it into her hand. "I'm not here," he said, holding onto the bill as she tried to take it from him. "Understand?" A tiny smile played at the edges of the girl's lips. Michael let the bill go.

Ensconced in his penthouse, wrapped in a bathrobe, Michael called for room service and texted Cee Cee: *I'm here.* The bellboy brought his food and stood nervously in the room. "Hey, I know you," the bellboy said with a drawl. Michael peeled another hundred dollar bill from his wad and shoved it in the bellboy's top pocket. "No, you don't," he said, backing the kid into the narrow entryway and up against the door. He had six inches and maybe seventy pounds of advantage. He let this truth sink in. Then, glaring with silent menace, he fingered the young man's name tag and said, "Brandon, is it?" Peeling off another crisp hundred, Michael shoved it in the young man's pocket. "Bring me a bottle of wine, Brandon. And if anyone comes to this door except you, or is waiting for me in the lobby, or in the parking lot with a camera, I'll come find you. Deal?" Michael flashed his blinding smile and pushed the young man out of his room.

Cee Cee joined him that evening and spent the next three weeks holding him in her arms as he shook uncontrollably, his nose running, his temperature spiking, his eyes burning. Every morning found either Cee Cee hunched over the toilet with morning sickness, or Michael hunched over it in withdrawals, heaving his guts out until they were empty, then heaving the emptiness until it felt like his lungs, kidneys, and intestines must surely fall out. His muscles seized in excruciating spasms. One morning he stumbled back to bed to find his mother lying in a pool of blood, her eyes glassy and dead, and Sam standing over her with a knife. The hallucination disappeared, and his head split with a pain that crushed the wide expanse of existence down to a pinhole of agony. All night he tossed and turned, soaking his bedsheets in cold sweat.

And then came peace. And with it, strength. He could hold down tea and toast. He could shower and shave. He could make love. For the first time in a year or more, Michael wanted his guitar. He felt like a man given new life. Under the cover of night, Cee Cee drove home to get it for him. She parked half a block away, avoiding the streetlights. Waiting up the block were three cars. She could just discern the outline of telephoto lenses pointed at his house. She opened the car door as quietly as possible, then, walking softly on the brittle earth, made a wide arc through the woods to the back door and let herself in as silently as a thief. The house was dark. In the moonlight, she saw evidence of Isabel: clean table, clean kitchen, clean floor, fat dogs. *I'll have to do something nice for her*, Cee Cee thought as she crept to the bedroom in the darkness, lifted his guitar from its stand, and left the way she had come.

Michael didn't sleep that night or the next. He put the television on low in the background and held his guitar like a long lost lover. He couldn't stop the music from coming. It seemed every time he got up to go to the bathroom or order room service, he'd come back with a song. His fingers worked of their own volition, gliding over the neck, stacking chords on chords, excavating a wealth of songs from the guitar like an archeologist in an unspoiled tomb.

By the end of two days, he had written six songs. They were different but familiar, country but bigger than country; bigger than Nashville too; bigger than Bucky, the Colonel, and Sam; bigger even than Michael. He could hear the arrangements in his head as clearly as if he were listening to the finished product on the radio. Michael wrote for Cee Cee. He wrote for the baby. He was in love twice: with her and with his unborn child. After wandering so long in the wilderness, he had finally found the path.

April came, and with it the first fragile tendrils of spring. Michael's head no longer ached. His mouth no longer thirsted for booze and pills. He continued writing, recording the songs as demos on his laptop while Cee Cee slept. He didn't want her to hear them yet. He wanted to give them to her for her birthday. He had a little speech planned, a way of thanking her for saving his life and for giving him a reason to keep living.

Meanwhile, Cee Cee began to show. She spent her days on the phone with Bobby Jones setting up her management firm, afraid to let Michael out of her sight. But two days before the tour was to begin, while Michael was in the shower, she called Martha. "Meet me at the coffee shop," she said. "The one on Twelve South." She put on an old pair of jeans and a faded flannel shirt, pulled her hair into a bun, and covered it with a baseball cap. Looking in the mirror, she realized that for the first time in her life, she needed a disguise. She felt a jolt of empathy for Michael. When the elevator doors opened in the lobby, she scanned the crowd, searching for she didn't know what: paparazzi? Bucky's henchmen?

No one gave her a second look as she slipped out of the back entrance, found the Jeep, drove to the coffee shop, and sat in the corner. Ten minutes later, Martha arrived.

"What did you want to see me about?" Martha said.

"Sit. Can I get you something?"

"Tea. Mint."

Cee Cee walked to the counter and ordered a mint tea and a cappuccino, then returned to Martha.

"You know, this is where Michael and I first met," Martha said.

"That's sort of what this is about," Cee Cee answered. "Anyone could have walked through the door that day. Michael is lucky it was you. You believe in him, Martha. I know you do. It's time to leave the Colonel." Cee Cee couldn't tell if the look on Martha's face was pleasure or pain. She continued: "I called Thomas Rhett yesterday. He's unhappy with his management and has an option on his contract in eight months. It took a little convincing, but if we can get out of Michael's deal with Bucky, he's willing to join."

"Join what?" Martha said.

"Us. Our empire. I've started my own label and management company. You'll be vice president, as we agreed."

Martha's face fell. She stared sullenly out the window. "He'll never let it happen."

"Who?"

"Bucky."

"How can he stop us?"

"He owns Michael's publishing. You can't release anything new without him."

"What does he want? Money? Michael has enough."

"He doesn't need money. And he said he wouldn't release Michael's music if it cured cancer. He wants to bury you. Both of you."

"I know," Cee Cee said softly. "So what's our move?"

"We don't have one."

"What if we just do it anyway?"

"Cee Cee, I can't be a part of this. Michael can afford lawyers. I can't. If I help you, Bucky will sue me too. I could lose everything."

Cee Cee thought for a moment. "No," she said. "Michael won't let it come to that. Neither will I. We need you, Martha."

Martha bit her lip.

"I'm sorry, Cee Cee," she said. "I've worked too hard to get where I am. I can't risk it all."

Cee Cee's phone buzzed: *Where are you?*

"It's Michael," she said. "I'd better get back. Please, just think about what I said."

45

GENERATION TO GENERATION

CEE CEE RETURNED TO THE hotel and felt the old tightness in her stomach as she entered the room. Then she sighed with relief. Michael sat waiting for her on the bed in a pristine white bathrobe, showered and shaved, guitar in hands, strumming and gazing out the window. While she was gone, he had ordered what seemed like all the peonies in Nashville and decorated the room with them. The bedspread was covered in flower petals.

Michael called her to the bed, undressed her, and gently pushed her onto her back. Flower petals stuck to her skin. He held himself over her, his weight on his sinewy arms. "You're the most beautiful creature I've ever seen," he said. Reaching over to the bedside table, he grabbed *The Kama Sutra* and showed it to Cee Cee with a twinkle in his eye.

He kept her up most of the night and woke her up the next morning for more. When they finished, Cee Cee fell on the bed next to Michael, panting and sweating. She rested her head on his chest and said, "Today is the last day. I didn't tell you this, but I made a deal with the Colonel. After the ceremony he's going to rip up your contract. It'll just be me and you, together."

"What about Bucky?"

"I took care of him."

"You did all that?" Michael said, playfully biting at her arm. "Wow. Passion in the sheets, business in the streets. Lead the way, my intrepid manager."

While Cee Cee showered, Michael bounced all the new songs from his computer and emailed the folder to her. In her purse he placed a note that read, "Check your email. This is our future." Then he watched as she stepped into the black cocktail gown from the night she first met Michael. She did her hair and painted her nails, then carefully ran a tube of bold red lipstick over her top lip and pressed her lips together.

"You better watch out," he said, kissing her neck, "or we're never going to leave this room."

As Michael began to unzip her dress, a knock came at the door. Cee Cee gave him a lingering kiss, leaving his mouth red with lipstick, then pushed him toward the door. He unlatched the chain and opened it.

"Hi, son," Sam said. "Can I come in?"

Pain shot through Michael's head. He felt the sick vertigo of a man who misses a step descending the stairs. It was a betrayal of expectation. Michael felt he had lost control of his body as he stepped back and made room for Sam to enter. Sam walked in and saw Cee Cee.

"Hello," he said, casually glancing around the suite and whistling through his teeth. "Quite a place you got."

Cee Cee pulled on her high heels and walked to Michael, placing herself between him and Sam like a shield. She glared at Sam, her eyes shining.

"What the hell are you doing here?" she said.

"I was hoping Michael and I could talk," Sam said. "Alone."

"You got a lot of balls, Sam," Cee Cee said. "After what you've done—"

Michael placed his hand on her shoulder. "It's okay," he said quietly to her. "I can handle this. I need to do it. Why don't you go on ahead? I'll meet you there. Be right behind you."

"Are you sure?"

She looked at Michael and saw the clarity in his eyes. Standing on tip-toes, she kissed his chin. "Call if you need me," she said.

Sam watched her leave, then selected an easy chair on the far end of the suite, plopped down heavily, and opened a small bag at his feet, from which he pulled a shining gold statue. "Your Grammy," he said.

"You left it. I thought you should have it." Michael made no motion to accept it, so Sam laid it on the carpet near his chair.

"Will I see you tonight at the ceremony?" Sam said.

"I'll be there. For her, not for you."

"Michael, I owed you time to sulk, and pout, and hate me, and whatever else you needed to do, but I want that to end now."

"Why?" Michael asked.

"Hell, I wouldn't have a career anymore if not for you."

"That's all I am to you?"

"Now come on," Sam said. "You know what I mean."

"I don't, actually," Michael said. His face was an impenetrable mask of defiance. "Want me to get you on the cover of *Rolling Stone* again?"

"I remember what it was like to be where you are," Sam said sadly. "You think it's never gonna end. Then it does. And the other side ain't pretty."

"If the other side looks like you, I hope I die before I get there."

"You're just as stubborn as your old man," Sam said. "Must be in the blood because God knows you didn't learn it from me."

"I didn't learn anything from you."

"I seen you up there on stage. I'd say you learned just about every damn thing you know from me, boy."

"Why are you here, Sam?"

"I told you. I want to bury the hatchet. I want us to sing together tonight and be good. This is the Hall of Fame. It don't get bigger than that."

"So I brought you back from the dead, and now you're afraid if I don't come make you look good, they'll realize you don't deserve it."

"That's what you think?" Sam said. "I don't deserve it?"

Michael nodded.

"And what about you, huh?" Sam said, his anger smoldering. "Why'd you come here? It's a big world. Why'd you come all the way to Nashville?" Michael began to reply, but Sam cut him off: "You wanted to meet me, didn't you? You wanted to profit from my name, didn't you? You wanted to step on my back to reach that next rung of the ladder. Didn't you? You're the same as me. We do whatever it takes to stay on top."

"I came because of my mother—the woman you betrayed."

"I didn't even know your goddamn mother," Sam shouted. "You know those women you fuck, then kick out of bed and never think of again? That's what your mother was to me. A piece of ass. You understand? Hell, don't you have a son out there kickin' in someone's womb?"

"She told you?" Michael said, wondering when—and why—Cee Cee would have told Sam. But as he watched Sam's face turn red with the realization, he knew she had kept the secret.

"Not Cee Cee?" Sam gasped.

Michael nodded.

"I'm going to be a grandfather?" Sam said, his anger dissipating.

"You have to be a father first to be a grandfather."

Sam put his face in his hands. "I'm sorry I said that about your mother," he said.

"Why didn't you visit me in the hospital?" Michael blurted, his mask of defiance cracking to show the hurt of a little boy. "After everything I did for you, you didn't even come see me. I'm your son. I could have died in there."

Sam sighed. "The Colonel didn't think it was a good idea."

"Why not?"

"I didn't ask."

"You just let him keep us apart like that? Again? Without even asking why?"

"He's been telling me what to do since before you were born."

Michael stared out the window for a moment lost in thought, then looked at Sam with his mask intact again. "My whole life, I wanted to know my father. I never thought the truth could be worse than not knowing. But my mother was right to keep it from me. I see that now."

A tense silence filled the room. Finally, Sam said, "I like you, Michael. If you want someone to write some songs with, make some money, go on tour, chase some ass, have some fun—that's me. If you want someone to help you learn to ride a bicycle, hold your hand while you cross the street, tuck you in at night, well, sorry kid. That ain't me. Never was. Never will be."

"I don't want anything from you," Michael said, struggling to control the emotion in his voice. "I did fine without you. My kid will too. I'll give him everything you could never give me."

"We ain't givers, you and me," Sam said. "We're takers. We take what we want. Music. Money. Women. We take it because they let us take it. I took your mother. You took Bucky's wife. And now, what, you think you're going to settle down and live a nice little life with your nice little family in a nice little house? That ain't you, Michael. Trust me. That baby will be born in sin just like you were, and when he needs you, you'll be on the road somewhere, and one day he's gonna grow up and throw it in your face, just like you're doing now. Maybe then you'll understand. You can't break that circle."

"I think you should leave," Michael said. "And after tonight, maybe we shouldn't see each other again."

Michael walked to the door and opened it. Sam stood. He looked ancient, his face careworn and creased like old leather.

"Good luck, Michael," Sam said. "I hope you do better than me. But you won't."

Michael stopped him as he walked through the door.

"Take your statue," he said.

"It's yours," said Sam.

"I don't want it."

Sam looked at the Grammy, looked back at Michael, and left without another word.

46

HURTS SO GOOD

MICHAEL'S HEAD PULSED. HE PACED the suite, trying to calm himself. The pain in his head grew somehow worse. He couldn't see. He picked up the Grammy and threw it at the wall. It took out a chunk of plaster and clattered to the ground, broken. Then the panic set in. He couldn't go to the ceremony like this. He needed his pills—just once more to get through tonight, then he'd stop for Cee Cee and the baby. He stumbled to his suitcase and dug to the bottom, only to remember again that Cee Cee had thrown them all away. He texted his dealer: *Delivery, ASAP*, then called room service for a bottle of wine and downed half of it in five long gulps.

The wine numbed him just enough to wait until the knock came at the door. His dealer had sent a girl, a little blonde with blue eyes swimming in black pools of makeup and tits so perfect Michael could almost feel them just by looking at her sweater. She had a tattoo of an infinity symbol on her left wrist. She was no more than a teenager by the looks of her, yet she already seemed to have been discarded by the world.

"How old are you?" Michael slurred as she took his order out of a leather satchel.

"Mind your own fucking business," she said, handing him three bottles of pills.

Michael downed an Oxy, and his body immediately relaxed like a little boy safe under his favorite blanket. Something switched in his brain, and he wanted more. "I need to know," he said, calmer, clearer now. Peeling off a hundred dollar bill, he held it out to her. "I want vodka," he said. "But I'm not sure if you can get it for me."

"Get it yourself," she said sullenly.

"You don't know who I am."

"Some rich asshat."

"There's a liquor store around the corner," Michael said, leaning back in a chair, the druggy warmth spreading through his body. He liked the girl. She had spunk. "Buy me a fifth of vodka. Any kind, doesn't matter. Come back within fifteen minutes and there's another of these in it for you." He handed her the hundred-dollar bill and held up another for her to see. She took the money and left in a hurry.

Ten minutes later, the girl was back. She entered the penthouse, huffing. "Jesus, you didn't have to run," Michael said. His head was beginning to hurt again. He took the vodka from her and poured two glasses. "Care for a taste?" he said. "I don't like to drink alone." It was a lie, but it worked. The girl took the glass and curled into one of the plush easy chairs like a feral cat, ready to spring to safety at the slightest provocation.

"So, you really don't know who I am?" Michael said, pulling his chair toward her but staying far enough away not to threaten her.

"I'm not an idiot," the girl said.

Michael grinned crookedly. "What else have you got in that bag there?"

"You paying?"

"Of course."

The girl took out a baggie of weed. "Fifty bucks," she said. Michael nodded, and she rolled a joint with the speed and precision of a Cuban *torcedor*.

"Do that again," Michael said eagerly. The girl rolled another joint, then lit one, took two deep puffs, and handed it to Michael. He inhaled and lost himself coughing until he thought his lungs were bleeding.

"Rookie," sneered the girl, taking the joint from his fingers, inhaling deeply again, and blowing smoke rings at Michael.

He composed himself, then went on another coughing jag, then composed himself again and with a sly arch of his eyebrow said, "So, what do you want to do?"

The girl inhaled the joint down to her fingers, then uncurled herself from the chair and walked to the window. "This place is nice," she said through a cloud of smoke. "Makes me want to break something." She took a corner of the silk curtain in her hands and looked back at Michael. He nodded, and she ripped the curtain from the wall. Michael rose to join her, and for a few madcap minutes, the room was a tornado of ripped silk. When they had finished with the curtains, Michael said, "What next?"

The girl walked to the piano and said, "Can you play this thing?"

Michael sat on the bench with the ceremony of a maestro and clumsily played the few chords he knew. The girl shut the piano lid and climbed on top. She stood unsteadily, reached up for the chandelier, and climbed like a monkey until she was dangling in midair over the piano. Michael began singing, "When the bough breaks, the cradle will fall, and down will come baby…." The chain holding the chandelier snapped with a whip crack, and the girl thudded down on the piano, protecting her face with her arms as the chandelier fell after her. It hit the piano and the lightbulbs shattered, sending shards of glass flying. Michael stepped on one as he rushed to the girl. His cut foot bled into the carpet. He couldn't feel it.

"Are you okay?" he said breathlessly. The girl's body shook with what Michael mistook for sobs but soon realized was laughter.

"Holy shit," she said. "That was incredible."

Her sweater had risen to her ribcage, exposing the soft pink flesh of her stomach. Michael bent down and kissed it. She sat up, and her mouth was on his, and her hands worked feverishly at the buttons of his shirt while he lifted her sweater over her head and marveled at what he saw, worked at the button of her jeans, then ripped off her underwear, then his pants and underwear.

Michael kissed her neck and let his mouth linger on her nipples. He ran his tongue down her stomach, and she lay back on the piano while he continued down the sleekness of her, touching on everything from hip to toe, then settling to work until her back arched in ecstasy.

Michael gave her no respite. He lifted her over his shoulder, laid her on the bed, and stood above her. "Are you ready?" he asked.

The girl reached out her ivory foot and rested it on Michael's chest. She was so young. He wondered what her parents had done to her, how they had hurt her to make her end up here, and then it hit him with the force of an epiphany: *I'm going to be a father.* For the first time in his life the girl lying on the bed was more than a plaything. He owed it to Cee Cee, to the baby, to be better than this.

"I'm really sorry," he said. "But I can't do this."

"I want to, if that's what you're worried about," she said.

"So do I. You're gorgeous. That's not it, though. I'm sorry, I just can't."

She bit her thumb and held Michael's eyes while, with her other hand, she trailed a finger down the elegant line of her neck and around the pink plenitude of her nipples, raising goosebumps on the soft flesh of her stomach, and finally coming to rest in the fine golden hair between her open legs. "You sure?" she said.

Michael fought with his desire as he watched her clothe her exquisite body. She planted a last passionate kiss on his lips as she left the room. The feeling lingered on Michael's mouth. He swayed woozily in the darkness of his penthouse, searching for a release. His head hurt again. He lit the second joint and smoked half of it, but it didn't help. He called for a car to pick him up in half an hour, then turned on the television and ordered a pay-per-view video titled *The Wetter the Better.* Scrolling through his pictures, past hundreds of nameless partners in various stages of undress, he found the one he wanted: Cee Cee sleeping in his bed, her left breast exposed, her golden hair spread on the pillow like a halo around her head. She looked so still and beautiful.

Michael rose from the bed in the sweet agony of desire, stumbled to the coffee table, found his pills, fumbled with the bottle cap, and swallowed two. The sensation spread through him like warm honey. Tripping over dirty clothes strewn about the floor, he went to his suitcase and dug out the snakeskin belt. He knelt on the bathroom tile, made a loop and put his head through it, closed the door, wrapped the belt around the handle and made a knot, then propped his phone with the picture of Cee Cee on a pile of towels and tightened the belt around his neck.

It was not his hand that touched him, but her body. She was with him. He felt the euphoria and held it off. He wanted to push it further than ever before. Timing the moment required precision. The pressure built. Yes. His body trembled; she would heal him. His face went purple. Black spots clouded his vision. *One more second...*

47

THE CIRCLE BROKEN

CEE CEE SAT IN THE darkened CMA Theater and dabbed her eyes. The final chorus of "Will the Circle Be Unbroken" reverberated off the walls and slowly died. It must have been the baby making her so emotional, she thought. She checked her phone one more time to see if Michael had texted. He hadn't. She felt sick. Was that the baby too?

Everything else was finished—the all-star tribute to Sam, the film of his life and career, Reba McEntire's induction speech, the unveiling of Sam's medallion. Now came the grand finale: Sam's big performance with Michael, the last step between Cee Cee and freedom. But Michael wasn't here. She wondered what had happened between Michael and Sam at the hotel. Most likely, she thought, Sam had pissed him off and Michael had refused to perform. She'd probably find him back in the hotel in his white bathrobe, strumming his guitar. She smiled to herself, knowing that even though she'd try to stay angry at him, he'd charm his way back into her good graces.

Cee Cee stood and excused herself from her row, treading on the hem of Lucinda Williams's bell-bottom jeans as she gained the aisle. She walked backstage where Sam stood with the Colonel, Martha, and Bucky. Their faces were tight and mean. Cee Cee took a deep breath and approached them.

"He isn't answering his phone," she said, before the Colonel could even start yelling at her. "I don't know where he is. Sam saw him last."

"Beats the hell outta me," Sam said. "He told me he'd be here."

"I can go back to the hotel and get him," Cee Cee said.

"No time," the Colonel said. "Sam's going to have to perform it himself."

Cee Cee wanted to slap the smirk off Bucky's face. He was clearly enjoying this. Then she thought of her future and remembered Bucky didn't matter anymore. She wouldn't fight him. As long as she and Michael were free to begin their life together, he could have the rest.

"Have you heard from him, Martha?" Cee Cee said, but Martha had had a last-second change of heart and decided to stay with the Colonel, and she could not even look Cee Cee in the eye.

Sam waited until the last minute, then stepped onstage and performed "Father and Son" by himself. During the second verse, Blake Shelton sneaked on stage and took over Michael's parts, saving the performance. The song ended to a five-minute standing ovation, and then the crowd shuffled out of the theater and back to the rotunda for a celebration.

Cee Cee wanted nothing but to jump in her car and speed to the hotel to check on Michael, but she had to swim through the crowd to get to the door, and it seemed everyone wanted to speak with her take a picture, or thrust a glass of champagne in her hand and propose a toast to the great Sam Rogers. The noise of the revelry swirled around her head.

She saw Sam floating in a crowd of admirers, drowning in slaps on the back and kisses on the cheek. She saw Bucky and his young girlfriend, standing next to each other but seeming miles apart. She saw the exhaustion in Bucky's eyes and knew that once they finished the divorce, he would keep getting older while his girlfriends kept getting younger, leaving between them an unswimmable ocean of time. She almost pitied him.

Then came the Colonel, trying to sneer through his Botox.

"You got lucky," he said. "I'm still going to rip up the contract."

"What?" Cee Cee said.

"I can't manage a dead man."

"What?" she said again.

The Colonel turned on his heel and found Bucky standing by the far wall. He whispered into Bucky's ear, and Bucky's jaw hung open. His eyes grew wide and wild. He let out an insane laugh. He struggled through the crowd and stopped Cee Cee with a cold smile.

"I win," he said.

"Get out of my way," she said.

"Gladly," he said, then muttered, "By the way, you might want to start watching what you eat. You're getting fat."

"I'm pregnant," Cee Cee answered, suddenly furious.

Bucky's face turned white. "Bullshit," he sputtered. Cee Cee tried to push past him, but he held her arm. "I already told you I'm not taking you back, so don't expect me to help," he said.

"Don't worry. It's not yours."

Bucky stared at her stupidly. Then the dawning spread across his face.

"You haven't heard, have you?" Bucky said, smiling like a wolf.

Behind him came Martha, staring at her phone and crying.

"Martha, are you okay?" Cee Cee said, escaping from Bucky's clutches.

"I'm so sorry," Martha said, sniffling. "I wanted to join you, but I just couldn't. I hope you understand now. And I hope you find a way to move on. I know you loved him."

"Who, Bucky? I couldn't care less what he thinks."

"No," Martha sobbed. She frowned and held up her phone. Cee Cee seemed to watch herself from outside of her body as she looked at a picture of the Thompson Hotel on the *People* magazine website and read the headline: "Superstar Michael Jennings Dead at Thirty-One."

"This isn't funny," Cee Cee said, certain someone was pranking her. She turned to Bucky. "This is a sick joke, even for you," she said.

Martha pressed the phone into her hands and Cee Cee read the article: "Michael Jennings, the country music phenomenon who burst onto the scene a few short years ago with his record-breaking hit 'Don't Change,' was found dead in his penthouse at the Thompson Hotel one hour ago. The cause of death was strangulation. Police are ruling it a suicide. Check back for updates as more information is released."

Cee Cee's knees buckled.

"If there's ever anything I can do for you," Martha said, but Cee Cee wasn't listening. She elbowed through the crowd to the door and pushed it open. A light rain had begun to fall. She ran to her car and broke down in choking sobs. It couldn't be true. She refused to believe it. She typed "Michael Jennings death" into her phone and found breaking news items from the *New York Times* and *USA Today*. She closed the tab, opened a new one, and typed "Michael Jennings death hoax," hoping still that this was just some elaborate joke. The search results returned more breaking articles about Michael's death, from CNN, *Rolling Stone*, and *Billboard*. The tears fell harder, smudging her mascara down her cheeks. Searching in her purse for a tissue, her hand fell on Michael's note. She pulled it out and read: "Check your email. This is our future."

Cee Cee's hands shook as she opened her email, found the folder of new songs, and downloaded it. She connected her phone to her car's Bluetooth and sat in silence, wondering whether or not she could handle hearing the music now. Suddenly she felt the need to move. She backed out of her parking spot and drove to the highway, not knowing where she was going, just that she needed to be somewhere, anywhere else.

She hit play.

Michael's voice filled the car, more powerful than she had ever heard it before, set to the haunting strains of his acoustic guitar. The music seemed to come from inside of her. Every note was a dagger to the heart, but she couldn't turn it off because here he was, alive and beautiful, forever.

The world seemed to shrink to a pinpoint. Nothing existed but her, Michael, and the sound of her tires rolling over the slick road. As the music played, she thought of the first time she saw him, of the first time he kissed her at the T.J. Martell dinner, of the arrogance and confidence he had to send his boss's wife lingerie. She thought of him on

Christmas, sitting like a child in front of the tree. She thought of the lips she'd never kiss again, and the body she'd never feel again against hers. She remembered the way he held his guitar, lovingly, the same way he held her. She saw the life ahead of her and wondered how she'd survive it without him. She knew she had to do something with this music. It was too good to keep to herself. Michael was right: it was their future. He would live on through it, as would their love. The last song ended. As if by magic, the rain stopped. Cee Cee exited the highway and realized that, without thinking, she had been driving to the only place that felt like home—Michael's house. She grabbed her phone, scrolled back to the beginning, and hit play. Michael's voice filled the car again.

For the first time, in rhythm with the music, she felt the baby kick.

ACKNOWLEDGMENTS

I WOULD LIKE TO THANK Adam Chromy, Travis Atria, Adriana Senior for believing in this story, Gretchen Young for publishing it, and Michael Hutchence and Martha Troup for helping to inspire it. I met Michael in 1987 while working as secretary to Ahmet Ertegun, chairman of Atlantic Records. Michael was a larger-than-life man, and much deeper than his rockstar persona. I also met INXS's manager Chris Murphy, and Michael's manager Martha Troup. Chris's vision brought the band to America. Martha was the first female manager I ever met in the music business. I want to acknowledge her dedication and tireless work for Michael and INXS.

A special thank you to Jason Owen, the King of Nashville.

ABOUT THE AUTHOR

DOROTHY CARVELLO IS THE AUTHOR of *Anything for a Hit: An A&R Woman's Story of Surviving the Music Industry.* Her book was reviewed by the *New York Times, Kirkus,* and *Publishers Weekly.* She is from and still lives in New York City. She is a graduate of Marymount Manhattan College.